London Calling

BOOK I IN THE LONDON ROMANCE SERIES

by Clare Lydon

custard books

First Edition April 2014
Published by Custard Books
Copyright © 2014 Clare Lydon
ISBN: 978-0-9933212-6-9

Cover Design: Kevin Pruitt
Copy Editor: Gill Mullins
Typesetting: Adrian McLaughlin

Find out more at: www.clarelydon.co.uk
Follow me on Twitter: @clarelydon
Follow me on Instagram: @clarefic

All rights reserved. This book or any portion thereof may not be reproduced or used in any manner whatsoever without the express written permission of the author.

This is a work of fiction. All characters and happenings in this publication are fictitious and any resemblance to real persons living or dead, locales or events is purely coincidental.

Also By Clare Lydon

London Romance Series
London Calling (Book One)
This London Love (Book Two)
A Girl Called London (Book Three)
The London Of Us (Book Four)
London, Actually (Book Five)
Made In London (Book Six)
Hot London Nights (Book Seven)
Big London Dreams (Book Eight)
London Ever After (Book Nine)

Standalone Novels
A Taste Of Love
Before You Say I Do
Change Of Heart
Christmas In Mistletoe
Hotshot
It Started With A Kiss
Nothing To Lose: A Lesbian Romance
Once Upon A Princess
One Golden Summer
The Christmas Catch
The Long Weekend
Twice In A Lifetime
You're My Kind

All I Want Series
Two novels and four novellas chart the course of one relationship over two years.

Boxsets
Available for both the London Romance series and the All I Want series for ultimate value. Check out my website for more: www.clarelydon.co.uk/books

Acknowledgements

There are many people who've helped me along the way with this book, so here's where you get a nod of gratitude. Thanks to my first readers: Jamie Cootes, Sheryl Scott, Rachel Batchelor, Shelley Morris, Holly McRae, Annella Linton, Valentina Zanca & Emma Young.

Thanks to the support and feedback of fellow authors Angela Peach, Cindy Rizzo and Kiki Archer. Three cheers also for my fantastic cover designer Kevin Pruitt; Gill Mullins who saved the day with her final proof; and Adrian McLaughlin for his publishing advice.

And of course, thanks to Yvonne for putting up with me on a daily basis and reading the manuscript a gazillion times (approx) without moaning too much.

For Yvonne, caffeine & sugar.
I love you all.

SEPTEMBER 2009 - SYDNEY
Chapter One

The sun's rays were sliding down the roof of the train like molten lava as it rattled into view. Tonight the city was scorched, melting. I stood on the platform and watched, rolling my neck back in a semi-circular motion, feeling my tired bones click and the stress of the day seep out of my body. That the sun was still out was good news as it meant I had time to get home, change and make it to the pub for a drink before the last shards of daylight pierced the horizon and evening draped itself across the city.

Enjoying a cold beer on a warm evening was still one of life's pleasures that filled me with fizzy, carbonated joy, and I'd been looking forward to it all day in between trying to sell advertising space to small businesses. This afternoon had been particularly trying after my colleague Dan had microwaved last night's leftovers for lunch, leaving the office smelling of warm fish.

During my quest to flog said space I'd consumed three chocolate TimTams and three cups of strong coffee, none of which were doing my system any favours on the kick-start front. Mind you, the term kick-start seemed to me more suited to motorcycle competitions or the side of cereal boxes, not actually involved in your life. It's when you tried to shoehorn such phrases into your day that the problems and retributions began. I needed a new job, that much I knew. Along with some willpower to stop eating chocolate biscuits.

The train lurched forward as its weary metallic hulk shuddered to a stop but I was standing in exactly the right spot for the doors as this was a journey I did regularly. 37 steps up, across a smouldering asphalt bridge, down the opposite 37 steps to platform 2 and walk to the third bench. The doors hissed 'hello' and I got on, selecting the nearest seat from four available and feeling the nylon sizzle under my thighs as I sat down.

Today was Karen's 30th birthday and we'd arranged to meet with friends at our favourite pub in Newtown before heading out for Thai food and dancing. Karen loved to dance and was thrilled at the recent proliferation of dance shows on TV – if there was one on, it was difficult to get Karen out the door.

She was coming to the pub straight from work and I'd told her I was too, but I'd left early so that I could get home, change and pick up her present. She wasn't expecting it and I couldn't wait to see her face. I'd searched everywhere for the perfect gift and believed I'd found it: some vintage earrings and a necklace I knew she'd love. Karen had style and these would adorn her beautiful features perfectly.

I looked at my watch – we'd arranged to meet at the pub at 5.30pm so there should be plenty of time. As the train pulled out I concentrated on not biting my fingernails as it was a habit Karen hated. Instead, I pressed both palms flat against my thighs and watched the hot Sydney afternoon slide by.

Three stops later and I was off the train, springing down the platform, my grey shoulder bag banging against my hip as I went. Even though I hated commuter mornings I was enthralled by the evenings, when everyone was far more relaxed and ready to kick back. I was much better at kicking back than kick-starting.

I called in at the shop to get a carton of milk, waving at Ken who was having a fag outside the bottle shop across the street. I let the milk hang off my left little finger as I fished in my jeans pocket for the flat keys and flashed the key fob over the access point: the door clicked obligingly open.

My flat (or apartment, as the Aussies would say) was in a building that housed 20 others, built in the '80s and starting to show signs of wear and tear. Today though, the lift glided swiftly up to the second floor, spitting me out onto the stained beige carpet in seconds. From there it was a short six steps to my thick white front door.

The lounge light was on as I made my way down the magnolia hallway – I must have missed it this morning. I told myself off and went through to the kitchen, making a mental note to wipe down the doorframe, which looked smudged.

Something wasn't quite right though. I could hear noises. My doctor flatmate Paula was working today so she shouldn't be here. I turned my head, feeling my heartbeat quicken and goosebumps break out along my arms as I headed back out into the hallway and towards the bedrooms. The noises got louder as I advanced and my stomach lurched – but they seemed to be coming from Paula's room, so maybe she changed her shifts. I stood outside her door and knocked lightly.

"Paula?"

The noises continued. There was a slap. It sounded nasty. Or perhaps she was having sex? But Paula didn't have a girlfriend and she wasn't the type of girl to bring someone home in the middle of the day. I took a deep breath, my forehead creased with concern and pushed open the door.

And that's when I came across Karen, kneeling over my supremely naked flatmate Paula, her hand raised to slap Paula's still-red butt cheek. In Paula's bed, not mine. On Karen's 30th birthday. My girlfriend, not Paula's.

Karen's face was flushed pink, her shoulder-length blonde

hair tussled – I knew that look, I'd seen it many times. Like this morning for instance, when I'd given her what I thought was her only birthday sex. Clearly I was wrong.

My brain tilted in my head as the full impact of this scene sunk in. This was not what I'd expected when I left work today. I wondered if I could get a refund on the earrings and necklace.

JANUARY 2010 – LONDON
Chapter Two

There had been no ice on the plane, which had seriously disrupted my plan of getting coolly plastered by the time we flew over Uluru. Since living in Australia I'd become allergic to warm alcohol, something I suspected was going to prove problematic back in the UK. Add to that the trolley-dolly attending me had croissant-like hands that flaked his skin over me with every move and it hadn't been a first-class flight – but you get what you pay for.

I sighed at the harsh implications of my monetary status and cast my mind into the future, seeing myself turning left at the plane door, receiving an ice-cold glass of champagne, a false smile, shiny cutlery, a plumped-up pillow. A girl could dream.

When we landed, Heathrow was as I remembered it: angular and cold. Plus, it smelt like a flat I'd once rented in Crouch End – part musty cupboards, part beige. Beige has a smell, believe me.

Even though I didn't step outside to get from the plane to the terminal, I could feel the winter air as soon as we landed. This was another aspect of my homeland I was going to have to get used to – the weather. Sydney had ruined me. I tugged my lightweight blue jacket closer around me but knew in my heart it was useless.

My right leg was still tingling with pins and needles from where it had been hastily wedged under the seat in front during the flight. I stamped it on the floor with a touch too much vigour and a woman behind me started like she thought I might produce a gun and put bullets through the rest of my fellow passengers. Plane travel made people jumpy. In addition, my short brown hair was stuck to my head, flattened by gravity and a sheen of other passengers' bodily fluids that hung wordlessly in the cloying cabin air.

One thing that had happened in my absence was that Heathrow loos had got better, with working locks, an abundance of paper and no handle to flush. Now when you were done, you simply waved your hand in front of a black dot on the wall. I hung my bag on the off-white plastic hook, checked its back pocket to ensure my wallet and passport hadn't made a break for it and sat down, sighing with tiredness.

Now I was back, the UK didn't seem quite as thrilling as it had back in Sydney. Now, suddenly the Australian city seemed like the exotic destination and London a place of defeat, where my family were, where I had no money, job or home.

I had a quiet word with myself as I washed my hands with pink liquid soap and squinted in the mirror, scanning my grey eyes for signs that landing back in the UK was a positive move. They were giving nothing away.

Once I'd passed the dead-eyed customs staff, I pushed my trolley through duty-free, out of the sliding doors and into the waiting throng beyond the long metal railings. As I was swept along I saw my parents standing near the end of the crowd in matching jumpers they'd bought from Debenhams – I remembered the phone call telling me this news. The jumpers were green and beige with jarring angular patterns that gave you a headache if you stared at them too long but were, according to my mother, super-warm and washed up a treat.

"Jess!" Mum yelped, seemingly more excited with every

step I took towards her. Despite my reservations, I felt a huge surge of warmth flood through me. It was the feeling of knowing that whatever else, I'd be safe here.

My mum swallowed me up in a flurry of excitable hugging and as I kissed her cheek I smelt her familiar floral perfume. At 5ft 3 she was a couple of inches shorter than me but we shared the same colouring and she'd passed on her blotchy skin tones to me too, something I never failed to thank her for. What's more, at 58 she was wearing well, her brown hair coloured with red to hide her grey, her smile untattered by age.

My dad gave me a more manly hug, squeezing me just a little too tightly so that I staggered slightly when he released me from his grip. Dad still had his slight paunch but also, amazingly for a man nearing 60, a full head of hair, with grey fighting his natural dark colourings for omnipotence. I surmised the grey was winning.

"How was your flight?" he asked, reaching past me to grab the handle of my trolley. We were on the move, my mum linking her arm through mine and grinning at me manically.

"It was fine, my legs are just about recovering."

"Well, you look great," Mum said, somewhat surprisingly. "I mean, your hair would look better if you let it grow but I've been telling you that for the past ten years..."

"Shirley..." Dad said.

"I'm just saying. Anyway, she knows we're thrilled to have her back. You know Maureen's son went to Australia for a year and never came back."

"He died?" I said.

"No silly! He met a girl and got married. Now she has a grandchild that she never sees, tragic. But she's on Facebook all the time and showed me pictures. She's going to teach me. You're on Facebook aren't you?"

I nodded.

"We can be friends!"

"Can't wait," I lied. There was about as much chance of Mum mastering Facebook as me turning straight.

"Oh, and I've got something else to tell you. Remember Phil?"

"Phil?"

"Yes, you know – *your* Phil…"

Phil was a guy I'd gone out with some 13 years previous, my last serious boyfriend before edging out of the closet for good. Mum still spoke fondly of him, as if he were the last hope of me ever settling down and having children. I didn't tell her that it's still possible to have children if you're gay – children with another woman wasn't on her roadmap and might just send her tiny mind into a tailspin.

"I think the statute of limitations on him being 'my Phil' might have run out years ago…" I said.

"Yes, well he called – lovely phone voice, you know – and he wanted your number."

"And you gave it to him?"

"No!" she said. "But I told him you were due back in the UK this week and told him to call back then."

"Great. You do remember I'm gay don't you, Mum?" My voice was sing-song. It didn't disguise my irritation.

"Of course! I just thought it might be nice to have a drink with him, that's all. No need to be so touchy about it."

What a lovely thing to look forward to – a phone call from Phil. Even if I hadn't turned out to be a card-carrying lesbian, I'm sure I would have split up from him, given the fact that while he was tall, solvent and not bad looking, he was also crushingly dull.

I felt an old surge of annoyance that even though my mum had known my preference for Martha rather than Arthur for over a decade, it didn't stop her stockpiling men for the rainy day when I realised my true heterosexual calling.

We trundled on and out into the airport car park, the

trolley rattling along the uneven concrete and my parents having an argument about which bay they'd left the car in, but Mum ultimately being correct.

So I was home – but had I done the right thing being run out of town by a broken heart? As I settled into the back seat and the English motorway spread out on either side of me, I felt at once at home but also like an imposter in my own country.

Chapter Three

I'd left England three years earlier and landed in Australia with only $5,000 in my pocket and a phone number on me. The $5,000 dollars lasted just long enough; the phone number got me a job selling advertising space with a local newspaper. I was soon spending oodles of Aussie dollars up and down the gay bars of Sydney's Oxford Street and Newtown, the bright lights burning a hole in my pocket and the Aussie dykes lasering my heart with their promises of a far-off future.

The first woman I met was Teri, an engineer from Newtown who doubled up as a drag king by night, airing twice a week as Butch Cassidy. Our relationship didn't last long; she dumped me when I took exception to her fucking other willing cowgirls waiting in the wings. Turned out, this was one cowgirl who couldn't be tied down.

After Teri came Alex, a truck driver who didn't consider it a day's work unless she had an oil stain on her clothes. I spent two consecutive nights in her multi-coloured sheets in Beverley Hills before sliding out on morning three. I left quietly with her cat Toby ushering me out the way I'd come in, a satisfied look on his grey, bony face.

My third conquest was Pat who worked in radio and was big on the Sydney lesbian scene. Pat was a hipster and no slouch in the sack, but when I gazed into my crystal ball it wasn't Pat I saw kissing me in the hall after a hard day, so we split after a couple of months, the search for love still on.

First to apply successfully and have her application rubber-stamped was Karen.

Karen, who was a major part of the reason I'd fled Oz and flown back to England. Gorgeous, blonde-haired, blue-eyed Karen, who crept up on my heart like some lesbian poster child. She'd painted a picture-perfect vision of our future together on a huge canvas in my head, before casually setting fire to it in a flaming haze of betrayal.

We were together for just over a year, time enough for me to buff up my heart for her and offer it as a shiny prize. She accepted without hesitation and together we embarked on a year-long love mission – we were astronauts, floating in our self-made bubble.

During the time I had Karen to myself I thought I'd never been happier. We spent the usual first three months in bed, both enthralled by the new body beside us. After three months in which I kissed every part of her countless times, we began to venture into civilisation, going to art exhibits, the cinema and sharing dinners out. After four months, I declared my love and she hers. Our friends got on, we were in love. With Karen, there was no standing on ceremony: I fell hard, with a dramatic and decisive thud.

We delayed the tried and tested co-habiting route, wanting instead to cherish our freedom as well as our relationship and not fall into the trap that so many of our friends had. So I kept a flatmate and so did Karen, only she ended up shagging mine and having an affair, breaking my heart into a thousand fragile pieces.

* * *

After the 'unfortunate birthday incident', as my friend Tom christened it, Paula had the good grace to move out the next week, only her temporary home was Karen's. I assured

Karen this was not a good move if she wanted to continue our relationship. She assured me she had no intention of doing that, and perhaps I shouldn't stop by our favourite haunt that Friday night because she'd be there with Paula and I might feel a bit uncomfortable and, well, single. I took her advice.

In the weeks that followed it suddenly became devastatingly clear that my happiness and Australia didn't appear to be compatible. Every time my heart and head fizzed into action, galloping towards a magical realm, an axe would fall elsewhere cutting the blood supply and killing the plan stone dead.

It was only after six weeks of drinking and heartache that I arrived home one night and realised what I was craving: home. Proper home. There was nothing to keep me in Sydney anymore. I'd tried the Aussie girls, we didn't seem to click and with Karen still fresh in my system I simply didn't have the energy to play the scene. So I'd fired up my laptop, looked up cheap flights to the UK and decided to alter the course of my life.

I began the farewell process, having goodbye parties with my workmates, my book club, my gay boys and finally my best friends – Tom and Tess. They were the first two I'd told my plans to three months previous and both had been aghast, doing their best to talk me out of it.

"All it ever does is rain!" protested Tom – he was originally from Manchester, so he knew.

"Who am I going to talk sport with now?" Tess had asked. But in the end, they knew they were fighting a losing battle and that my heart was made up.

The night before I flew they both came over to my now empty flat armed with sparkling wine, Chinese food and a goodbye playlist created by Tom. As Kylie played, Tom proposed a toast.

"To Karen. When I see you, you'd better hide because I'm going to slap you for running our girl out of town," he said.

I spat my drink out and smirked.

"You have my permission."

"To our girl Jess," Tess said, giving Tom a stern look. "I can't believe you're leaving us in February and not staying for Mardi Gras – what kind of a gay are you?!"

I laughed – Tess knew very well my contempt for all things Pride.

"You know, I saw Karen and Paula out at Love Lounge last week – I didn't know whether to tell you," she added. I shrugged with what I hoped came across as indifference.

"It's fine," I lied.

"Anyway, they didn't look happy – I flung them a death stare on your behalf."

"Good girl," said Tom.

We'd finished the evening with shots of Russian vodka and Tess reiterating she didn't know what she'd do without me. But there was no looking back now: the die was cast. I was 32 and going home with only a rucksack on my back and a wealth of memories and friendships to show for my time in Oz.

When the plane took off, I wondered what Karen was doing, if she was happy, if she knew I was leaving or wanted me back. Whatever, it was too late now. I was gone.

Chapter Four

My brother Jack was waiting at the family home when we arrived, along with his wife Vicky and their two sons, Luke and Freddie. The kids had no idea who this dishevelled woman their dad was so pleased to see was, being aged three and two and never having met me before.

"Meet your best new babysitter, boys!" was Jack's introduction as I kissed them both hello. Luke was the older of the two by 13 months and had fair hair, while Freddie was a walking shock of blond.

"If you're paying, I'm available," I said, scooping Freddie up in my arms. To my surprise he acquiesced without a murmur, looking at me quizzically with his big blue eyes.

* * *

Jack had met Vicky at university ten years earlier. Drawn by her way with a hockey stick and her frankly cracking tits, he'd successfully wooed her and somehow managed to persuade her to marry him four years later.

I'd been a reluctant bridesmaid, mainly because it involved wearing a lilac dress and slingback heels, both of which had no regular place in my wardrobe. My concerns were doubled by Vicky's sister Kate, also a lady of lavender and unaccustomed to wearing flowing gowns. Particularly when they had to be worn in front of a crowd and Jesus nailed to a cross.

"You do remember who you've asked to be your bridesmaids, don't you?" Kate had asked Vicky when she'd presented us with her choices at the first dress fitting. "Lilac isn't really my colour."

"Nor mine," I'd chipped in, both of us behaving like sulky teens, starkly out of place amongst the pearly white interior of the bridal shop.

"Just try the dresses on, play nicely and I'll buy you both lunch afterwards – deal?"

Since then, Team Bridesmaid had been a regular duo on the London scene pre-Sydney and I was looking forward to catching up with Kate now I'd returned.

* * *

"So how does it feel to be back?" Jack said as we sat down on our parents' cream leather sofa. Jack worked in the city doing something terribly clever with numbers and had inherited Dad's thick head of dark hair, which he kept very short. He was dressed in black jeans and a Ralph Lauren polo shirt, his feet encased in jauntily striped socks. His style was what the Americans would call preppy.

"Surreal," I said, taking in the new addition of a glass coffee table and numerous dried plants around the room. "And after a day on a plane, I'm feeling super."

"And how are you after Karen – Kate told us," Vicky said. She winced slightly.

She too was wearing jeans along with a cream lacy top that had slid down one shoulder, revealing her tanned skin. I shrugged.

"Okay, you know."

She gave me a concerned look as Freddie finally wriggled free from my embrace and toddled over to sit on his mum's lap. Vicky smoothed back his fine hair and kissed his head.

"Well, Kate says to call her for a drink very soon. She also mentioned that she knew someone who had a room near her. Have you got her number?"

"I do, thanks."

"And whatever the reason, we're very glad you're back," Vicky said.

"Thanks. But can you do something about the weather?"

* * *

A few hours later Jack, Vicky and the boys were gone, Mum and Dad were being happily entertained by some Sunday murder-mystery and I was lying in the guest room, exhausted but unable to sleep with my mind working overtime.

So I was back in London, seemingly for good. Plus points: roof over head, far away from Karen, back with family. Minus points: back with family, freezing cold, missing friends. You have done the right thing, I told myself. This is absolutely the best course of action. It makes total sense and this is the next chapter of your life. I lay having a pillow-fight in my mind for a couple of hours before it eventually shutdown and I drifted into a fitful sleep, dreaming of Bondi Beach, sharks and Karen. No need for a dream diary to untangle that one.

Chapter Five

The next morning my mum woke me at 9am, jetlag be damned. She also made me a bacon sandwich and chatted non-stop – all that was required from me was the odd nod and smile throughout mouthfuls of food and slurps of tea. Did I want to come with her to pilates later? What about bingo this evening? How about a slice of apple pie? I politely declined all three, which left her muttering into the washing machine as she filled it. I stacked the dishwasher and disappeared upstairs to call Kate.

"The wanderer returns with a broken heart. How's being back in the bosom of your family, girl?" Kate said.

"Strangely normal. How are you?"

"Same old same old – three years on and that's still the case."

"That's what everyone keeps saying."

"That's because it's true. People who do adventurous things make us all feel bad when they return and nothing in our lives has changed."

"Adventurous. Okay, I'll go with that." I paused. "Listen, Vicky said something about a room. Is it still going?"

"Unfortunately not. But come out for a drink later and I might have another option."

"Sounds intriguing. Okay, where should I meet you?"

"Athena in town, just off Greek Street. Google it if you're not sure. I finish here at 6, so let's say 6.30?"

"Perfect. And I don't have a phone yet so don't be late."

"Yes, miss. And wrap up warm. Remember, no thongs, you're not in Bondi anymore."

"Har de har."

My first foray back into London lesbian life. I put my parents' cordless phone on the bedside table and lay back on the guest double bed, the sheets still comfortably creased from my night's sleep.

The radio alarm told me it was 10.21am. I worked forward in my head to where they'd be in Sydney right now – 8.21pm, time for TV or Monday night beers. Tom would be out on Oxford Street, jeans fresh from the wash and tight T-shirt hugging his just-worked-out torso. Meanwhile, Tess would be sinking a schooner of beer in Newtown after a hard day teaching. The thought of Newtown made me feel sick.

That was what I knew and now it was my old life, in the past. I'd given it all up to come back to live with my parents in a magnolia room with my mum inviting me to bingo. I closed my eyes. I needed a plan of action to combat these thoughts and take my mind off the fact that I'd lost the love of my life and that, at 32, I was sleeping in a room with patterned pelmets. It was temporary, never forget.

My mum broke my maudlin thoughts with a timely knock on the door.

"Jess, can I come in?"

She poked her head round the door before I could answer, as was the pattern of my childhood. When she saw me still lying on the bed, she recoiled.

"You're not dressed yet! I'm going to the shops in a bit and wondered if you wanted to come too?"

"Into town?"

"No, Sainsbury's. Why don't you come with me and we can buy you some food. I don't know what you like to eat anymore and I want you to feel at home."

"Okay," I said.

"Jump in the shower then – half an hour?"

She closed the door and I knew she was right. I had to start moving and getting on with my life, not lying flat and procrastinating. I swung my legs off the bed and propelled my body upwards. First step in the process, food shopping.

I looked out the window to check on the weather – compared to Sydney, it looked like the ice age had cometh. I dressed appropriately in thick socks, T-shirt and my favourite red hoody. However, as soon as I stepped outside the front door and saw my breath running away from my body, I dashed back in and rescued my old work coat from the spare room wardrobe. It didn't really go with my casual attire but right now warmth was my priority, not fashion.

Chapter Six

I was early in town to meet Kate, full of the lasagne Mum had cooked and wearing a jacket that I'd forgotten I had. I was looking for some shoes when I came across it and it immediately took me back to working at the call centre and late-night drinking sessions in Soho with my mates. There was even a stain on the side that was testament to my amazing durability back then.

Getting on the tube again was an experience too, having done it every day for six years and then not at all in Sydney. But now I was back in London, I'd have to get used to it again – the crowds, the smells, the elbowing. As we pulled into Oxford Circus I was sucked into a swathe of commuters and swept along towards the neon way out sign. A minute or so later I was spat out into the swirling central London winter air, infused with the smell of cigarettes, traffic fumes and hot nuts sold from tiny metal carts.

Being 20 minutes ahead of schedule, I decided to find the bar first. Once inside, I ordered a Heineken from a surly bartender in a black vest top who wasn't as cute as she thought she was. I sat myself down at a table near the door so I wouldn't miss Kate, but it was also good for people-watching. I was curious to discover what, if anything, had changed in my three years away.

I dimly recollected that London dykes had been more standoffish than those in Sydney, with hair and attitudes that could do you some serious damage. Sydney women had been more welcoming – or perhaps I'd thought that because I'd got a shag within ten days of landing there.

But today was a different day, a different time and perhaps my luck was about to change. My mind flicked through my Karen album as I thought this, so I took a swig of beer in a bid to cleanse the images.

If I was looking for evidence of a better scene, this bar was proof. It was cool but charming with a smart wooden bar and they'd got the lighting spot-on, keeping it low and intimate. I shifted in my seat, watching a couple of lesbians walk by hand in hand in the early evening sun. I smoothed myself down in an effort to ensure I was presenting a positive face of lesbianism through the bar window.

I clearly was, because two minutes later a cute, dark-haired woman walked in wearing a T-shirt that said 'Treat Yourself: Take Me Home Tonight'. She flashed me a killer smile as she walked to the bar and I returned the favour. By the time Kate arrived 15 minutes later, I'd nearly finished my beer so I accepted her offer of another, along with a welcome hug.

"Great to see you – how are you?" she said. She set down two beers on the table before unwinding her enormous black scarf from around her neck. She slung a thick lumberjack-style jacket on the back of her chair before sitting opposite me.

"Surprisingly unjetlagged for now. How was your day?"

"Another day in publishing," she said.

Kate was tall, slim and boyishly handsome. I'd seen pictures of her in her teens with the same flowing locks that her sister possessed but that was in the days before she realised she was a dyke. As soon as she'd acknowledged that, she'd chopped it off. Her hair was now stylishly cropped and peroxide blonde, framing her stand-out cheekbones and piercing green eyes perfectly. She was wearing dark blue jeans, a green shirt and white Converse boots.

"You're looking well anyway – heartbreak obviously suits you. Or perhaps the Aussie climate? Whichever, give it a month and you'll soon be looking pale and grey like the rest of us."

"Try another week with my mum," I said.

"How is the lovely Shirley?"

"She's well. She sends her love by the way." I shifted in my seat. "And you must have done something right because she was not-so-subtly telling me earlier that I could do worse than you – you're a catch in my mum's eyes."

"She fancies me – I knew it!" Kate said.

"I think she might. If I went home tonight and told her it was on, she'd be thrilled."

"Well, I have a plan to tease her beyond her limits – her and our delightfully coupled siblings. Ready?"

I nodded.

"You can come and live with me."

"Okay – but you already have Roger the lodger if I'm not mistaken. And shouldn't we at least have a drunken shag before I move in?"

Kate grinned.

"You've seen through my dastardly plan. Yes, at the moment I do still have Roger – but not for long. Dear old Rodge has been saving like a demon and bagged himself a shared ownership place. He didn't think he'd have it for at least a few months but it's going to be ready in five weeks. So if you can wait that long, the room's yours."

I thought about it for a millisecond.

"Sold, you're a lifesaver. I'm sure I can cope at Mum and Dad's till then," I said. I pushed back my chair and stood up.

"Something I said?"

"Just nipping to the loo – beer runs straight through me."

"Some things never change."

When I got back, the cute T-shirt wearer I'd smiled at earlier was on her haunches chatting to Kate. When I sat down, she put her tanned hands on her thighs and stood up. She had short, dark hair, lucid hazel eyes and a transfixing smile. She was around 5ft 6 inches tall and wearing jeans that clung to all the right places.

I tried to stop my eyes assessing her too obviously but think I failed. I was gratified to notice that she seemed to be doing the same to me too, lingering on my breasts before raising her smile to my face. Kate made the introductions.

"Jess – this is Lucy. This is my mate Jess who's just traded in sunny Sydney for freezing London."

"Nice to meet you. You're from Sydney?" Lucy asked. I shook her outstretched hand.

"No – I'm a returning Brit."

"Well, good to have one back here – there are far too many Aussies in London hitting on our women and drinking our beer." She paused, then wrinkled her forehead. "Not that I'm complaining, some of them have been gorgeous…"

"Don't worry, there are plenty of Brits in Sydney doing the same thing."

She laughed at that.

"How long you been back?"

"Just landed yesterday."

"Really? God, you're doing well – I'd still be too jetlagged to even breathe."

I smiled at her. She was so animated when she spoke and I felt an instant pull towards her.

"I've just moved back to my parents' house so it tends to propel you into getting out and about a bit quicker."

"I'm going in a few days, so maybe I can get some tips from you?"

"To Sydney?" I said. To say I was surprised was an understatement.

She nodded and her grin showed up a cute dimple in the side of her cheek.

"Absolutely," I continued. "I can tell you where to go and, more importantly, where to avoid."

"Excellent," she said. A satisfied smile.

There was a slight pause in the world for me right there as I considered how she said 'excellent': it was warm and inviting.

"Anyway, I better get back to my friends," she said, turning, breaking me from my train of thought and flicking her head towards a bunch of women at the bar.

"I'll catch up with you later," she added to Kate, "...and get the Sydney lowdown from you," switching her gaze to me. "Nice to meet you, Jess."

"You too," I told her, to which she beamed.

I followed her retreating figure to the bar and she turned to smile at me, which made my stomach lurch. Recovering my poise, I took a swig of my beer and tried to adopt my poker face to Kate.

"So, how do you know her?" I asked. I wasn't sure it was working.

Kate crossed her legs and assessed me.

"She's a friend of Caroline's – we've been out for drinks quite a few times." She smiled at me before stroking her chin.

"She seems nice."

"She is. Single too. And very available from what I remember her saying."

I held up my hand, lying before I could stop the words tumbling out.

"I'm not looking – I'm off women, they're poisonous."

"Uh-huh."

"No uh-huh about it."

"Sure," Kate said.

"Anyhow, crashing on, I have a message for you from your sister. She told me to tell you to stop being a dick to this new woman you're seeing, who I take it is Caroline. I said I'd pass on the message."

"She did, did she?"

"She did. So spill?"

"I think you know most of it. She's called Caroline and she's a nurse."

"Handy for bedside manner." I put my elbows on the table. "Where'd you meet?"

"Bijou – a monthly night just off the Strand. Vic thinks we're serious just because I took her to babysit the boys last week but it's early days. So just because I haven't proposed marriage yet, she thinks I'm being a dick. I tell you, she's so desperate for me to get married since it's allowed now. I told her not everyone necessarily wants to do that but she doesn't listen."

"And how was the babysitting – did you get to first base?"

Kate rolled her eyes.

"Don't you start. I had Vic and Jack giving me wide eyes when they got back. I think they expected ruffled beds and hickeys. We actually watched CSI and had a takeaway."

"Did you touch her tits at least?"

"Enough! So anyway, you're on for the flat then?" Kate said. The subject of Caroline was officially closed.

"How much?"

"£500 a month all in."

"Sounds fine."

"To us then?" Kate said, holding up her beer.

"To us," I replied.

Chapter Seven

The next morning I slept through till 11, lulled by alcohol and the knowledge I'd left a note for Mum telling her not to wake me. Amazingly she complied so I awoke refreshed, if a little hungover. Kate and I had stayed at the bar till around 11 and Lucy had joined us for the last hour after her mates had left, where I'd discovered she was an optician by day and a wannabe drag king by night.

I told her about the Sydney shows and my ex and she was amused at the stories, although assured me that UK drag king shows weren't quite as advanced. Unbelievably, she was heading out to Sydney for six weeks for an extended holiday and to take in Mardi Gras – bad timing on our part if we wanted to get to know each other better. She seemed pained when she told me that both her evenings before she departed were already accounted for, but she promised to look me up when she was back and fill me in on her time in the Harbour City.

I hoped she wasn't lying as I could seriously get used to the way she looked at me, her gaze unerring as she listened intently to my stories, settling momentarily on my lips before looking me directly in the eye. Her raw intensity made me swallow down. Hard.

"Where are you staying?" I'd asked as Kate had got up to get the final round in as last orders rang out.

"I've got family near Bondi so I'm staying there at first,

then meeting up with some friends and we've hired a flat for two weeks in the city. I'm really excited – never been before and I've always wanted to do Mardi Gras." She'd paused to drain her beer.

"Is it as good as everyone says?"

"Mardi Gras?" I'd asked, stalling.

She'd nodded.

"Fantastic," I'd said. This wasn't the time to tell her I hated dressing up, parading and being proud. Instead, I'd described the Sydney party atmosphere, the vivid colours, the drink, the women. Actually, not so heavy on the women part, that was on a need-to-know basis.

"It's a shame you don't still live there. Maybe we would have met anyway," she'd told me, her dimple standing out as she'd flashed me that smile again. She was intoxicating.

"Perhaps we would. At least, I hope we would have."

Kate had arrived back with the beer, curtailing our flirting although Lucy's eyes carried on surveying me. When it was kicking-out time, we'd made promises about meeting up when she was back and had exchanged numbers. Her hug goodbye was firm and I knew I wanted to see her again.

"Keep in touch – and see you in six weeks I hope," I'd told her softly as we pulled away.

"Count on it," she'd told me, kissing me on the cheek. Her breath that close had made my blood race and we both knew something had shifted as we stepped slightly unsteadily out of each other's space, our gaze steady, our brains scrambled. I let out a deep breath remembering it even now.

As I lay in the guest room on day three of operation UK, the move somehow didn't feel so catastrophic. Thanks to Kate I now had somewhere to live and had received a timely ego boost from a sexy woman – how my mother would swoon over an optician. Actually, who was I kidding? I'd swoon too, although perhaps not so much over her occupation and more over her. My mother would have swooned over Karen's TV exec badge too, but that was not to be.

I reminded myself to concentrate on the present and not the past as I went downstairs for breakfast. As my self-help ahoy friend Kevin used to say, if you've got one foot in the future and one foot in the past, you're pissing all over your present. I certainly didn't want to do that.

Chapter Eight

For my next trick I had to find a job. Before I left for Sydney I'd been working in a call centre, having left my teaching career and then managing to drift with no clear plan. However, going back into teaching was the last thing I wanted to do, as were sales or being cooped up as a call-centre chicken. I wanted to propel my life story forward, not send it into reverse. 32-year-old graduate, own hair and teeth seeks gainful employment that won't lead to thoughts of topping herself. How hard could it be?

Seeing London through fresh eyes always made me wonder about its beauty. When I first arrived back, the city looked far too hectic, an oppressive haze of bodies, cars, buildings and sharp edges. But as soon as my senses became acclimatised after a few days, all the ragged lines, crime and poverty seemed to belong to elsewhere as the vibrancy, energy and architecture filtered into my being. It was a bit like Sydney in that respect – people from the country just couldn't understand what the pull of noise and concrete was. But somewhere beneath them was the buzz of life that just didn't happen in the suburbs and beyond.

Today, London looked lopsided, colourful and pulsing as I walked along the Euston Road, shivering even inside four layers of clothing. I hunched my shoulders and tucked my scarf in closer around the front of my neck as the wind razored through my clothing, slicing my skin. Cars glinted in the crackly, February demi-sunshine, boxy red buses ground along noisily and black cabs buzzed in and out of traffic with the cocky swagger of those that own the road.

When I'd first spoken about coming home, Mum had been full of all the new properties being built and how I should put my name down for a shared ownership scheme as soon as I was back. However, all the flats were outside zone four, outside the protective barrier of the inner city. In the sprawl where the grey concrete stopped sparking with life, where art was a dirty word, where being gay wasn't quite as revered. Jack and Vic had taken the plunge when they got married and moved out to be able to afford a house. But with two kids and an estate car, they'd been welcomed with open arms and nosy neighbours. When you're a friend of Dorothy, different priorities came into force.

All of this contributed to the fact that I was planning a move inwards when all of my straight mates were branching out in search of gardens and sash windows, married up with two-hour-long commutes. Not that I didn't covet all of those things – apart from the commuting. I was in my 30s after all, where thoughts traditionally turn away from beer and all-nighters to cocktails, wine and dinner parties. For now, though, a job was the starting point that headed towards that goal.

* * *

When I got home my mum had a surprise for me – a mobile phone with £30 of credit on it, telling me to contact my mates and give them this number.

"I saw Julia in the High Street today and she said she'd love to see you!"

For some reason, I'd been stalling on contacting my old mates. Kate was safe: she wasn't going to judge, plus we had family to laugh at together. Deep down, I knew all my other mates wouldn't judge either and would be happy to see me – they were on my side, after all – but my own judgement wasn't so forgiving.

I'd sailed off to Australia three years ago full of optimism about how my life might turn around out there. I celebrated my 31st birthday in a new lesbian strip club in Surry Hills with Karen on my arm, full of hope for the future. But by the time she'd rinsed my heart dry, I realised nothing was changing fast. Now here I was back home, living with my parents and somehow that felt like I'd failed. And my mum knew that. Perhaps she's wiser than I give her credit for. She was right about my friends, of course. And it wasn't true that I'd learnt nothing – I'd definitely learnt that you couldn't run away from yourself, no matter how hard you tried.

Julia was thrilled to hear from me, cancelled her plans for the next day and told me to come and meet her for lunch in town, her treat. Sarah, my mate from uni, booked me up for a night on the lesbian tiles on Friday, telling me that she'd round up the troops.

After that I called Adam, my best mate from my former dull job and the one good thing to come out of it. Adam was a straight-acting gay man at work, but once in Soho he got in contact with his inner glitter and had no trouble sparkling. Adam was still at the firm, although he was now bossing people like us around and still hating it.

"You did the right thing getting out – I can feel my soul withering by the hour," he told me.

He offered me some work which I politely declined, but he let me know the offer stood if nothing else came up. I asked about his love life and he told me he'd been laying off the scene of late. He'd just bought a flat in Tufnell Park and was busy nesting, spending every weekend either visiting Ikea or tending his balcony herb garden.

"A herb garden? I'm impressed," I said.

"Don't knock it. If you're trying to cook all of Jamie's meals it's a godsend to have all these herbs on hand."

"Are you turning camp in your dotage, dear?"

"I'm thinking of getting one of those lacy dolls to cover my spare loo rolls. Since turning 35, I see the point."

"I've got all this to come," I said. "All you need now is a husband to pick your herbs for you."

"Now that would be lovely."

Another few more calls and arrangements later, and it felt like my social calendar was booked up for a year. I prepared myself to tell the same stories of love, loss and surf over and over, then offered to make dinner which Mum readily accepted. She settled herself in front of the telly with tea and cake, watching a show about adult children coming home to live and how they bleed you dry.

"You can stay as long as you like," she said as I began chopping onions and garlic for my Bolognese. I told her she was too kind.

Chapter Nine

The next day at lunch Julia launched herself at me as soon as I walked into the fancy French bistro she'd chosen. She was taking a break from her job as a high-powered lawyer and her 5 foot 7-inch slim frame was suitably attired in a stylish grey skirt and jacket with a lilac shirt. Her face was done in that clever way where you make it up to look completely natural when it's actually caked with slap. Her dark hair cascaded over her square shoulders, her toned ankles barely supported in 3-inch shiny black heels. In short, she looked professional and stunning, and I told her so.

"Oh I've missed you and your lezza charm!" she said. "And I can't believe you've been home since Sunday and it's taken you this long to call – I thought your flight had been delayed or something."

My chair made an awful screeching sound as I pulled it out from under the table, making us both recoil slightly.

"No, just me working up the courage to come out of hiding. Plus it's so bloody cold here, I was thinking about just doing what tortoises do and asking Mum to wake me up when May arrives."

"You great berk," she said, helping herself to the basket of bread and butter on the table and offering it to me.

"You look fab anyhow – even a bit tanned. And I like your hair that length – suitably dykish. You're coming round for dinner soon so you can see Tom. Plus I have this friend I'm so setting you up with!"

"Can I catch my breath before you start your dating service on me again?"

* * *

I'd known Julia since secondary school where we'd become close friends due to our love of music and drinking. When school ended, Julia and I went on to the local sixth-form college to do A levels and had kept in touch through university, pooling our shared experiences over summer and Easter drinking sessions.

Julia had met Tom at uni, had moved in with him six years ago and she was succumbing to marriage in a few months' time. She had one of the sharpest minds I knew and, to top it off, had those elusive qualities that I failed spectacularly on – drive and ambition. What Julia wanted, Julia got.

I, on the other hand, came out, graduated, hated teaching and then proceeded to drift from job to job, going through a belated adolescence where I actually wanted to sleep with people before I eventually settled down with a blonde named Maria. We'd lived together for three years before drifting apart a year prior to my Sydney jaunt. She'd since married some woman called Abby – I'd been invited but declined from the other side of the world.

* * *

"So how are the wedding plans coming along?" I said. I tilted my head to one side like a question mark.

"Nightmare – let's not talk about it. I'm boring myself so I'm sure it's thrilling for everyone else around me."

"That's what you're meant to do though, isn't it – bore the pants off everyone? Two girls in my office in Sydney were getting married last year and it's all they talked about for 12 whole months. In the end, I had to hand it to them – their persistence was impressive."

"Let's just say it's all done as far as I can tell. Apart from the huge pile of stuff that I keep ignoring. Tom's parents are still peeved it's not happening in a church and he keeps wilting, until I remind him that it's our wedding and not theirs." She breathed out an exasperated sigh.

"Then there's my mum and her constant bleating about a theme – what is it with weddings and themes? I told her the theme was us and wasn't that enough? I think she'd be happier if I announced we'd both be dressing as Elvis, expected the guests to do the same and hired an Elvis tribute artist to perform. I honestly think it's more trouble than it's worth but it's too late to pull out now, as I keep reminding Tom. I'm a hopeless romantic, what can I say? You've saved the date, right?"

She tugged on her cufflinks as she asked me, smoothing her shirt on her right arm.

"Logged in my brain. I might even buy a new tie for the occasion."

"Oh, splashing out!" She paused. "I tell you though, I'm certainly only doing it once – it's tedious in the extreme and bloody expensive. I'm sure if we'd just called it a party and not a wedding we could have slashed the cost in half. As soon as the W word is mentioned, companies start painting zeros on the end of their bills and they know you're going to pay for it because that's what you do."

"Glad it's such a time of joy," I said.

"There's the honeymoon though – I'm looking forward to that. Three weeks on safari – it's the only thing that's keeping me going."

I leaned back as the waiter brought our starters – butternut squash soup for me and goat's cheese salad for Julia.

"Fantastic, I'm starving. No breakfast this morning, just a hugely dull meeting," she said, tucking in with gusto.

"So how is the world of lawyering?" I said. "Have you turned into Ally McBeal yet?"

She shook her head sadly.

"I still feel let down – it was the only reason I became a lawyer. But when I got there nobody wanted to do karaoke and nobody wanted to have sex on a desk or lick my wattle."

We both laughed, knowing this was half-true – Ally McBeal really was Julia's inspiration for being a lawyer.

"It's good to see you – I missed this," I said. I took a mouthful of soup and winced as it burnt my tongue.

"Me too," she replied.

"So is this a regular haunt?"

"Yeah, it's good for lunches – and by the way, this is on me. Or rather, on Hall & Turner."

I picked up my glass of wine.

"Well here's to Hall & Turner."

Julia chinked and we both drank.

Half an hour later we both had our mains of salmon and a refilled glass in front of us, and I'd filled in Julia on my heartbreak. She was stoic about the whole situation, claiming I'd had a lucky escape discovering Karen's spinelessness so early on.

"It could have happened five years in and then you'd have felt much worse. Better to get it out of the way within the first year if it's going to happen, right?"

"Is that looking on the bright side?" I said.

"No such thing as a bad experience, just an experience," she said, a sage look on her face.

"So says the woman who's never had her heart broken."

"I've read books!" Julia said. She paused to take a swig of wine.

"By the way, have you heard about Maria?"

"*Maria* Maria?" I said.

"The very same."

"No. What?"

"Pregnant."

"What?" I almost shrieked, before recalling where we were. "But she hates kids!"

"Not anymore."

"I can't believe it." I shook my head, disbelief coating my mouth. "I at least thought she'd get the other one to do the dirty work. Still not tempted?"

"To be a lesbian or have kids? I think Tom would say no to both, unless he could watch of course."

Myself and Julia had always been steadfast in our ambition to avoid having children, if for very different reasons. Julia was a lifelong child-phobe and so had spent her entire adult life pumped full of hormones designed to stop the joining together of her eggs and any errant sperm. Injections, IUDs, pills – you name it, she'd used it.

For me, the story was more one of 'it's not likely to happen by accident and I haven't met anyone who's changed that view'. Our lives had continued on a path of spare income, dinner parties, nights out and weekends away with no thought given to babysitters or child-friendly venues.

"Anyway, back to you and your single status – I have a woman for you and she's perfect!"

I thought about Lucy from the pub the other night and wondered if she'd be as perfect as her, but then put her out of my mind and forced myself to concentrate on the here and now. Besides, she'd probably meet the woman of her dreams in Oz and decide to stay there for good. She might even meet Karen. Oh god, don't let her meet Karen...

"Hello? Earth to Jess?" Julia was snapping her fingers in front of my face.

"Sorry," I said. I put myself firmly back in the room.

"I was talking about setting you up on a hot date with the perfect woman and you drift off..."

"Didn't you say that about the last two?" I said.

"This one is for real though. Tom and I both fancy her but we're leaving her for you."

"For a supposedly straight woman, you know an awful lot of single dykes."

"She's not a dyke, honey – she's a lesbian."

"The difference being?"

"About 50 grand a year."

"I'm a dyke right now then," I said.

"It's fine – everyone likes a bit of rough every now and again. As for knowing so many, what can I say? Moths to a flame, I'm like a lesbian pied piper. Perhaps they're all drawn to something they know they can't have," she said.

When it came to lesbians Julia certainly did seem to be some sort of siren, towing along a never-ending conga line of ladies all willing and eager. I wasn't complaining, though – if she considered them a prospect and the timing was right, she set me up with them instead.

Julia had succeeded twice with me. Once with a mind-blowing three-night-stand with a Kiwi named Helen; and once with a two-month fling with Gwen, who claimed to be a Russian princess. Gwen was so tall she kept banging her head on my doorframe every time she left my bed to go to the loo.

On the plus side, mine and Julia's taste in women was astoundingly similar so I trusted her judgement – looks-wise at least. Personality-wise, she'd got it wrong on a couple of occasions but her batting average was still fairly healthy. After all, I'd never have shagged a princess if it hadn't been for Julia.

* * *

Later that day after a slightly boozy lunch, I was once again left to my own devices in the big city. Julia hadn't left before booking me in to meet up with her new matchmaking prospect who was called Angela. I'd baulked at the name but she'd assured me she wasn't like Angela from our school who used to stutter and pick her nose in class.

"As far away as can be – open-mindedness is the key," she told me. Easy for her to say. "Plus, Ange is a lawyer," Julia added. "So if nothing else, think of the money, honey."

Chapter Ten

After a slightly more prolonged time in the family bosom than intended – nearly two months since I landed – I was finally settled into Kate's flat. Mum had been a little teary at my parting but had sent me on my way with fresh crockery and a cake – everything a girl needs.

So now I had a room of my own – Virginia Woolf would be proud. The next task was to find a job, which wasn't proving as easy as I'd imagined. Adam's offer was lurking in the back of my mind and I was close to calling – two months into my London resurgence and I was growing weary. Still, at least the weather conditions had stopped being quite as arctic and spring was showing signs of coming to life, with our next-door neighbour's window box housing some stunted mini-Daffodils. Not quite a riot of yellow but a gentle hint at what was to come.

Plus, by my reckoning Lucy should be just about home by now. I decided to give her some space to settle back into life but hoped she'd been looking forward to seeing me as much as I'd been thinking about her. She'd sent me a couple of texts from Sydney telling me about her bar and sunshine-filled exploits. However, when you don't know someone that well, it's difficult to strike the perfect text-flirt balance, especially when the texts came through when I was just going to bed and vice versa. I hoped that now we were back in the same time zone things might progress.

I was pondering this while heading home after a walk in the park when I saw an ad in a café round the corner from the flat advertising for staff. It was one of those cool, bright and airy cafés that were springing up all over London, even offering flat whites for all our Aussie friends.

There were around eight wooden tables, an abundance of natural light dancing in through enormous windows and local artists exhibiting on the walls. Chalked specials above the counter announced Thai Salmon and Asian Veg, home-made quiche & salad, mushroom & asparagus frittata, as well as baguettes, cakes and pastries displayed on metal and china cake stands under domed plastic casings. Surely working in a café was better than working in an office all day?

Before I knew what I was doing I was pushing the door open. Five minutes later I was sitting down on a comfortable wooden chair with a cup of tea opposite the owner, Matt. It turned out Matt also used to work in an office until it all got too much for him, so he used his redundancy payout last year to open Porter's.

"There was nowhere round here that I'd want to go for lunch, so I thought I'd open my own place," he said. He fiddled with the empty sugar packets that he'd just stirred into his tea.

Tall, fair and almost handsome, Matt was the kind of bloke my mum had had in mind for me since birth. He had a full head of wavy hair which was unusual in men over 30 and I put Matt at around the 35 range.

Rather than being an interview, our chat turned into a counselling session as I poured out my tales of workplace woe and how the thought of going back into an office filled me with dread.

"I got back from Australia two months ago and I've been applying for tons of office jobs, but if I actually got one I think I might feel a bit sick," I said, screwing up my face.

"So don't get one," Matt said, leaning back in his chair

and smiling at me. "Have you ever worked in a café before?"

"No, but I worked in pubs when I was a student and I really enjoyed that."

Suddenly, all my doubts about getting a job melted away. Taking this, I wouldn't have to be a commuter, work in an office or call Adam. Even the thought of telling my mum that her graduate daughter was working in a café didn't put me off.

"Well you seem sane and I need someone who can start straight away – how about a trial tomorrow?" Matt said, crossing his strong arms across his chest.

"Sounds great."

Matt beamed.

"Triffic. I should get back." He flicked his head towards the counter before standing up and we shook hands.

"Glad you came in," he said. "See you tomorrow – 7 o'clock?"

I gulped down the shock of the early start time.

"See you then."

* * *

Working with Matt turned out to be better than I could have ever imagined – even the early mornings didn't deter me, plus they were balanced by finishing mid-afternoon. It helped that I only had to get out of bed at 6.45am, being able to walk to the café in two minutes, and also that I could eat breakfast when I was there.

Matt and I clicked from the first day and doing something practical was a welcome change from staring at a computer screen all day long. This was real life and seeing people come in for their morning coffee and gearing themselves up for the day ahead made me glad I wasn't doing the same.

The only caveat was that I wasn't making the salary I

was used to – in fact, I wasn't making a salary at all, instead getting paid weekly in a brown envelope in a similar manner to when I was 15. But with some savings still intact this job was perfect for now, and the fact I wasn't dreading getting up for work more than made up for the shortfall of cash. Well, almost.

On the plus side, my cooking skills were coming on a treat and my customer service was second to none. Kate was astounded when I told her, but also slightly envious that I'd stepped off the treadmill.

"So I could come in and you could make me a bacon sandwich?" she said. She was leaning on the kitchen doorframe, chewing the inside of her cheek.

"If you paid me £3, absolutely."

"I might just do that. Do you get to make coffee too?"

"Yep – espresso, Americano, latte, the lot."

"I've always found that strangely alluring – all that banging, refilling, slotting and pouring." She enacted doing just that with her hands while she stood there. I frowned.

"You're weird, you know that don't you?"

"It's been said before."

* * *

The daily routine involved either serving coffee and breakfasts at the counter or preparing the daily lunch menu. Matt got into work every day at 6am to get the breakfasts cooked and assembled – we didn't offer a full fry-up but rather fruit, porridge, pastries and bacon or sausage baps with or without eggs. But what people wanted most was a coffee to wake themselves up and kick-start their morning. Suddenly, I was the queen of the kick-start – who would have thought it?

For the first week, Matt had me serving customers, making coffees and heating food – not too taxing. He also employed his cousin Beth throughout the week, who rocked up from 8am–2pm to tend the counter too.

While Matt was tall, Beth was short and round but carried her excess weight well. She had brown hair that she tied into a ponytail and never sat still – a constant bustler as my mum would say. My mum liked bustlers. Matt also had an army of part-time non-related hired help who wafted in and out on a rota system that was a mystery to me but it seemed to work. Most were mothers who wanted extra money and café hours suited them perfectly.

The height of the rush was from 12.45pm for an hour, where queues often snaked around the side of the whitewashed building, people coming to eat inside or take out in our New York-style brown cardboard food boxes. Matt had not only done a great job with the food but also with the packaging and, after only a little time working there, I must admit to a strange pride at the loyal customer-base he'd built up.

Porter's also attracted a clutch of Polish workmen from a nearby building site and seeing them eating their quiche and salad or home-made soup amused me no end, bucking my builders stereotyping with some style. They were also always unfailingly polite, which is more than could be said for some of the office workers.

Beth and Matt knew them all by name and Beth had taken a particular shine to Artur the site foreman, who was all muscles and sandy hair with a twinkly smile. Every time he came in she scuttled out the back looking for some important item, which Matt and I teased her endlessly about.

Beth was stern in her defence that she had no idea what we were talking about and that it was a good job somebody round here handled the job with some professionalism and didn't behave like schoolchildren all the time. We weren't fooled, though.

Chapter Eleven

After a week of working at Porter's I was surprised to find I was getting to know the customers – those who came in before 7.30am, those who rushed in late at 8.45am, those who came for lunch early at 12.20pm or breathless at 2pm. By Friday of the first full week I was also dead on my feet – another thing about working in a café is that it keeps you moving constantly. I had been pondering joining a gym when I could afford it but now it felt like I might not need to.

Beth didn't head off at 2pm on Friday, instead popping into the kitchen to whip up a batch of her banana and carrot cakes for the beginning of the following week. Matt and I ate together, shutting the café doors slightly early at 3pm and discarding our aprons for coffee, minestrone soup and wedges of bread.

"So how's your first full week been?" Matt said. He dipped his bread and licked the drips from the side.

"Exhausting," I said. I mirrored his bread movements, eating quickly as I was famished.

"Being on your feet all day does that to you. But I still prefer it to sitting all day." He paused. "Do you fancy a pint after we shut up here? My treat – staff morale and all that. It's normally just me and Beth, but now we're expanding..."

"Sounds great," I said. "And you have to give me the recipe for this soup."

"Trade secret," he winked.

We decamped to the local pub at around 4.30pm but it was already filled with swathes of office workers glugging back pints of lager and glasses of wine, their volume getting louder as the afternoon wore on. We managed to get a seat in the corner and Matt got the beers in, proposing a toast when he was back sitting with us.

"To our new team – welcome, Jess!"

We all chinked pint glasses but, instead of drinking, Beth put hers down, feeling in her pocket for a tissue.

"Drink!" I said. "If you cheers and then don't drink, it's seven years' bad sex."

Beth immediately grabbed her pint and gulped down a mouthful.

"Even bad sex would be preferable to no sex so I don't want to jeopardise my chances of either," she said. "And where are the crisps, Matt?"

"We just ate lunch," he said. A sigh.

"An hour ago," Beth said. She tapped her watch and tutted. "God, you're a rubbish boss," she added over her shoulder as she got up, her grin wide. "No no, you stay there, I'll get them..."

"My mum warned me to never work with family," Matt said. He flicked some imaginary dirt from his jeans. "So are you out tonight?"

"Not sure – I might tag along with my flatmate somewhere. You?"

"Nah – I have to get up early tomorrow to get the food order for next week and then I've got my son overnight."

"Son?" I repeated.

"Yeah, Charlie – he's six."

Matt fished out his iPhone from his jeans, tapped the photo icon and up popped an image of his son.

"This is his school photo from last year – he's a bit bigger now."

"He's lovely," I said. I leant in to see a gap-toothed Charlie grinning back at me, his brown hair cut slightly wonky at the front.

"Is that my little Charlie?" asked Beth. She put two packets of crisps on the table, one salt and vinegar, one cheese and onion.

"I wasn't sure what you liked so I got a mix," she told me. "Are you seeing him this weekend?" she said, turning her attention to Matt.

Beth sat astride a stool and ripped opened the salt and vinegar, carefully tearing the packet down its spine to open it out flat on the table so the crisps were easily accessible.

"Tomorrow," Matt said.

"Do you want me in then?"

He shook his head. "Nope – he wants to do some baking so I'm going to take him in and do a bit myself."

"Okey doke," Beth said, putting another handful of crisps into her mouth and not waiting for them all to evaporate before addressing me.

"So is this one of your locals?" she said. A crisp part whizzed past my left ear and I pretended not to notice.

"Not really – I haven't lived here long enough for a local. Could be a contender, though."

"Serves beer and crisps but it could do without quite so many of the city idiots," she said.

"Don't knock them, without them we'd be out of business," Matt said.

Beth made a 'humph' noise, then took another sip of her pint before fixing me with an inquisitive stare.

"So Jess, any boyfriend?"

"Beth!" said Matt. "At least wait until the second pint." He shot me an apologetic look. "Sorry, she's not known for her subtlety."

"What?" Beth said, rolling her eyes. "I was only taking

an interest in our new staff member and I've held back all week which is a miracle in itself I'm sure you'll agree." She paused.

"So, any boyfriend?"

I shook my head.

"Girlfriend?"

At that Matt grimaced and put his hand up to his forehead, shaking his head. Beth slapped his arm in rebuke.

"Matt. We're all enlightened adults here. And you might be very set in your ways and dating purely the opposite sex but that's not for everyone. I've been thinking about maybe trying women lately – men certainly haven't done it for me so far. Anyway, off the point – girlfriend?" she asked me with a fixed stare.

This was the moment I always expect whenever I met new people – the ever-rolling coming out process. Straight until proven innocent. At least Beth was making it pretty easy for me and she seemed like she'd be positively upset if I told her no. I didn't like upsetting people. A thought of Lucy briefly flitted across my brain but I quickly dismissed proclaiming her as my girlfriend, seeing as we'd met once, texted three times and had yet to kiss. The definition of a girlfriend she was not, especially as I still hadn't worked up the courage to call her or vice versa.

"Not at the moment," I said. I blushed despite myself.

"You see!" Beth said. She put both palms on her thighs and leant back smiling.

"Am I that obvious?"

"Not really – just a hunch. And well, if I fancy lurching to the other side I know where to get some tips don't I?"

"I wouldn't take any tips from me. I don't have a girlfriend, remember?"

"Join the club," Matt said. He looked glum. "Perhaps we should start speed-dating in the café during the evenings.

Free slice of carrot cake for every punter who gets off with one of the staff. Definite winner I reckon."

* * *

Later that evening back at the flat, I heaved a box up onto the bed and sliced it open with some scissors, cursing as I cut the top of my right index finger. Inside was Australian stuff: letters, photos and accessories, including a beautiful purple glass fruit bowl that Karen had bought me for my 31st. I'd dithered as to whether or not to bring it home but it was something I'd coveted for weeks before I opened it and so I was resolved to cleanse it of any Karen association through use and love.

I put it on my chest of drawers for now, then opened a pack of photos that showed Karen and I on a weekend away in Melbourne, arms around each other on St Kilda beach in the summer sun. Although the photos looked idyllic and still made my heart lurch as I looked at Karen's tanned face and stunning blue eyes, I knew that later on that evening we'd had a huge row at a restaurant after Karen decided to flirt outrageously with the waitress.

It wasn't an isolated incident, either – our rows had been getting deeper, longer and more constant towards the end of our relationship and it wasn't until a few months later that I knew what had changed. I put the photos back in the pack, considered throwing them out but then thought better of it. I wasn't quite ready yet. It was now nearly seven months since the split and I felt almost cleansed of Karen, but not quite.

Chapter Twelve

A few weeks later the weather changed and only for the better. It was mid-April, so still spring, but it felt like an early summer's Saturday – the last two days had been alight with heat. Pavements cracked, plants withered, hosepipes snapped into life as their owners swung them around their gardens rodeo-style.

This morning had begun with a torrential downpour though, which was typical seeing as this was the start of the weekend. All week long I'd been staring out the window as the sun bounced along the street shaking hands and ruffling hair; now it was rain that was stinging the pavements and dampening spirits. However, the forecast was for sun later and as I breathed in the smell of warm, damp tarmac through the windows of the flat I knew that would be true – the wet was temporary.

I pulled my duvet cover up the bed and jumped in the shower, using some fancy new shower gel that Kate had bought recently that smelt of lemons. After a leisurely breakfast I dressed and headed to Porter's to whip up some delights for the early part of the week ahead – it was my turn for the Saturday baking, which I'd come to love.

I was also planning to use the time to make a dessert to take to Julia's for my blind date later. She'd called earlier in the week while I was gulping down some fresh air outside the café, pondering life. It was at times like those I wished I smoked, then at least I could puff away while contemplating and look a bit French and deep in thought. I was stubbing out my imaginary cigarette just as my phone went. It was Julia.

"Hello, it's me – where are you?"

"Being contemplative."

"Oh dear – what's up?"

"Don't ask," I said. So she didn't.

"Okay. Well I have some news to brighten your day. Remember Angela?" Her tone had risen as if she was on a children's TV show.

"My future wife – how could I forget?" I leant back, putting the sole of my foot flat against the wall of the cafe.

"She's coming to dinner on Saturday and so are you. Me and Tom, Jason and Andy, you and Ange." I could hear the note of triumph in her voice – Julia loved it when a plan came together.

"You're too modern, Jules: straight, gay and lesbian couples. Shouldn't you chuck in a tranny and a bi couple to complete the set?" I said.

"That's next weekend. Besides, we can only seat six at the table. So are you on?"

"Do I have a choice?"

I pushed myself off the wall and stretched my neck into the sunshine.

"I'm offering you a hot lesbian – can you afford to turn me down?"

"If I did would it make any difference?" I asked.

"Stop answering questions with questions." She paused. "Shall we say 6, then? Then we can have a chat before everyone else descends."

"Sounds perfect."

"See you then, hot stuff." And with that, she was gone.

* * *

So here I was with live football screeching out of the digital radio Matt had recently bought for the kitchen, with a batch of chocolate, coffee & walnut and lemon drizzle cakes on the go. Working in the café sans customers and anyone else was strangely alluring, like sneaking back into the office when nobody was there. I resisted the urge to strip naked and run around – this always worked better in films and sitcoms than in reality – and baked methodically instead.

Baking was something I'd discovered a talent for and whoever knew it was so therapeutic? All this time I'd been trying yoga and pilates, when really what I'd needed was butter, eggs, flour, sugar and an oven. I mixed together the flour, sugar, baking powder and bicarbonate, whipped up the eggs and melted the chocolate in a glass bowl over low-bubbling water, marvelling as I always did as it dissolved into a puddle of silky brown gloss.

I allowed myself a brief fantasy about licking some from a pair of pert breasts – perhaps Lucy's? – but then realised that would involve getting chocolate in places I'd rather not. In my experience, sex and food rarely mixed in a fun, clean way, or perhaps I was just a little bit anal. I wondered again about Lucy: was she back from Sydney yet and had she had a good time? I hoped so but not too great, obviously.

When the chocolate was glossy, I folded all the ingredients in together, pausing to wipe some residue mixture on the Wonder Woman apron Matt had bought me the week before. A couple of hours later and all the cakes were sitting obediently on their wire perches like show dogs at Crufts.

It was after lunchtime and I heard my stomach rumbling so I decided to make myself a sandwich and a coffee, taking it through to the counter so I could sit down while eating. This always confused passers-by as they could never work out if this meant the café was open or not. My plan was to keep my head down and shake it sorrowfully at any hopeful knocking on the glass. Today, I was not open for business. Not until later at least.

I settled myself at the counter with my chicken sandwich and latte, licking my index finger to turn the page of yesterday's paper. An engine's roar made me look up briefly as a huge lorry rumbled past Porter's making the café door vibrate in its lock. When its long body slithered from view, I was astonished to find myself looking directly at Lucy who was walking past the front window oblivious to my stare. She had no idea I worked here and I instinctively picked up the paper to cover my face.

But Lucy wasn't alone. She was walking along the path with another woman, smiling and chatting. The woman, who was not unattractive with long blonde hair, leaned in and said something to Lucy. She threw back her head laughing. I felt winded. It was as if someone was filming them purely for my benefit but this was one vignette I didn't particularly want to see.

I dropped the paper, realising they weren't looking in my direction. My neck turned with a heavy crunch as I followed Lucy and her plus one walking down the street, arms now linked. Perhaps that's why she hadn't called. We had only met once after all, but I hadn't forgotten her. Perhaps the feeling wasn't reciprocated. My face fell into a frown. Perhaps she'd met the love of her life in Sydney who just happened to live in London and here they were, doing that couple thing on a Saturday of walking around the city looking smug.

I'd lost my appetite and pushed away the second half of my sandwich, chewing on my bottom lip. I might be jumping to conclusions but then again, my eyes could normally be trusted. I felt the hot stab of disappointment.

* * *

Back home, I got down to ironing my party shirt for the evening ahead, not quite managing to vanquish the image of Lucy and her mystery woman from my mind. While I was getting ready, the phone went.

"Any job news yet?" It was my mum. She sounded breezy.

"I've got a job, I told you."

"Yes, but a proper job," she said. Her tone had now changed to that special type she reserved for telling off her children.

"This is my proper job for now."

"But you've got a degree…"

"That'll get me a job in sales and I am all out of sales pitches. Besides, I like this job." I began to chew my left thumbnail.

"What kind of café is it? And are you cooking? I just never saw you in a café. Is it like on EastEnders?" I could hear the frown in her question.

"Not quite. It's just around the corner, run by a lovely guy, sells posh quiche and cake."

"What's his name?"

"Who?"

"The fella."

"Matt. He's from Guildford. Makes a mean cheesecake."

"Is he single?" she asked. Her excitement at me spending all my days with an eligible straight man was barely concealed.

"He is. 35, solvent, own business and hair. So if you know of any single ladies, throw them my way and I'll sort them out."

There was a pause on the other end of the line as she took in the fact I wasn't including myself in that category.

"I'll bear that in mind," she said. Vaguely contrite.

"Actually, I'm being set up tonight with a lawyer." Where had that come from?

"Oh – what's his name?" Scrap contrite.

"Angela. You do remember I'm gay, right?"

"I was just joking," she said. She wasn't. "Where's that then?"

"Julia and Tom's."

She spent the next few minutes waxing lyrical about Julia and Tom, declaring them a "super couple". During her cascade of words I was able to select my jeans and shoes for the evening and unpack a bag of toiletries I'd bought on the way home.

"What's rustling?" she said.

"Nothing," I lied. I walked from the bathroom to my bedroom and opened my wardrobe.

"When are they getting married?"

"June."

"You'll have to remind me to send a card. Dave and Vera's daughter married Gary Holmes last weekend – do you remember him from school?"

"No." I sighed.

"I'm sure he was in your year," she said. "Anyway, she looked lovely."

"I'm sure she did." I wondered if she picked up on my sarcasm. "Listen Mum, I have to get ready."

More sighing.

"Send Julia my love. Are you coming for dinner tomorrow?"

"No. Kate and I have the boys and we're taking them to the zoo."

"Ooh, lovely. Say hi to Kate. A Sunday soon then?"

"I'll call to confirm." I selected some socks from my top drawer.

"Make sure you do – and bring Kate too!"

Maybe she did fancy Kate.

Chapter Thirteen

I arrived at Julia's bang on six to be greeted by Tom flicking one of the corks on his sunhat, worn in my honour.

"To make you feel at home, Sheila," he said. He leant in and kissed me on my right cheek so that I felt the bristle of his stubble. When Julia had met Tom at university ten years ago he'd had a full head of hair but now his brown thatch was decidedly thinning. In my absence he'd also put on some weight which he was hiding well with a black T-shirt, but he was still the same warm, welcoming Tom.

"So have you met this woman I'm being paired up with tonight?" I said. I kissed Julia from behind as she was busy de-veining a bowl of prawns with some cocktail sticks. I screwed up my face at the sight – I loved eating shellfish but not so much the preparation.

Julia was ready for the evening in green trousers and white shirt, covered right now with a black apron. I could tell from the way her dark hair was still a little static that she was fresh out of the shower and recently coiffured.

"No, but I've seen a photo and she looks just your type – tits, breathing, you know," he said. "You look lovely by the way," he added to appease me, which worked a treat as I accepted an ice cold bottle of Stella from him.

"He's right – you look very presentable," Julia added. She turned to appraise my jeans and posh shirt combo fully, before nudging the tap with her right wrist and rinsing her hands.

"Suitably lesbian but not too dykey?"

"What's the difference?" Tom said, picking a bit of stray food from his bare foot and then grabbing the counter for balance.

"She's going to be wowed," Julia said. I hoped so, because my Plan A was probably making dinner with her new blonde-haired squeeze right now. I sighed anew but then slapped my mind back into the present and hoped that Julia's comment proved to be true.

I spent the next hour and a half watching Tom and Julia expertly doing the dinner party waltz, preparing prawn cocktails, lamb rack, veg and dauphinoise while also preening their table until it looked like it had just stepped out of the pages of a glossy magazine. I pondered on the fact they were so grown up while I was, well, not, but then decided I had to get into the headspace of being Mrs Available & Attractive for my date. Attention.

While they prepared, I drank and chatted which meant that by the time the doorbell went signalling the next guests, I was a touch squiffy. I ran to the loo to check my hair and ensure that none of Tom's crostini had taken up residence in my front teeth. They hadn't. I heard Tom greeting male voices, so rushed out of the loo to say hi to Andy and Jason, a gay couple I'd spent many an evening being fed and watered with.

"You're back!" squealed Andy, kissing both cheeks before holding me at arm's length. "Looking gorgeous too, you fox!"

I loved Andy, he always said the right thing even if it was a total lie. He once told me he loved my hair and I believed him until I realised we were speaking on the telephone.

"Another set-up for you tonight, Jess," said Jason. He followed up with a double kiss. "Let's hope she's as good as the last one – I could do with a laugh."

Andy and Jason had been together as long as I could remember and they were Julia's go-to gay couple. Apparently they hadn't always looked like each other but as tends to happen after a while they'd now managed to morph into one goateed, dark-haired whole, both with flat stomachs, pressed jeans and shiny shoes. They also both owned a ridiculously sharp sense of humour and spent most of the evening laughing at one another's jokes. Truly a match made in heaven.

"I'll bring the champagne out as soon as Ange arrives – she's running a bit late," Julia said. She ushered us into the lounge.

We all sat down on the dark grey sofas as Tom came in carrying cold beers to accompany the nibbles, then he rushed out again in a blur. In between the boys arriving, Tom had changed into a grey shirt with black piping, very on-trend. Jason moved a coaster along the coffee table towards me, knowing Tom would have a cardiac otherwise.

"So you," Andy said. He nudged me in the ribs. "How are you? How's being back?"

"It's good," I said, through a mouthful of crisps. "You know, challenging at first but I think it was the right move."

"But what happened with that girl? When we were round here last you were all set with some Aussie, Julia told us – TV exec?"

"I was…" I said. "But I'm not anymore."

"Well I guessed what with you being here," he replied.

"So is this move for good?" Jason asked.

I smiled. "Yep – you're stuck with me now, like it or not."

"I like! And now we can get back to normal after a break of a few years, right?" Andy said.

"Absolutely – what is a Saturday round here without me being on a blind date?"

"Not a fun one," said Jason.

Twenty minutes later the doorbell rang and I put down my Stella, ran my fingers through my hair and took a deep breath. I needn't have worried.

Ange turned out to be a hot brunette with cascading shiny shoulder-length hair and someone I would never approach in a million years. She was slim, just-so jeans, designer shirt and stilettos. Heels and jeans always made me flustered and tonight was no exception. I swallowed hard and shook her hand, gratified as I looked into her darting hazel eyes that she seemed just as nervous as me.

"I've heard a lot about you – Julia should go into PR," she said. I liked the feel of her hand – a firm handshake but soft, cared-for skin.

"Neither of you need any PR, the raw material's so good," Julia said. "Right, now that's the awkwardness out of the way. I just want you to know that I don't expect you to sleep together tonight but I do expect to be a witness at the wedding, okay?"

Ange laughed and I rolled my eyes, to which Julia looked thrilled.

"I'm glad we're in the same firm, Julia. With logic like that, I'd hate to come up against you in court," Ange said.

"Piff and paff," she replied, picking up a bottle. "Now then, champagne?"

* * *

My blind date turned out to be witty and good company, laughing at my jokes, refilling my glass and having a sense of humour about her chosen profession. She managed to charm the boys as well as me and made all the right noises about my chocolate cake when it came to dessert, declaring she'd always fancied dating a chef – "sex and food on tap, what more do you need?" I blushed, which Julia took great satisfaction in pointing out.

One thing Julia hadn't mentioned though and I was sure she would have noticed was that Ange had one distinct drawback – her voice was shrill with a matching laugh that reverberated around my skull longer than it should.

I knew after the first sentence when her voice soared through the octaves with excitement while she was chuckling at a well-known TV advert that anything that transpired between us would not be permanent. I like to talk and I like to listen, but not to such a piercing cry as hers. My inner judgement had already decreed this was a non-starter. Shame, because she was hot. It looked like Plan A and Plan B were out the window and I'd have to come up with a Plan C. I hoped we wouldn't have to chug too far through the alphabet until I hit the magic letter.

We moved on to the cheese course, Tom fetching the port to go with it. Jason asked what we'd score the evening if it was on Come Dine With Me. Unanimously we all plumped for 10, apart from Tom who said we were all far too polite and a ten needed a constant flow of champagne all night long.

He fished out some Spanish brandy to round off the consumption and offered the boys cigars. They declined, but Julia and I grabbed them, plonked Tom next to Ange and made our excuses. Once outside, Julia was almost bursting with excitement.

"So?" she said. She grinned and was hopping from foot to foot while also pulling on her cardigan to shield her from the breeze. The barmy day had turned into a typically frigid night and the wind seemed to possess teeth, biting us through our skimpy attire.

"Do you like her?"

I lit my cigar and sucked, then coughed abruptly.

"Are you really going to smoke that? I thought it was just so we could go outside and have a sneaky chat," Julia said. She looked pained.

"Good point," I said, coughing some more. "Looks cool though, doesn't it?"

Julia slapped my arm.

"I didn't think anyone actually smoked cigars?"

"They don't. Just idiots like me." Still coughing, face turning red.

"Stop avoiding the question!"

"Er, in case you hadn't noticed, I'm dying here."

"Well die a bit quicker so you can answer please," Julia said.

"What was the question again?" My eyes were streaming now.

"Jess..."

I eventually stopped coughing and gulped in the fresh air, its chill searing my throat. I was going to have to check my make-up on the way back in too.

"God. Yes, she's great. Perfect even. Apart from..."

Julia raised an eyebrow.

"Apart from?"

I looked a bit sheepish and put the cigar to my lips again.

"What are you doing?" shrieked Julia. She swatted it away.

"You know," I said. I nudged her arm with my elbow.

"No, I don't. I mean, she's sexy, well off and she's clearly into you. What am I missing?"

I pushed myself heavily off the wall and sighed.

"Her laugh."

"Her laugh?"

"And her voice. They're a little shrill don't you think?"

"I knew you might think that..."

I shrugged. "But she is hot, you were right on that one."

"So a non-starter?"

"Depends if she talks while she's having sex."

"You're such a bloke sometimes," she said. She slapped my arm and feigned outrage unsuccessfully.

"Pot, kettle," I replied.

"And there was me thinking this was a sure thing."

"Never say never."

We both shivered.

"Anyhow, can we go in now, I'm cold," she said. Disappointment coated every word. "You never know, though – I don't think it's a deal-breaker…"

"We'll see," I said. I kissed her cheek, stopping en route to make sure I didn't look like a drowned panda. I didn't – turns out waterproof means waterproof. When we went back in we found Tom in the kitchen lining up cocktail glasses on the counter.

"I was thinking espresso martinis?" he said. He had a cocktail shaker in one hand, vodka in the other.

"And this is why I'm marrying you." Julia squeezed him from behind.

"I take it we all want one?" he asked, looking at me.

"I might want three but we'll start with one," I said. Tom grinned.

From the lounge we heard Soft Cell's *Tainted Love* get cranked up and Andy and Jason singing at the top of their voices. Julia and I exchanged grins and went to investigate.

* * *

Two hours later we were three martinis and a vat of tequila down and putting the world to rights. The Middle East, religion, The X Factor, psychologists and noisy neighbours were just some of the topics that had been covered in-depth, along with the impressiveness of my cakes which Ange was keen to labour.

"That was, honestly, the best cake ever," she kept repeating, looking into my eyes. I knew it was the booze but suddenly her voice didn't seem quite so grating. Now, all I could hear were her eyes, her neck, her breasts sitting perkily in her shirt.

Julia came back into the room from the kitchen and sat in Tom's lap, looking suitably glazed. I put my hand on her knee and looked at her fondly.

"And after all our chat, we haven't even talked about the most important thing," I said, rubbing her knee. "Your wedding! And you too, Tommy. I mean, fuck! How did that happen?"

"I dunno man," Tom said. "One minute we're just Tom and Julia, the next we're going to be man and wife. Scary stuff. Give us a few years and we'll have two kids and a station wagon."

"For some reason, every time Tom talks about having kids he turns American. It's an estate car darling," Julia said. "Besides, they'll be no children here, remember."

"Oh I remember," he said, putting his arms around Julia's waist. "It's just, I have this recurring dream that once we're married, we're suddenly going to start producing children against our will – it's just something that's going to happen and we won't be able to help it."

"Tom's convinced I'm going to turn into some kind of Stepford wife and we'll move to an American suburb where all I want to do is iron and all he wants to do is mow the lawn and play with power drills. I put it down to an overdose of American films and dramas." Julia raised her hand to ruffle Tom's hair and he leant into her embrace.

"It could be worse – at least he's not watching Shameless," Ange said.

"Oh I watch that. I just choose my fantasies carefully," Tom said.

"Well if you do pop out a couple, be sure to name them all-American names too," Ange said. "Brad, Maddy, Chip, that sort of thing."

The thought of children made Julia shudder and Tom pulled her close, kissing her left shoulder as he did.

"You've got so many contraceptives pumping through you babe that nothing could get through," he said.

The music changed from some hip new group to Duran Duran's *Rio*, which made us all look over at Jason standing by the iPod.

"Sorry, couldn't resist – final chance to dance!" he said, sweeping Andy off his feet and into the middle of the lounge.

"One for the road?" Julia said. It was a statement not a question as she picked up the tequila and poured us all another shot. We slammed at speed then, clearly energised, Ange got up too and yanked me out of my chair to dance. Julia joined us too and I looked over at Tom who was sat back taking it all in, a contented smile on his face.

Three songs later, the tequila had been drunk and the clock had edged itself around to nearly 3am. Ange didn't want to leave the dance floor though and twirled me into Julia, who tumbled into Jason and Andy and there was a smash as a wine glass was dislodged from the table. We all twirled, stopped and held our breath.

"It's fine everyone, carry on!" trilled Julia over the music. "Just mind the glass."

Tom was down on his hands and knees picking up the larger pieces and Andy turned on the top light and joined him. Ange, however, took Julia at her word and put her other hand around my waist, turning my body into a slow dance against the music, our breasts touching, our thighs in hot proximity.

Close up, she was around 4 inches taller than me in heels, with glossy hair and fantastic lips that smiled down at me. I accidentally kicked Andy, still on his haunches collecting stray glass, as my concentration went walkabout as a consequence of being railroaded by Ange. Perhaps Julia was right – if she didn't open her mouth she'd be almost perfect.

The boys all scurried out to the kitchen with the glass in their hands, leaving Ange and I alone in the lounge. She pulled me closer then twirled me away, like we were a couple on Strictly Come Dancing. Then she spun me back and as I landed against her warm body I felt a familiar jolt between my legs. High pitch or not, my libido was kicking in because a tall, attractive stranger was dancing with me.

If we'd been in a club I guarantee you we'd have been snogging by now. I think the same thought crossed her mind as she realised where we were and we both pulled back, the bright overhead lights of the lounge becoming too glaring. Out of sight, we could hear the others clearing up in the kitchen.

"And then there were two," I said. My voice was husky and I was aware of the electricity in the air.

"It seems that way," she said. "I think that might be a natural end to the evening anyway, what with it being nearly three o'clock." Her eyes were slightly bloodshot. "We live the same way. Fancy sharing a taxi?" Here was an invitation.

"Sounds good," I said. We both shared another conspiratorial smile and then picked up some glasses from the table to busy ourselves and break the moment. In the kitchen, the three boys were stacking the dishwasher, with Julia sitting on the black counter-top dangling her feet.

"No more dancing?" she said. Her words were slurred.

"Simon said stop so we did. Anyway, we were thinking of ordering a cab – unless you need help here?"

"No, no, no, you go," Julia said, jumping down from her vantage point. "We've got this all covered haven't we boys?"

General murmurs of agreement from the boys as Tom brushed past us with a hand-held hoover to deal with the breakage.

I went to retrieve the coats from Julia's bedroom, who hastily followed me in while dialling a taxi on her mobile. She shut the door just as she was connected.

"Yes, hello. Can I order a cab from Braemar Road please? Yes. Going to..." Julia turned to me. "Going to?" she said.

"Going to my flat and then to Angela's who lives in Stoke Newington – remember?"

"Going to Old Street, then Stoke Newington," she said into the handset. There was a brief pause. "Great, thanks." She clicked the red button. "Five minutes."

"Stop smirking at me like that."

"I'm not smirking. This is me being smug about one of my plans coming together."

"We're just sharing a cab because it makes sense, goddit?" I said.

"Uh-huh, whatever you say."

I opened the door. "Is this Ange's coat?" I asked, holding up a black jacket not too dissimilar to mine.

"I think so," Julia said.

I walked down the hall and handed the coat to Ange who was waiting in the kitchen doorway, chatting to Jason. Hugs, kisses and goodbyes followed, accompanied by more slurred smirks from a rather worse-for-wear Julia and then there really were just two.

As we walked out to the cab, the night air threw a blanket of chill over us and we both shivered as we hurried out of the gate and into the waiting taxi. Sitting next to each other, my breathing seemed very loud and laboured although it was probably just in my head. The sky outside was jet black as I looked upwards, the stars shrouded by clouds from the London gloom.

"It was a great night wasn't it?" Ange said. Her voice was still too shrill but that didn't stop me finding her attractive right now. For one brief second I wished it was Lucy sitting next to me but it wasn't so I had to live in the moment.

"Yeah, those guys can cook. The lamb was amazing."

"The chocolate cake wasn't bad either," she said.

I smiled at her and she put her hand on my leg, causing a frisson right up my body. It seemed the feeling was mutual.

The back seat suddenly seemed far too small for the two of us. I put my hand on top of hers and we exchanged a look as the cab turned into Old Street.

"Jason and Andy are great, too," Ange said, squeezing my hand. Squeaky, high-pitched still, but the booze still roaming my system wasn't listening. My mind was playing a game with my libido now. This was going nowhere, but it could tonight.

"Do you want to come up for a drink?" I said. I wasn't quite sure who was asking this daring question as the words slipped out of my mouth, but it seemed to be me.

"I'd love to," Ange replied. No hesitation. And with that, our fate for the night was sealed. The cab pulled up and I got out and paid the driver, waving away her offer of cash. I breathed in the fresh air as the taxi drove away, pulled the keys out of my jeans pocket and opened the door, ushering Ange in but also putting a finger to my lips as I did so.

"Flatmate," I whispered as she walked up the stairs in her slinky heels. She nodded and did exaggerated walking on her toes up the stairs, which caused me to giggle, then her, and before long we were making far more noise than I ever intended, she of course slightly more shrill.

I had a momentary battle with my conscience who was choosing this moment to point out that while I may be attracted to this woman, her voice and laugh repelled me. I tussled with the thought for a good few seconds before guiding her into my bedroom. I knew if we did the usual drink-and-sofa-foreplay my conscience would never shut up. Right there and then, Ange had willingly come home with me and it had been a long time since that happened.

"I really want you," she said, pushing me onto the bed. It was meant to be sexy I know, but once again, the voice jarred in my head. It was too late to pull back now, though – so said the rest of my body anyway.

Within moments we were naked, but the little voice in my

head wouldn't shut up. With every kiss to my breast, stomach, inner thigh and back they were silenced, but when I had to return the favour it resurfaced. I wondered when I'd become Ms Morality.

Ange seemed to be suffering no such qualms – when I slid my hands down her body, kissed her breasts and touched her she was wet and wide open for me – invitingly so. When I fucked her, which wasn't hard, she came within minutes, grinding against me before sitting up with me still inside her and thrusting her tongue into my mouth.

Nevertheless, when she laid her naked body on top of mine, I didn't say no. Neither did I try to stop her when she sucked my breasts, scratched my back, slapped my arse or buried her head between my legs. And I was powerless to stop the resulting orgasm when her fingers slid inside me and she played me like a pro. I didn't fake, I didn't have to. In that moment, she was perfect.

Chapter Fourteen

It was, of course, a different proposition when I awoke the following morning with a hangover, short on sleep and the prospect of a day at the zoo with Kate and my nephews in store. Ange was still asleep when my alarm went off at 10am and I managed to turn it off before she was disturbed. I wondered just how you went about evicting a gorgeous woman from your bed of a weekend morning without hurting her feelings or making yourself look like a complete and utter berk.

I reached over to my bedside table, wondering if Ange had thought me remiss not having a table and lamp for her, too. If she did, she hadn't said so. I had one text and knew it would be from Julia. I was correct.

'So – have we both woken up with a lawyer in our bed this morning?' She's so bloody clever that one. I sighed again and replaced my phone on the bedside table, managing to knock my keys off in the process which caused Ange to open her eyes, squinting at me and holding her head.

"Morning," she said. She rolled over and kissed my shoulder. "Ugh, my head."

"Morning," I replied. I realised what an impossible situation I'd got myself into and briefly wondered how many other people up and down the country this Sunday morning were waking up similarly. Perhaps I should start a Facebook support page for us drunken one-night standers, although I'm not sure the Daily Mail would completely get it.

London Calling

* * *

"So, last night was great, but the thing is, your voice and laugh are way too high-pitched for there to ever be anything between us. So while you're attractive – and I have to say, you really are – and you wear jeans and heels incredibly well, this is what it is. A one-night stand, pure and simple. I hope that's all right for you – I had a great time. But now I really have to throw you out because I'm taking my nephews to the zoo today. So would you mind leaving quickly? You can use the loo if you need to but a cup of tea is out of the question. We can keep in touch via Facebook if you like."

"Sure no problem, I completely understand. I'm going to voice therapy to try to lower my voice issue – should I call you if it's successful?"

"Absolutely! With that sorted I think we could have a great relationship."

"I'll let you know. Last night was amazing, thanks again."

We shake hands. The end.

* * *

This, of course, is not at all what happened next, but wouldn't it be a sane and great world if we could all be that honest and accepting? Instead, Ange tried to instigate conversation to which I was fairly mute. She looked confused and she had a right to be.

"Sorry, am I missing something here?" she asked. She propped herself up on her elbow, her breasts looking gorgeous in my bed and it took all my strength not to reach out and touch them.

"We had a great night, you invited me back, we had sex and now you're being, shall we say, a little frosty. You are single, right?" she said. Her eyes clouded over with doubt.

"Absolutely!" I said. Now it was my turn for my voice to go up an octave. "Single, young, free and... well, not so young, but you know."

"But now you're... not interested, is that it?"

"Well... it's not you," I began.

She put up her hand as if stopping traffic.

"You don't need to say anymore..." she said. She vaulted out of bed and began hastily putting on her pants, followed by her bra and shirt. She shook her head as she was doing so.

"You know, Julia says you're one of her best friends so I'm not sure why you'd do this to another of her friends."

"I'm... it's... I thought I was available. I really did enjoy last night and you're amazing..."

"Yes, I know – it's not me, it's you." She shot me a look. I deserved it.

"It really is. I just feel... I don't know. Maybe I'm not over my ex quite yet."

"Spare me the dyke drama."

She tried to put on her jeans but her co-ordination failed her. In trying to pull on one leg, she lost her balance and crashed into my wardrobe, putting out her hand to stop herself falling over. I looked down graciously but had to bite my inner cheek to try not to laugh. My sense of humour quite often didn't match the moment.

"Are you okay?"

"Fine," she muttered. She steadied herself, finally getting her jeans on and scooping up her watch and rings. "Is my coat in the lounge?"

"Yes – I'll get it for you."

I jumped out of bed realising this situation was turning into a car crash and that Julia would kill me when she found out. I got my dressing gown from the back of the door and threw it on hastily, aware that being naked was not what the occasion called for. As I went to open the door, I heard her take a deep breath.

"You know, for what it's worth I really liked you. We got on well and I thought that the sex, be it drunken, was a good start..."

She put her head down and breathed out heavily, her hair cascading, the wind suddenly knocked out of her sails. When she moved her head back up I could see tears glistening in her eyes. She reached up and tucked her hair behind her ear out of habit and breathed deeply to stop herself from crying. I felt awful and incredibly shallow. Injustice had a shape and a texture that now seemed to be weighing heavily on Ange's body.

"I'm really sorry," I said. Even I knew it sounded lame.

My stomach fizzed with despair and an acrid taste crept into my mouth, which I swallowed down. Maybe I wasn't as ready as I thought, starting to believe the web of lies that I'd spun. Or maybe I was just incredibly shallow and should never have invited Ange back if I was just going to reject her as I knew I would the following day. I hung my head in shame.

"I'm going to get my coat and go. See you around," she said.

She opened the door and walked down the hall and into the lounge where Kate was sitting watching TV in green shorts and a navy blue Gap sweatshirt.

"Hi," I heard Kate say as we walked in. Ange picked up her coat and looked at me, then back at Kate.

"This is my flatmate Kate," I said by way of one of the most awkward introductions in the history of the world. Kate though, as is normal in these situations, got up and offered Ange her hand. And Ange, polite to the last, shook it and smiled weakly.

"Nice to meet you," she said.

All three of us stood looking at each other, Kate not

quite knowing what was happening. Ange eventually broke the silence.

"I've got to go. I can find my own way out," she said. Dignified to the end.

I walked after her to the top of the stairs but managed nothing apart from a weak smile as she looked at me for a final time. She in turn gave me a death stare, as was her right, then took the stairs two at a time, nearly crashing into Kate's bike at the bottom and slammed the door shut so hard the whole flat shook. I gripped the bannister and breathed out hard, then looked up to see Kate staring at me.

"And what the fuck was that?"

"That was a very hot lawyer named Ange."

"I could see that. But what was *that*?" Kate's eyes widened.

"That was me fucking up spectacularly."

"How so?"

"Can we talk about this after I've had some coffee?" I said. Kate walked up and put an arm around my shoulder.

"Absolutely. I'll put some on now, shall I?"

* * *

Half an hour later we were still on the sofa, me onto my second cup of coffee while Kate was still laughing about the whole situation.

"Her voice didn't sound that squeaky when she said goodbye, you know."

"She wasn't in a super-chatty mood though, you'd have to agree," I said. I started to bite a fingernail.

"Well no, that's true." Kate said. "Poor old Ange."

"You're not being very helpful."

Julia had already sent another text but I wasn't up to giving her the full story just yet.

"I'm sorry, but this is so not you. You're so bloody fussy

about women normally, but then this," Kate said.

"I know, I'm a bad person."

"I didn't say that."

"But that's what you meant."

"No it's not." She shook her head from side to side before leaning forward, a fluffy red cushion falling from her lap as she did.

"You're not the first person who's brought someone attractive home to sleep with after a night out, then woken up and realised it wasn't for them. It's not the crime of the century."

"But I feel awful." I covered my face with my hands and leant back.

"Could that be to do with the wine, vodka and champagne you drank too?"

"Ugh, you forgot the tequila," I replied through my fingers.

"So you fucked someone you had no intention of having a relationship with. And you told them so the next morning. It's called a one-night stand. You didn't invent it."

"Thanks for the sympathy."

"Sympathy?!" Kate said. I actually heard a snort. "I wasn't the one that got laid last night by a power lesbian in heels. You'll find it's in short supply here." I managed a weak grin at that.

"That's better," Kate said. "Now, stop feeling sorry for yourself and get in the shower – we have a zoo to tackle today in case you'd forgotten."

"Do we have to?"

Kate gave me a look and I hauled myself off the sofa.

"Will you at least make me breakfast?"

She smiled and took a sip of her coffee.

"I will, but only because I love you, unlike Ange. Now go and wash your guilt off in the shower, you harlot."

Chapter Fifteen

Kate was good to her word and handed me a bacon sandwich 20 minutes later along with a fresh cup of coffee. I was still weighed down with woe, but I did at least feel a little more human after a shower and clean clothes, although looking at my bed had me replaying last night. I made a mental note to change the sheets later before going to bed.

"Can I have some pills too, please?" My voice was laced with self-pity.

"What did your last slave die of?" Kate said. But she got up and got me two ibuprofen and a glass of water anyway. She'd got dressed in the interim period into jeans and a dark blue shirt. Coupled with her white leather shoes and just-so hair, she looked like an ad for modern lesbianism.

"Thank you, dearest," I said. I sighed heavily before popping the pills with the water. "What did you do last night anyway?"

"We went to some club that Caroline's mate was DJing at. It was a bit lame but I was the dutiful girlfriend."

"And where is she now?"

"Working – we both went home alone last night unlike some people. I didn't drink either as I volunteered to drive, so my head is a cool, calm environment this morning." She gave me a broad smile.

"Aren't you a saint?" I said.

The doorbell interrupted our conversation. Kate got up and I heard voices and kissing in the hallway, then zips being undone, coats being hung. A moment later Kate ushered in Luke and Freddie, with Jack and Vicky close behind. They were the picture of a traditional family: two cute kids accompanying my metrosexual brother alongside Vicky, whose eyes told me she couldn't wait to be led to her first glass of wine.

"Morning sisters – and I mean that in every sense of the word," said Jack. He chuckled heartily at his own joke. "How is Sunday in non-married childless land? Hungover?"

"She is," Kate said. She lifted Luke up and kissed his forehead. "I'm saintly, you know that Jack."

Vicky came over to kiss me but even her lips hurt my head.

"Sure a trip to the zoo is exactly what you need to feel better," she said.

"Just what I thought when I woke up this morning," I lied. "But it'll be fun to bond with my two favourite nephews. Isn't that right, Freddie?"

Freddie stared at me uncertainly but I picked him up and sat him on my lap anyway where he stayed, quite content.

"What are you up to?" I said. Small talk didn't come easy this morning. My mouth felt claggy.

"We're going to the Tate Modern first and then for a posh lunch. Food cooked for me and wine poured by handsome waiters. Heaven," Vicky said.

"Speaking of which, our reservation's for 2pm so we should get going if we want to look at art first and be cultured." Jack was up on the balls of his feet and tapping his watch.

"Do they always run off this quickly?" I said.

"Every time," Kate said. "We'll feed the kids – pick them up when you like."

"Thanks, ladies – text you later," said Vicky, kissing her sons in turn.

As soon as the door shut Freddie's lip began to quiver so

Kate used a distraction technique which involved a packet of Custard Creams along with promises of ice cream and tigers at the zoo. It worked a treat.

"You've done this before," I said, as the boys chatted excitedly about tigers and forgot all about their missing parents.

"Yes, but it's nice to have a partner in crime," she said.

"Right then, you two. Let's go to the loo before we get coats on and go to the zoo!"

The kids clapped their hands in excitement and I joined in, laughing. Maybe this wouldn't be so bad after all.

* * *

Drained and zipped up, we grabbed buggies and expressed the boys to the tube. As I was soon to learn, children and buggies slow you down monumentally and I had a whole new respect for the mums I sometimes tutted at on the bus or tube. Not having been around the boys for so long, it was still amazing to me how small Luke and Freddie were and how cute – tiny hands and shoes and huge eyes looked up at us as we scooped them out of their buggies.

"Are we going on the tube, Aunty Kate?" asked Luke. His fair hair was blowing into his eyes at the top of the tube steps.

"Yep. You ready to go on a train?"

Luke nodded his head furiously.

"You good with the buggy?" Kate said, seeing me juggling it while grasping a two-year-old. I finally kicked the right bar and it collapsed, trapping my fingers as it did and causing me to say a word not yet in the boys' vocabulary. Or maybe it was with my brother as their dad. Kate laughed as she stood beside me, Luke's hand in hers and her buggy already tamed.

"This is what comes of being the stay-in-England aunty – buggy skills," she said.

"I'm sensing that."

We cleared the barrier and made it onto the escalator, me holding Freddie tightly as I was suddenly aware of the big drop down to the bottom and how tiny he was. A few stops and an unnecessary amount of steps later we arrived flustered and out of breath at the zoo with two kids in need of a wee and two aunties in need of a drink.

"How's your head?" said Kate. We were washing the boys' hands post-loo, holding them over the sink as they wafted their tiny hands under a fiercely icy faucet.

"Cold!" screeched Luke with understandable horror – I'd suffered it myself two minutes earlier.

"Child-focused," I said, lying wildly.

However, much as my mind did keep wandering to Ange, I had to admit it felt like I'd done the right thing in ditching her. Last night had felt fine in the moment but nowhere else. The next time I got together with somebody I wanted to be sure it was going somewhere – for her and myself. Kate consulted the map, jolting me from my thoughts.

"What do you think – monkeys first?" she said.

"Sounds like a plan."

* * *

Luke was quite taken with the monkeys, especially the squirrel monkeys who ran around their cage as if performing to some secret tunes playing in their heads. We had to leave the red-faced spider monkeys though after Freddie burst into tears when one lunged at him after showing us its arse. I could understand Freddie's fears: they were odd-looking creatures who squawked too much for my still-delicate head.

Both boys got a bit freaked out by the darkness of the reptile house – they weren't alone. However, the big hit of the day was the aquarium where we did indeed find Nemo, much to the delight of all four of us.

After an hour and a half of wandering round the zoo we all needed a break. Kate spied one of the outdoor cafés and we grabbed one of the wooden picnic tables beside it, feeding the kids chips and cokes while we added hot dogs to our orders. All around us parents and kids were eating additive-laden foods and planning their next animal adventure.

As I wiped some ketchup from Freddie's mouth and helped him out of his jacket, I caught the eye of a lesbian couple passing by. We exchanged the lesbian look – it's a bit like when bus drivers acknowledge each other, albeit with fewer buses. I smiled, before swallowing down some more headache pills with a swig of Coke.

"Still feeling it?" Kate asked from across the table.

I nodded, while she grinned at me.

"You do know we're presenting as the poster alternative family unit here don't you?" I said.

"It's crossed my mind," she said. She kissed the top of Luke's head as he ate his chips with utmost concentration. "I think we make a great-looking unit. Ever thought about having some?"

"Not really," I said, wrinkling my nose. "It's the pushing them out that scares me."

"Yeah, but when they turn out as cute as this – and let's face it, yours or mine stand a good chance of looking fairly similar – it might be worth it. I fancy it in a few years." She shielded her eyes from the sun as it dipped out from behind a cloud.

"Besides, you could always get your other half to push them out – advantages of being a lesbian no.37," she added. I chuckled as Kate grinned at me, giving Luke another squeeze. Then a razor-sharp smile zipped across her features and she shot me a look.

"Oh, by the way – I forgot to tell you." She shook her head. "I can't believe I forgot to tell you."

I looked confused as I took Freddie's chips from his tiny hands and replaced them with a drink. He looked happy with the swap. I wrinkled my forehead.

"Tell me what?"

"That Lucy was there last night. With all the Ange excitement this morning I forgot."

"Lucy? Where?" My attention was caught.

"At the club. She just got back from Oz last week. She asked after you. That was of course before she knew you were a toxic heartbreaker and to be steered clear of. But she wasn't to know, was she?"

"What did she say?" I was sitting up straight now, my interest piqued as my entire body flooded with warmth. When did I turn into such a harpy? Luke chose this inopportune moment to jump off Kate's lap and hop around, clutching his trousers. Kate held up her hand.

"Let me take him and I'll be back."

"Kate…" I whined as she disappeared to the toilet with Luke. It was wrong to be chastising my nephew for a toilet break but I couldn't help it. Two minutes later and they were back.

"So?"

"Hmmm?"

"Kate…" I said. She sat Luke back at the table. "Was Lucy there with anyone?"

"Yeah, her cousin I think," she replied. "Quite cute actually. Why?"

"No reason. What did she look like – her cousin?"

"Why?"

"Did she have blonde hair, long?"

"Yeah she did," Kate said. She arched an eyebrow. "Hang on, are you interested in her cousin now?"

A wave of relief washed through me. It was her cousin, not her new girlfriend. Her cousin. That'll teach me to jump to conclusions.

"So what did she say?" I said. I couldn't stop a huge smile lighting up my face.

"She asked how you were, if you'd found a job – she asked more questions than she needed to, let's put it that way. Caroline agreed and she's known her a long time. Her face had that slightly odd look on it when she was asking about you. The same one you're giving me now when you're asking about her. A bit goofy," Kate said.

I pursed my lips then smiled.

"But she had a gorgeous voice if I remember correctly."

"Heartless wench."

"I still got it, though," I said.

"LL Cool J you are," she replied.

I paused while Freddie slurped the last of his Coke. Lucy still liked me. Thank you, love gods and goddesses.

"You finished, Freddie?" I said. He nodded, a man of few words.

"What about you, Luke? What was your favourite thing so far?"

"I think the chips," he said, putting another in his mouth.

"Chips!" said Freddie, clapping his hands and kicking his tiny heels against my shins. It hurt quite a lot.

"Aunty Jess?" Luke said.

"Yes?"

"I love chips – do you?"

"Course I do – you'd be mad not to. Only a stupid person wouldn't love chips."

"That's what I think!" Luke said, smiling at my answer. It was definitely a bonding moment. Fifteen minutes later we were all chipped up and ready for more zoo.

"Well let's get ready to go then – and if you're good, Aunty Kate might buy you an ice-cream." I winked at Kate.

"You better be good then, hadn't you?" she said to me, before plonking Freddie in his buggy.

As we walked off towards the hippos with Luke and Freddie jibbering to each other in their buggies, I felt a stirring of familial satisfaction. This was definitely something London offered that I couldn't get in Oz – family bonding with my nephews and dyke-in-law. Today was just what the doctor ordered and I'd managed to scramble through it admirably. I thought about Ange but shoved that thought to the back of my mind. Then I thought about Lucy and grinned anew. Perhaps this weekend hadn't been such a blowout after all.

Chapter Sixteen

Julia turned up at the café the following week for lunch, her face carrying a vaguely cross look which dissolved as soon as I gave her a sheepish one. She was wearing a Columbo-style mac that seemed to be the choice of the modern-day professional when the weather took a turn for the better.

To soften her mood I sat her down with one of Matt's speciality goat's cheese & red onion tarts, along with a glass of posh fizzy orange I knew she loved simply because it had a French name. It certainly worked as Julia's eyes lit up at my offerings. However, I knew I wouldn't be off the hook for long.

"So when you said you didn't mind sleeping with her so long as she didn't open her mouth, I thought you were kidding," she said, tucking into her lunch. I could tell she wanted to be cross but the tart was working its magic.

"This is really good, by the way," she said. "You didn't make this, did you?" She shovelled another forkful into her mouth and savoured.

"No – this one is Matt's speciality," I said. "And don't speak with your mouthful."

She looked over at Matt serving behind the counter.

"He's single, right?"

"Yes Miss Matchmaker."

"Well you can mock all you like but it wasn't me who messed it up." She paused. "I might just have someone for

Matt. Would he be interested in dating?"

"He's desperate, so I'm guessing yes."

She shook her head.

"How can he be desperate? I thought there was a shortage of eligible straight guys. He's got his own business and a full head of hair – you'd have thought people would be queuing up to grab him."

I shrugged.

"Leave it with me," she said and then waggled her finger in my direction. "But you're not off the hook. It's a good job Ange is not in my department, that's all I can say."

"Better to be honest though, eh?"

"Or just not to shag them and leave them? I'm not giving up, though – it's my mission in life to get everybody happily coupled," she said.

"But we can't all be like you and Tom now can we?"

"God forbid," she laughed. "Look, I have to run as soon as I've finished this," she said, checking her watch.

"So you just came in to berate me?"

"Yes, but I don't have time to do it properly – I have a wedding to organise, remember? You have got the hen do booked out, right?"

"I have it stained on my eyeballs. When I try to look forward, that's all I can see."

"Just the way it should be," she said.

* * *

Lying on my bed later on, I texted Tess on the off chance she'd be around to Skype. Her text came back at lightning pace, saying she had BIG NEWS in capital letters. I logged on, sitting up and making sure neither me nor my room looked a tip. But then I reminded myself I wasn't talking to my mum or the Queen.

Tess appeared on the screen in jeans and her favourite blue T-shirt, waving in an animated fashion as people tend to do on Skype. It's a strange facet of human nature.

"Hey Jess, how are you?" she asked from the other side of the world.

"All right. You're looking very chipper for 8am."

"I couldn't sleep so I've been up for three hours. I've cleaned the bathroom and done some ironing. It's actually nearly lunchtime in my body clock."

I laughed.

"So what's the big news that needed capital letters then? The suspense is killing me."

Tess sat upright on her sofa, re-balancing the laptop. It made no difference whatsoever but it seemed to please her.

"Can you see me okay?"

"Yep, fine."

"Well – I was out at Ghetto on Monday with Tom…"

"Oh I miss those nights!"

"You hated going out on a Monday," she reminded me.

"You know what I mean."

"Well anyway. I was out at Ghetto and I ran into Jan. Remember Jan, Kevin's friend?"

I thought for a minute.

"Blonde hair, buggy eyes, gobby?"

"Exactly that. Still blonde, still buggy and still very gobby. And she informed me that Karen and Paula are no more – Paula dumped Karen and ran off with another woman."

I was shocked.

"I know, right!?" said Tess. She took in my stunned face, captured in grey, grainy magic on my laptop's tiny webcam. I blew out a breath.

"Well, I didn't see that coming."

"Neither did Karen. Karma though right? What goes around…"

"There is that. I don't know what to say really."

"Serves her bloody right, something like that?"

"That'll do," I smiled.

However, part of me couldn't help thinking 'poor Karen'. I hoped she was all right but I was still pleased at the news – there's nothing worse than being dumped for someone and then that couple staying together for years on end. You want the person who dumped you to go through the same pain and it appeared I was getting my wish.

"Did Jan say anymore?"

"Just that Paula has already moved in with this woman in true lesbian fashion, being that she was living with Karen and couldn't very well carry that on…"

"Who is she?"

Tess shrugged.

"Someone she worked with apparently. But anyway, enough of my news – tell me about high-pitched Ange. That sounds like a story…"

I settled on my bed and began the tale.

Chapter Seventeen

The following Saturday was slowly baking so I decided to go for a walk. As I clicked the door shut the clouds were parting to reveal patches of blue beneath, while underfoot the ground steamed as the sun pounded the streets. I said hi to a street cleaner who looked oddly at me as if I were about to assault him and headed down to the canal, through the Van Gogh Estate and out onto the Kingsland Road.

As I walked, I breathed in the smells of Vietnamese and Chinese cooking as I passed by the myriad scruffy Asian cafés packed solid with wilted white plastic chairs and chipped tables. A little further down the road a Tesco Express had just opened, propping up a new set of flats in an old building that used to be a factory. At its side the small customer car park was almost melting with a hazy shimmer hovering over the grey tarmac, the world above it wobbling from side to side as if in a Hanna-Barbera cartoon. A few more steps and I was on the canal path.

London's canal network never failed to thrill me and it was where I often headed on sunny days – either there or down to the Thames itself. Being by water always afforded me time to think - it was like putting my thoughts and feelings on a daily wash cycle and spinning them round until they were rinsed thoroughly.

Today, top of the list was 'do I need to buy more eggs?' Second was 'I really should book a dental appointment'. The further I walked, though, the more these thoughts cleared from my brain and allowed the more buried ones to appear. Things like, 'I wonder what Lucy's doing today?' and 'I wonder if Karen's thinking about me now she's been dumped?' I grinned at the sweet-tasting justice of it all.

Walking up the canal I could feel the sun soaking into my face. My new shades were also working hard to save me developing squinting wrinkles and I decided to stop at a pub that had people spilling out of it, all flocking to the water for beer and reflection.

After waiting for an eternity at the bar I took my pint of cider and sat on the towpath, levering myself down into a cross-legged sitting position and managing to shield my cider from the sun. All along the towpath, couples, friends and solos like me sat reading books, drinking, chatting, laughing. The relaxed atmosphere of a Saturday in the city crackled right along it – the time was only 2.30pm after all, with the whole day ahead of us.

I'd decided to save myself last night after the usual two Friday pints with Matt and Beth and had told Matt to do the same as Julia had set him up on his blind date tonight with a woman called Natalie. I smiled thinking of my workmates and of how these people had become such a big part of my life in such a short space of time. I'd only been working at Porter's for the past seven weeks but already it felt like a lifetime, like this was what I'd been waiting for all my life. A café, who would have guessed?

I took another sip of my cider and pondered which shops to hit after my drink when my train of thought was interrupted by a shadow looming over me. I squinted up into the sun and turned to see a woman on a bike peering down at me.

"Jess?" she said.

"Er, yeah." She had a helmet on so I had no idea who it was.

"Lucy – friend of Kate's? We met in town a while back."

I twisted, steadied my weight on one leg, leaned on it and straightened up fully to match Lucy's height, brushing the back and front of my jeans of any excess gravel they'd acquired.

"Hi!" I said. I tried to control my voice. "You made it back then?"

"Yep. There and back alive." She gave me a shy smile. "Good to see you again."

"You too." I said. "Nice bike."

"Thanks. I've just cycled from Little Venice – could do with a drink actually."

Her bike looked like it meant business being silver and shiny, my two criteria for judging such things. Also, if the toned cut of her calf muscles were anything to go by, she was no stranger to it, either.

"Well join me," I said.

"You sure?"

"Positive. I can guard your bike while you get a drink if you like."

"That'd be great." She laid her bike delicately on the floor beside me. "Do you need one?" she asked, unbuckling her helmet strap underneath her chin before taking it off completely and ruffling her short dark hair. I smiled and cleared my throat.

"I'm good."

"Back in a tick."

I couldn't help a huge grin spreading across my face as I watched this attractive woman disappear into the pub. This Saturday was definitely full of possibilities. When she returned just minutes later – she either flashed the bartender a killer smile or was one of those people who trampled old ladies to get a drink – I noticed again what I'd noted the first time around: gorgeous dark brown eyes and adorable smile.

Dressed casually in T-shirt, cut-off jeans and trainers, Lucy looked great. She sat down beside me with a pint of lager and we clinked glasses.

"Gorgeous weather, isn't it?" She ran her hand through her hair. "Excuse the helmet hair – it probably looks a right state."

"Looks fine," I said. She smiled and I noticed her cute dimple again.

"I was out your way last night – I hoped I might bump into you," she said.

"I was knackered last night so didn't have a big one."

"Same here, I didn't stay." She paused. "I've had a killer week."

"Lots of eyes?"

"Everywhere you look," she smiled. "So I thought I'd ride it out."

"Good plan."

I decided not to declare my hatred of towpath cyclists right at that moment – strategic planning.

"So tell me about your trip to Sydney – did you meet any cute women?"

Why in the world had I asked that? Lucy snorted.

"I was beating them off with a stick. Or is it a boomerang in Oz?"

"I'm not sure either would work."

I paused, regaining my composure.

"Okay let me try again. Did you make it to Bondi?"

She nodded enthusiastically.

"It was ace. And I even took some surf lessons."

"Now that is amazing. I was there three years and never got beyond putting on a wet suit and splashing about in the sea with a board. Fear of sharks."

"Right," she said. "Well I can't say I was a pro but it was fun – and the instructor was cute too."

"Now we're getting to the bottom of it," I said and she laughed. Even at one of my bad jokes. Interesting.

"What about Newtown?"

"Ah well, that's a whole other story. Oh, and I saw that drag king – your ex, what was her name?"

"Teri?" I said, stunned. I often find my mouth running away with me and telling people stories of my life, safe in the knowledge they're never going to run into the lead characters who are safely tucked away on the other side of the world. Until now.

"Yes, Butch Cassidy!"

"Oh my god, now I'm really embarrassed…"

"No need. I was really impressed with her – she's still doing the act with the black dildo by the way…"

I blushed phone box red.

"And it's just like you said – very realistic shall we say…"

Lucy began to laugh as I gulped at my pint for something to do.

"Hmmm. I'm not sure I could have made you feel much more uncomfortable," she said. I smiled and flicked my hand nonchalantly.

"It's fine. It's just, you know, a blast from the past brought up by someone who's here and now and I've only met you twice. But I'm glad you enjoyed the show. Whatever else she is, Teri's definitely a pro."

"Agreed."

Lucy closed her eyes and stretched backward, arching her body into the sun, straining every muscle to allow the sunshine in. I caught myself staring but turned away quick enough so that when she opened her eyes, I was looking into the water. Smooth, I thought.

"So do you come here often?" she asked.

"Good line," I said.

"I got them all."

We both laughed.

"But in answer to your question, yeah I do. I love the water so I walk along the canal or the river, whichever one I fancy."

"Me too – apart from I bike it. Have you done the Thames Path?"

Her eyes raked my body as she waited for an answer. I felt goosebumps prickle my skin and hoped she wasn't looking too closely as I evidently couldn't be cold.

"The bits around London – but I'd love to do the whole thing all the way to Gloucester."

"Me too." She paused. "Perhaps we should do a section one day."

"Maybe," I smiled. Lucy smiled back.

"I just hope you're not one of those cyclists who nearly knocks pedestrians into the water at every opportunity."

"Not me, I was a girl scout," she said. She leaned over and rang the bell on her bike. "I always ring and always say thank you."

"Good to know," I said.

I discovered that Lucy had really enjoyed Sydney and had gone to all my favourite bars, which made me feel homesick and missing my friends. She asked why I'd moved back.

"I had my heart broken and I didn't want to settle down so far away from my family and friends – plus it just seemed the right time."

She nodded. "Sometimes the fates conspire to tell you something don't they?" She indicated my empty glass. "Can I get you another?"

"I'll get them," I said. I was up and walking before she could say no.

At the bar, I wondered where all this was going and also marvelled at how random it was too. I turned back when I got to the bar and she was watching – when she saw me turn she abruptly looked the other way. We were getting on really well and the spark we'd shared on our first meeting was definitely still there. I tried to locate the feeling that was growing in the pit of my stomach and settled on excitement mixed with fear – not such an unhealthy response to the first woman who'd flicked a switch since Karen (bypassing the ill-fated Ange).

But I still wasn't sure I was ready for this, still wasn't sure I didn't have too much baggage to carry from the last relationship into the next. Whenever I'd flipped the coin of love before it'd fallen pain-side up. Could I trust that the odds would be stacked in my favour sooner rather than later?

However, that was all in the future. Right now, I wasn't in a relationship with Lucy and all I was doing was having impromptu Saturday lunchtime drinks – nothing more, nothing less. As I walked back to where she sat I sipped my pint to stop it from spilling and tried to look nonchalant. I sat down giving her a full-beam smile.

"So tell me about your heavy week and your new job..." she said.

We sat together chatting for another 45 minutes before parting and confirming numbers, promising to meet up for a drink soon and this time sans bike and perhaps even inside a bar. As she cycled away, turning back to wave once before her legs swung into motion, I hoped she was as buoyed by our meeting as I was. I knew one thing – I had better hit the shops to take my mind off of things before my thought process spiralled out of control and I was married to her with two cats.

Chapter Eighteen

I got home later that day having been successful in my shopping quest, managing two new tops and a pair of jeans. I'd also had a smile glued to my face the whole afternoon.

I let myself into the flat and went up the stairs to be greeted by Kate singing loudly along to Pulp's *Common People*. I could smell onions and garlic on the stove as I hung up my coat in the hallway and walked towards the pastel-blue kitchen. Kate was completely unawares, topping up her wine glass and stirring her food. I tapped her on the shoulder and she screamed.

"Jesus!"

"No, Jess."

"You scared me you moron."

"Turn the music down then. Lucky I'm not an axe murderer."

"I didn't give them any of my keys," she said.

I lowered the volume on the radio that was placed next to the juicer Kate had bought six months ago in a fit of health. It had yet to be introduced to the art of juicing.

"And you've turned into Nigella in my absence I see."

"Jamie actually. This is his new spag bol recipe which reckons it needs to simmer for over two hours, hence the early start time."

"Sounds great. I'm off for a shower."

"I'll pour you a glass of wine," she shouted. I retreated

down the hallway and heard the volume get turned back up, along with Kate's singing voice.

I particularly liked the bathroom in Kate's flat, decorated in classic black and white with a walk-in shower big enough for two. She didn't have a bath but I wasn't really a bath person so that didn't bother me. Once inside the huge shower I lathered up my hair and body, standing under the jets of water for far longer than necessary and enjoying the feeling of them hitting my skin.

So, I'd had drinks with a new woman – not quite a date but I hoped there would be an official one. Perhaps we would go out to dinner and she would make a big show and insist on paying for me and I'd be embarrassed but secretly love it. Despite myself and no matter that I was a devoutly deconstructed post-modern feminist and all that jazz, my deepest darkest desire was to meet a woman who worshipped me and was rich enough that I could lead the life of leisure that I should surely have been born into. Even someone buying me dinner made me giddy.

My stomach and further below moved slightly as I thought about Lucy and what little I knew of her. Short dark hair, cool clothes and seriously kissable lips. I wasn't sure where the catch was because there had to be one. Attractive, solvent, available women didn't normally show an interest in me. Apart from psychos like Karen and, of course, Ange, and Julia was giving me a hard enough time about that as it was. But Ange was history.

I dried off and went to my room, pulling on my white towelling dressing gown and settling onto my cream duvet. I turned on my laptop and pulled up Facebook: on the right-hand side was a box entitled 'Friends you might know'. In that box was a picture of Karen smiling out at me. 'Add As Friend' said a tag below. Sometimes, social media needed a clip round the ear.

Kate's spag bol was smelling delicious as I returned to the kitchen freshly cleansed and dressed in jeans and a black T-shirt. She passed me a glass of wine that was standing on the counter and we chinked glasses.

"That must have been the longest shower in human history."

"I was very dirty," I said. "Plus, I had to catch up on the book of face and what was going on in the world. Nothing as usual in case you were wondering but it has to be checked."

I dipped a spoon in the Bolognese sauce and tasted it. I winced as it burnt my tongue.

"You're being a very good wife to me so far you know."

"Well my other wife's coming for dinner too so don't let on, she might get jealous."

"I'll let her know you save your special sauce for her."

"Please!" Kate said.

"Did I get any post today?"

"Nothing – think they might still be on strike. Or rubbish. Or both. By the way, I'm doing starters too, so don't eat too much," Kate said as I opened the fridge.

"You're definitely getting a shag tonight."

"From you too?"

"Ha ha," I said. My mind instantly flicked back to Lucy and her gorgeous smile – clearly my face gave me away somewhat. Kate threw me a quizzical look as she opened the cutlery drawer and took out three knives and forks. I took them from her.

"I'll do that."

She blocked my way out of the kitchen.

"No, you're not running away. You've got a funny look on your face. Tell me what's going on."

"Nothing."

"Jess…"

I was suddenly very shy and didn't want to tell her, but I knew I might burst if I didn't.

"I walked to Angel today along the canal."

"And?"

"Guess who I bumped into."

"Who?"

"Guess."

"Karen – she's flown over from Australia begging you to take her back."

"No – I think you might have heard about it by now if that had happened. Guess again."

"Ange wielding a knife?"

"It's a positive thing."

"I don't do positive," she said. "I dunno, tell me."

"Lucy," I said, matter-of-factly as if it happened every day.

"Luuuucyyyy!" Kate said. Her voice was sing-song and bore more than a note of triumph. "And?"

"And nothing – she was on her bike, I was drinking, she stopped and had a drink too."

Kate raised her eyebrows at me.

"And you didn't ask her out, let me guess."

"Why would I ask her out?"

"Because she's good-looking, clearly interested in you and you're gagging for it."

"How do you work that one out?" I said. Then I pouted. "And I am not gagging for it."

Kate laughed.

"Are too. But really – she stalked you to the canal, that's a clue isn't it? Do you think she could possibly like you too?"

"Har de ha."

"You can't just brush this one off. You get on right?"

I nodded.

"You fancy her?"

I smirked.

"She clearly likes you. Tell me you at least exchanged numbers?"

"We confirmed our numbers, yes."

"Hallelujah. There is hope! Just make sure you call her and seal the deal."

"You're truly the last of the romantics, you know that?"

"I have been told. Now set that table, woman, and don't think this is the last we'll be talking about this tonight."

"Perish the thought," I said.

* * *

Caroline turned up half an hour later and we sat down to our parma ham, rocket and mozzarella starters at the table. She was shorter than Kate with dyed red hair and skin so pale it seemed to be paper-thin, almost translucent. She had a couple of piercings at the top of both ears along with one in her eyebrow and Kate had confided they weren't her only ones. I wondered if she rattled when she was treating her patients – you don't come across many super-pierced nurses after all, or at least I hadn't. Caroline was also from up north so her conversation was somewhat sing-song, her vowels truncating and stretching as if she were playing some kind of accent accordion.

In addition, perhaps because of her job or maybe her age – she was 36 – she seemed more sorted and somehow more grounded than most people I knew. Somehow, Caroline exuded calmness and authority and I could see that was one of the qualities that drew Kate. My thoughts were broken as Caroline leaned in and took Kate's right hand in hers.

"This is gorgeous, babe," she said, kissing Kate's knuckle. I saw the blush rise in Kate's cheeks and told them to get a room, at which they both laughed.

"Perhaps we should – although then you won't hear what you're missing and you might not be prompted into action," Kate said.

"What's this? What have I missed?" asked Caroline. Kate filled her in on the Lucy drinks-by-the-canal scenario and she seemed to be of the same mind as Kate that this meant something.

"You don't stop on canal paths and have a drink with someone if you're not interested," she said bluntly. "She could have just cycled on by and you'd never even have known. Besides, I know Lucy and this means she's interested."

"She is?" I forked another piece of cheese and ham and swirled it around in olive oil and balsamic vinegar. I had no plans to eat it but I was trying to play it cool. Caroline nodded.

"Plus, she was asking after you the other night, too. She did it casually but we both detected that she might have been slightly aggrieved you weren't there with us. She wasn't nearly so pleased to see us, was she?"

Kate pulled a sad face and shook her head.

"So do what I told you and call her. You're in your 30s now, you know, there's no time to be sitting around and wondering about these things. Carpe diem and all of that," Kate said. She raised her fist to emphasise the point.

"Easy for you to say," I said. "You didn't just have your heart smashed into tiny pieces by your last girlfriend."

"True," Kate said. "But that was about ten years ago..."

"Er, nine months..."

"Time enough," she said. "It's time for you to get back out there. You need some excitement in your life – something fun and less heavy on the heartbreak. You've made it back from Australia, you've got a home and a job – now you just need a girlfriend and a cat and you're living the lesbian dream. Am I right?" she asked Caroline.

"Bang on, babe," she replied.

Kate got up to collect the starter plates.

"Hang on, when do we get a cat then?" Caroline's eyes followed Kate as she left the room.

"I'm only interested in one type of pussy," Kate shouted over her shoulder as she disappeared to the kitchen.

"She's such a charmer," Caroline said. "But she's right, you know. Why don't you call her? What have you got to lose? The worst she can say is no." She raised a pierced eyebrow. "But I guarantee she won't. I know Lucy."

"How long have you known her?"

I was intrigued – Kate hadn't suggested that Lucy was an old friend and that Caroline might be a useful information source.

"A while – nearly ten years. We met at a friend's party."

"A party?" I repeated. I rested my chin on my palm. "Just friends?"

I let the question hang in the air, not really understanding why I asked it in the first place. Caroline cleared her throat and batted it away.

"Briefly more but that was a long time ago – we're far better as friends, believe me. But don't let that put you off…"

Right. Zero degrees of separation but even that didn't deter me. This was the lesbian world, after all.

"Bottom line is Lucy's lovely – she even put me up in her spare room when I was homeless a few years ago. Plus, she wants a relationship – she's been single a while now. So if you do too, I'd say this was a goer."

This was a lot to take in. A thought passed across Caroline's face and she snorted. I gave her a quizzical look.

"Plus, if you do start going out with her you'll meet her family, too. More northern than me if you can believe it. And they like to sing. Oh my, do they like to sing…"

"Is she seeing sense yet?" Kate shouted through.

Caroline fixed me with her gaze.

"I don't know. Are you?"

I smiled. "We've got a connection that's for sure, so I'd like to get to know her better. I'm not sure about the singing though…"

Kate brought in the Bolognese and I managed to steer the conversation in other directions, both of them silently acknowledging they shouldn't push me too much on this if they wanted a positive resolution in the end.

So we talked about Caroline's amusing patients and the idiots at Kate's work who say words like leverage and synergy with a straight face. We also waded into the customers who came into Porter's and sat there all afternoon when clearly they should be at work.

But eventually, as we drained another bottle of wine and Kate brought in shop-bought chocolate fondant desserts to accompany the next red she uncorked, the chat came back around to me. Specifically, me and my need to put myself back out there, to lay the ghost of Karen once and for all.

"But what if I'm a curse on all relationships?" I said.

"God, you think highly of yourself – Jess the spirit of doom?" Kate laughed. She filled my glass with the fresh Malbec.

"You know what I mean," I said. "All my other girlfriends seem to have gone on to have successful relationships after me, some of them even marrying and settling down with kids. I'm the common denominator in all of the stories, the one clanking link that somehow never seems to fit. What if I'm simply incapable of having a healthy, happy relationship? I don't know if I want the responsibility of making someone else unhappy again. I mean, look at what happened with Ange."

Kate was having none of it. "Absolute rubbish and you know it." She put down her dessert spoon and licked her lips. "Maria and you didn't break up badly, you just drifted out of love. And Karen was an absolute moron to not know how great you are. And Ange was a one-night stand, so get over it. You need to get better at spinning yourself, you know."

She took a slug of wine and then put on her serious face. "How about considering the fact that you bolted from all of these relationships because you knew they weren't right and you were saving yourself from even more hurt in the long run, did you ever think about that?"

"No," I mumbled.

"No, I didn't think so," Kate said. "You need to look in the mirror and see what a catch you are. Plus, now you're a master-baker, how much more of a catch do women need?"

Both Caroline and I laughed out loud at that and, sensing a receptive audience, Kate continued.

"I mean, imagine it. You take a girl out, you charm her, you put the moves on her and then the next day, you jump out of bed and rustle up some muffins." She sat back in her chair, revelling in her humour as Caroline snorted.

"Attending to muff, then muffins, all in one morning," she said with a sage nod of the head. "A dream date, clearly. Do you want me to check if Lucy likes muffins? I can text her now…"

"No!" I screeched. Cue raucous laughter.

We ended the evening with me grudgingly admitting I was somewhat of a catch which seemed to satisfy the other two. They also made me promise to think about calling Lucy tomorrow, which I agreed to. Apparently there was a three-day window to act on these things and I was already into day two seeing as it was now officially Sunday. Tick-tock went the clock.

Chapter Nineteen

The next day dawned just as sunny as the previous. I awoke with a slightly fuzzy head to a text from Jack telling me to come over to theirs for a barbecue if I had no other plans. I didn't and as I could feel the sun beating through my window even from under the covers, a day soaking up its rays in the suburbs sounded just dandy. Kate and Caroline were also invited but declined, so I left them to spend the day together and got on a microwave-hot train to the suburbs.

I fiddled with my phone the whole way there, scrolling through to Lucy's number, hovering my finger over the green 'call' button but not being able to bring myself to make the move. I understood the clock was ticking but reasoned I'd do it later – I didn't want to look too keen.

To take my mind off it I scrolled through the rest of my contacts and marvelled at the paucity of them, it being a new phone and me having not acquired a whole lot of numbers as yet. Lucy was one of only three names listed under L. She was by far the most attractive in that category.

As I was smiling at my phone, it beeped and a text came through. It was from Kate.

"Call her," it read.

She wasn't giving up on this was she? I put my phone away and wiggled my feet in my flip-flops, glad I'd chanced wearing them as the day was baking.

Jack and Vicky lived in the burbs. "Still on the tube map,"

Vicky had countered when I'd mentioned the fact. "Zone five sweetheart, social suicide!" I'd replied.

As a trade-off for living on the far reaches of the Northern line, however, they'd been able to afford a three-bedroom house on one of those new-build estates that were full of young couples and small people playing football against any available wall. Also, they'd made a bunch of good friends in their neighbours, quite a few of whom were coming along today.

Jack gave me a hug and seemed genuinely pleased to see me when the cab dropped me off, which always threw me a little because we fought so much when we were growing up. That fighting had somehow evolved into an easy brother-sister-almost-friends-even relationship over the years, no doubt aided by Vicky but also by my absence. He was also grateful I was back now to share some of the parenting duties that Shirley and Ian required.

"Are Mum and Dad coming?" I said. He took my beers and plonked them on the side as I followed him into the kitchen.

"Other plans," he said, raising his eyebrows. "They'd already been invited to dinner at some friends I've never even heard of. Apparently Mum met the woman at some course she did and now they're spending Sunday afternoons with them. Sure Dad's thrilled about that seeing as Arsenal are on the telly."

"Poor old Dad," I paused. "Is there room in the fridge?" I picked up the bag of beer.

"I'll take them outside, we've got a beer bath out there. Come on." The bottles clinked as he grabbed them.

If the house had appeared empty, that's because everyone was already outside in the surprisingly large garden at the rear of the house, mainly given over to grass with a raised patio near the house and a Jack-built barbecue area to the right behind the garage.

Jack and Vicky had one of those dark wooden garden furniture sets that are always on the front cover of home supplements and all six chairs were taken with ladies sipping white wine. Showing great understanding of gender stereotypes, there were also three men poking meat on the barbecue and another five men sipping from their bottles of beer in close proximity, just to be sure their masculinity wasn't in doubt. Intertwined in this domestic scene were seven kids, all under five, zipping in and out of adult legs.

After eating some seafood, a home-made lamb burger and a slew of salads, I unwisely played football with my nephews. I lasted two minutes before deciding I should let my food go down first, and cajoled two of the other little boys into taking my place.

After extricating myself from the field of play I fell into place beside Jack's mate, Daniel, who I'd known for as long as Jack and Vicky had been together. Daniel was shorter than I remembered but still a sweetheart and a well-dressed one at that. He was wearing cut-off jean shorts, faded T-shirt and flip-flops. To all intents and purposes, Daniel really should be gay as I'd told him on many occasions, to which he always laughed and told me he just couldn't get over the stubble. That, and the other cock.

Daniel was newly single, fucked over by his former girlfriend, so we commiserated and tutted at the state of womankind. But then I let slip to him about Lucy and he seemed to be on Kate's side.

"You like her?" he said.

I nodded.

"Then you should call her. Simple as."

"It's not though is it?"

"Isn't it?" he said, giving me that questioning face that had been a favourite of Kate and Caroline last night.

"No it's not. What if it ends badly like all the others? Plus, I have trouble pressing the green button on my phone when her number's involved."

Daniel waggled his fingers in a 'come hither' gesture, palm facing up.

"Give it to me."

"What?"

"Your phone."

"Yeah, right."

"Seriously. I'll press the green button then all you have to do is talk."

He was still holding out his hand. I laughed and smacked it away.

"You're not getting it, I'm not that drunk. Yet." I paused. "Do you know about the three-day window?"

He took a swig from his bottle of Peroni and nodded.

"It seems to cut across sexuality lines, that one – all my friends, straight and gay have been telling me the clock's ticking."

"They're not wrong," he said.

"But why three days? Can't I call her in a week?"

Daniel shook his head and laughed.

"And there was me thinking gays were sensitive."

"That's gay men, darling," I said, patting his hairy arm. "I'm a lesbian remember – I'm butch and tough and spend my evenings fixing bikes and smashing things."

"I know, I'm lucky you're not beating me senseless right now," he said. His smile revealed a dimple in his right cheek, all of which only served to remind me of Lucy even more. "But anyway, call her. If you don't call her within three days then you clearly don't think very much of her do you?"

I thought about that.

"So you'll call her?"

"I thought you were down on love?"

"That's my own – I'm still in the beat-myself-up stage. But you know me, I'm a romantic at heart. I'm for love – and for sex. And if you've got a chance at both then I'd say it's worth a shot, even if you end up getting shot down. Which I'm sure you won't."

"I hope not."

"God loves a trier," he said.

"But hates a fag apparently."

"That's only because he's still not over the fact that his only son was gay," he said. "And you'd think after all this time too…"

I shrugged my shoulders. "Parents always take it the worst."

We both laughed.

"So you're going to call?" Daniel persisted.

"Oh. My. God. Yes, I'm going to call. You're worse than my mother."

He smiled. "How is the lovely Shirley?"

"Still mad."

We both smirked at the thought of my mother with Daniel. Put frankly, Mum had a bit of a crush on him and Daniel did nothing to dissuade her.

"Say hello for me."

"Far too dangerous. She'll think that means you want to whisk her off from Ian and ravish her."

"There's a thought. Would you and Jack be comfortable calling me daddy?" he asked.

I shuddered.

"What, too far?"

"Way too far," I said.

Chapter Twenty

The next day at work, Matt described his date Natalie as "perfect". He'd taken her for dinner at his favourite bistro and they'd got on brilliantly.

"And she's got a kid too, so she wasn't put off by mine."

"So you're seeing her again, I take it?" I said, taking a load of coffee cups from the dishwasher and swearing because they were still red hot.

"I hope so," he said. "Want a hand?"

I nodded, sucking my slightly singed fingers and he started unloading with me. Matt made light of the scorching crockery.

"That's great, I'm really pleased for you."

"Can you tell Julia thanks for me?" he said, piling up a stack of saucers.

"I will, or you can tell her yourself next time she's in which won't be long. She's a big fan of your quiches."

* * *

Turns out also that Kate and Daniel needn't have worried about me. I was just about to have my lunch after the rush had died down around 3.30pm when a woman walked in wearing a crisp black shirt, black jeans and biker boots, resting her helmet on her hip. She smiled at me as she walked up to the counter. It was Lucy.

My stomach did a flip and all the spare blood in my

system pumped rapidly down my body. My breath caught in my throat as I tried to keep my poise and not melt on the spot.

"Hi," she said. She smiled at me and ran a hand through her hair. She went to say something but the words seemed to stick in her throat. I knew then that perhaps Lucy had been scrolling to my number all weekend too.

"Hi," I said. "We really must stop meeting like this."

I honestly said that without anybody putting a gun to my head. Luckily, Lucy laughed.

"We must," she said. "How are you? Nice weekend?"

"Lovely, ta." I paused. "Can I get you a drink? Coffee? I recommend the chocolate cake too, it's delicious." I was babbling, never a good sign.

"A latte's fine, thanks."

"Grab a table and I'll bring it over."

She fished in her pocket for some money but I waved her away.

"My treat," I said. She blushed. This was going well.

I looked over at her as I steamed her milk and felt something stir inside. Don't bugger up the latte, Jess. Matt appeared in the doorway, watching me.

"I thought you were taking a break?"

"I was – but Lucy's over there," I said, nodding towards her. "So I thought I'd make her coffee."

"Well make yourself one and go and join her – go on," he said. He put the lid back on the milk. "Better still, take that over to her and I'll make yours."

I began to protest but he pushed me gently out from behind the counter.

"Take it."

I picked up the latte and walked with as much poise as I could muster to where Lucy was sitting reading that day's Evening Standard, her motorbike helmet sat on the chair beside her. She smiled up at me as I approached.

"Anything interesting?" I said.

"Not remotely, apart from the fact that Pantene are two for one at Sainsbury's. Must remember that."

She had a gorgeous smile and I was suddenly aware that I was wearing an apron. I hastily put her coffee down and untied myself from the back, lifting the neck string over my head, feeling it ruffle my hair as I did.

"So do you work around here?"

I sat down at right angles to her and ran my fingers through my hair before folding my apron on my lap. Anything to take my mind off the sudden attack of butterflies flitting around inside me, threatening to fly out of my mouth, eyes or nose, they weren't fussy. We locked eyes and I felt slightly sick as Matt approached with a tray carrying my Americano, a jug of milk and some home-baked cookies.

"Ladies," he said. He set down the tray, his eyes flitting between us. "Enjoy."

"Thanks, Matt."

I offered Lucy a cookie. She took one but then instantly put it down on the table.

"In answer to your question – not really. I mean, I don't work a million miles away but there are nearer cafés."

"Right." I picked up a sugar, put it down.

"But I wasn't coming in for the latte particularly..." she said. She trailed off and looked around, slightly embarrassed. "God, this doesn't get any easier does it?"

She stumbled on, rubbing her hand up and down her right thigh.

"Thing is, I didn't just come in here to say hi. I was also wondering if you fancied having dinner sometime?"

I tried to control my face from being too surprised, but probably only succeeded in portraying evidence of constipation or trapped wind.

"I'd love to."

If I looked odd, at least I was sounding normal. Decisive even.

"Great," she said. She looked painfully relieved. "That's great." Double-great. This *was* going well.

"When were you thinking?"

"How does Friday sound?" She crinkled her face like that might be the worse day in the world to have dinner.

"Sounds brilliant," I said.

Did that sound too eager? Should I have consulted a diary? I made another mental note to buy a diary. Lucy beamed at me. A woman I used to work with in Australia tried not to smile too much in case it gave her wrinkles in the future. Lucy, I was pleased to note, was not one of that breed.

"Now let's try to have a normal conversation now that's out of the way."

"Do you think that's possible?" I said.

"We could try."

She stayed for 20 minutes and for every second of it, all I wanted to do was kiss her. Instead though, I drank my coffee, ate my biscuit, tried not to stare at her too much and marvelled at the fact that such a hot woman had come in here and asked me out. In my head, a choir was singing a hallelujah chorus but I persuaded them to keep the sound down so she couldn't hear. Not just yet anyway.

When she left, I told her I was really looking forward to Friday and she smiled shyly and told me she was too, causing my body to purr once more. I took a deep breath and saw her out the door, waving with a cheesy grin on my face. When I picked up the cups and walked back to the counter, Matt gave me a knowing look.

"Someone looks happy."

I blushed again.

"I just got asked out on a date." My voice cracked with excitement.

"We are smoking in this café this week!"

He returned my grin and put his hand up for a high five.

"That we are." I smacked his palm with a satisfying thwack.

* * *

Kate was, obviously, cock-a-hoop when I filled her in that night. She was also impressed Lucy had respected the three-day window.

"At least one of you did at any rate," she said. "So I take it you're pleased then?"

I nodded and leaned against the counter-top.

"You know, all that doubt, all those worries – they didn't enter my head when Lucy asked me out. It was a simple question: would I like to have dinner? And my overwhelming response to that question was yes. Pure and simple. Perhaps it wasn't just Ange's laugh that was the deal breaker, eh?"

"You think?" Kate said, rolling her eyes to the ceiling. I tutted and walked out.

Chapter Twenty-One

Friday at work I was all fingers and thumbs, not concentrating on what I needed to do, giving out Americanos where lattes were needed, cutting overly generous lumps of cake for punters and generally being "a little absent" as Matt gently put it.

"It's like you've got something on your mind," he teased me, brushing his wrist across his tanned forehead. Matt was one of those people who stepped outside and got a tan whereas my skin was not quite so obliging. Here in London, the weather was unseasonably hot for May and we were all suffering with the heat. As Beth pointed out repeatedly though: "Sweat means calories burned – let's get to work!"

Seeing my agitated state, Matt gave in trying to persuade me to come for one drink with them after work. Instead, he insisted I leave as soon as the lunch rush was over.

"If you're anything like the women I know, you'll need at least three hours to get ready."

I was amused and somewhat touched that he put me into the same category as his exes.

"What about you?" I asked. "Don't you drink too much either – you've got a lady to impress," I said.

"A quick one after work won't hurt. Dutch courage…"

* * *

We met outside Cosmo Bar which was handily just around the corner from the flat. Comically, despite my protestations Matt had been correct with his approximations of how long it would take me to get ready. I'd spent 45 minutes trying on different outfits – tie or no tie? – and a further 45 minutes trying to perfect my make-up. Plus, there was shaving, scraping, moisturising and plucking to be done, it's amazing how it builds up in just a week. Not that I was planning to sleep with her tonight but you just never knew where life might take you.

When I was satisfied there was no make-up on my chosen top and that my face gave the illusion of minimal or no make-up, I presented myself to my full-length mirror for the verdict. Not bad. Patting my pockets for keys and money, I pulled the door to and walked out.

I was bang on time, she was early. This was a good sign. This particular Friday the bar had a cool buzz building as punters slotted into their seats to kick-start their evenings and we were no exception. Behind the bar, three male and two female bartenders in grey shirts were busy mixing, slicing and shaking.

As I approached, one of the women caught my eye and shot a piercing smile my way. Either she was desperate to pour me a drink or I was giving off come-get-me pheromones. I hoped Lucy was picking them up as I walked her way.

"Hi," she said, leaning in for a kiss. Cheek or lips? I panicked, turned my head and she ended up kissing my ear. Not a terribly smooth start.

"You look good," she said. Was it just me or had her voice got huskier? The hour had thrown up jeans, my special shiny red shoes and a paisley shirt that always drew compliments and action – Tom and Tess had christened it my pulling shirt but this was its first real outing in the UK.

"So do you," I replied. And she did. Glitter-flecked top,

fitted jeans, black shoes and alluringly shiny hair – she looked edible. I didn't take my eyes off her lips as she spoke.

"Tempt you into a cocktail then?" she said. "I was considering a Long Island Iced Tea but it might send me a bit loopy."

"What's that?" I indicated a glass already in front of her.

"Just water – I wanted to wait till you arrived to order proper drinks."

"Well, it's not a first-date drink but if we both have a Long Island Iced Tea then we're on even ground aren't we?"

"Or not so even."

She gestured to the bartender that we were ready to order. I smoothed myself down as I tried to find a comfortable position to assume while also coming across as sexy and alluring – no mean feat on a bar stool. The cute female bartender had been replaced by a cute male bartender who was equally smiley as he took our order.

"I think he fancies his chances," Lucy said as he zipped down the bar to retrieve a cocktail shaker.

"I don't blame him."

"So," she said.

"So," I repeated, smiling gently.

"I'm glad you came."

"It would have been rude to just leave you here alone, wouldn't it?"

She laughed.

"Very."

"It was a bit of a trek from my house, though."

"Oh yes, I imagine. At least a minute?"

"At least."

The drinks arrived and I handed the bartender a £20 note.

"Cheers," I said. We chinked glasses.

Lucy tasted hers first and made a face that suggested the drink was loaded with alcohol. I had a taste and made the same face, dimly recalling some show on lovers and how they mimic what the other does. Mental note to self.

"I know you really shouldn't drink these but I always think it's the best-value cocktail – all those spirits and the same price as a drink with only half the combinations. I think it's my Irish budget-driven upbringing," she said. When she laughed her eyes seemed to glitter like her top and her dimple made her look delectable.

"So, how was your day?" I asked.

She exhaled before she replied.

"Busy. Packed schedule and I had to refer one of my patients to a hospital as I think we detected cancer on a routine eye-scan. Horrible to do but good that we caught it early."

"That's a bit rubbish."

"It happens. At least she'll hopefully catch it before it does lasting or fatal damage. Cheery start to the conversation eh?" she said. "How was your day?"

"Not quite as dramatic. Unless you count the guy who came in wanting some quiche, a sandwich *and* a slice of cake – that's a lot of food for one person." We both laughed.

"Did you work in the café before you went to Australia?" she said.

"No, never done that kind of thing before. I worked in bars at university but I'm too clumsy to be a waitress and never really saw myself as the service type. But it beats working in an office hands-down – I never thought I'd take to it like I have. Plus, I can now bake a mean cake and offer free coffees to cute women who happen to come visit, which is always a winner, isn't it?"

"Certainly is," she said. "I admire that, you know."

"What?"

She shifted slightly on her stool and leant forward.

"That you had the guts to change things, get out of a job you didn't like. I did it too but it takes a lot. Tons of my mates are stuck in jobs they don't really like but they're too lazy or scared to trade them in for something else. They get used to the money and the lifestyle and then before you know it, you're 40 and stuck somewhere you don't want to be."

"I know plenty of people like that," I said. I sipped my drink and looked over to a group of girls who'd just come into the bar. They'd obviously been drinking for a while.

"I'm not sure I set out to change things as much, it just happened," I said. "When I came back from Oz I didn't want to just fall into my old life like the intervening three years never even happened. Porter's were advertising and I thought 'what the hell'? The worst that could happen was I didn't like it and then I could look for something else.

"But actually, it's been a breath of fresh air. Sometimes I'm amazed this is what I'm being paid to do. I'm even pretty good with customers and I've always thought I hated people secretly. Probably not something I should admit on a first date, right?"

Lucy laughed out loud. "I know what you mean – occupational hazard."

"You get people coming in looking sad, worried, happy – people buy coffee and cake in all different moods. And some of them, the people who come in mid-afternoon who are clearly bunking off work and needing some time – I want to go over and put an arm around them.

"I remember being them, remember being stuck in an office with artificial lighting. My last job in the UK, I never even knew what the weather was like outside because my window was too high to see out of."

Lucy nodded, stirring her drink with the black plastic stirrer.

"Life's too short."

"You changed career too?"

"Yep. I was going to be a lawyer."

I thought about Angela, my short-lived brush with the legal profession.

"Wow, that's quite a change."

"Yeah. Nobody in my family ever went to university and when I started, I wasn't really sure what I wanted to do. My parents were just amazed I was going and pleased to fund me a little. But I had to choose a subject and so I plumped for law."

"Far more sensible than my choice."

"Oh?" she said.

"International Relations."

She chuckled. "You were curious about the world and wanted to save it with your diplomacy, right?"

"Exactly that."

"Well, I was the opposite. I thought if I'm going to university, I'll do something *big*," she said, raising her voice slightly for the last word.

"So I did law. But after a while I realised that everyone on my course seemed really serious about it and I... Well, not so much. So I had a word with my course people and started all over again the following year but this time training to be an optician."

"And your parents were happy to support your decision?"

She nodded. "Yeah, they're quite chilled and they trust me, which helps."

I shamelessly leaned in closer to her, brushing my hair out of my eyes and looking upwards.

"So what's your expert opinion of my eyes?"

She put her hand up to my face, clutching my chin with her fingers on one side and her thumb on the other. She studied my eyes closely, which made my heart race that little bit faster. My whole face seemed to heat up at her touch.

"Deep, clear, brooding," she said. "Oh, I think you can see out of them too."

Her face was so near to me I was sure she could hear my heart, beating like a kick drum. I briefly considered leaning in to kiss her – it would have been so easy – but decided that wasn't first-date etiquette. Instead I leaned back, studying her collarbone, her breasts, her lips. Which really didn't help matters. I cleared my throat before speaking.

"I bet you say that to all the girls."

"Only the ones I'm interested in," she replied.

* * *

Half an hour later and we were in Nha Trang, my favourite Vietnamese restaurant which also turned out to be Lucy's, too. It wasn't a fancy place – if you go to an Asian restaurant that is, leave immediately. However, if you looked beyond the church hall chairs and white paper table cloths it had incredible food, although if you were expecting a smile you might be disappointed.

Once we were settled with our beers and prawn crackers, I began to babble. I also remembered to ask about her life and family, which I knew Julia would have given me a gold star for. Apparently in pressure situations I turn into a one-woman stand-up show, which is amusing for a while until I realise it's a monologue not a dialogue and it's all been about me. Tonight, I was performing well.

Lucy told me she was from an Irish Catholic background, the second of four kids. She'd grown up in Yorkshire where the rest of her family still lived but she'd decided to give London a go.

"Really, you're from Yorkshire?" I said.

"Yep."

"So why don't you sound all ee-by-gum?"

"I moved to London for uni and when I discovered nobody could understand a word I said or that if they did, it was the subject of great hilarity, I changed it. It still comes out when I'm drunk and in certain words but that's all. My family consider me a traitor but they'll get over it."

I also discovered she'd had three previous long-term relationships, one just tipping two years, and she'd been single for the past nine months. She also owned a flat in Bow and worked at an opticians in the city.

"Caroline tells me that I have to meet your family but I was a bit scared when she mentioned it might involve singing," I said. Lucy looked horrified but then burst out laughing.

"I can't believe she told you that," she said. She shook her head and smiled ruefully. "Don't worry, you don't have to sing until at least your third visit. And if it comes to it we can work out a song for you, no problem."

She must have seen the slight hesitation in my laughter because she reached over and stroked my arm.

"I am joking," she said.

I grinned with relief. "Yeah, I knew that."

"My family would love you – that's not the problem. It's whether you could take my family." She chuckled at her own joke. I noticed she had remarkably regimented teeth too, all stood to attention in a perfect white line.

In return, I told her an abridged version of my history, light on the heartbreak, heavy on the humour, glossing over the Karen question as if it hardly mattered and leaving out the key elements of betrayal. Even I knew never to get into past relationships on a first date.

"So are you pleased to be back in the UK?" Lucy asked after I'd painted Australia as a sunshine-filled playground.

"Things are certainly looking up," I said.

For the rest of the meal we chatted easily. She wasn't into football but apart from that she seemed almost impossibly perfect. By this time we were well into our second course and Lucy had mixed beansprouts, basil leaves and lime into her noodle soup, before adding more chilli than I would have dared.

"You like it hot," I said.

"I do," she replied. I felt a blush rise in my cheeks and tried to regain my cool. She looked amused.

"What were we talking about? My week... To be honest, I've just been working and looking forward to tonight," she told me, fixing me with an intent stare.

Bold, I thought. And sexy.

"Me too," I said.

* * *

When we finished Lucy insisted on paying and my heart duly swooned. I felt her hot hand clasp mine as she led me out the door and down the street, the night air still balmy to touch. We walked with just the slap of our soles on the pavement and the hum of anticipation in the air.

"Where we going?" I said. Lucy squeezed my hand.

"You'll see."

She took me to a bar I didn't even know existed – through a dark door and down into ultra-low lighting which caused my eyes to recoil. Once they adjusted, I saw Lucy was leading me to a booth with red leather seating. A waiter appeared and kissed Lucy on the cheek before holding out his hand to me.

"Max," he said. "Nice to meet you."

Max was only a few inches taller than me but he wore it well, his confidence and generous smile making him seem taller.

"Jess," I replied. I shook his hand. "I assume you two know each other?"

"Max is an old friend from university who's just opened this place. You like it?" Lucy put her arm around Max's shoulder and pulled him close.

I nodded. "It's great."

Max gave me an easy smile.

"What can I get you?" He ran his hand through his close-cut ginger hair, a pen wedged between his middle and index finger. "On the house of course."

"You're not going to make a mint that way sweetheart," Lucy said. We agreed on gin and tonics with Max waving away Lucy's money. When the drinks arrived Max put them down with a flourish, telling us to enjoy.

"Here's to a great evening," Lucy said. She winked at me and I melted on the spot.

I sipped my perfectly poured G&T, deciding I'd definitely be back if this was the standard of drinks.

"God, these are good," Lucy said, as if reading my thoughts. She put her hand on my leg and stroked it for a few moments, which caused a shiver right through my core. When were we going to kiss? I drifted off somewhere thinking about this and only zoned back in to catch the end of Lucy's sentence.

"...really great. Live music most weeks. Perhaps we could do that sometime soon?"

I blinked. I'd been so busy imagining our first kiss I'd faded out of the conversation. And she'd given me her full attention. I tried to style it out.

"Here?" I hoped that was the right answer and I'd got away with it. I had.

"Yeah. They've got a band I fancy coming along to soon, Violet Eyes. They're a bit new-wave disco kinda sound. Do you fancy coming with me?" She paused, looking at me expectantly and drawing her body back as she got slightly defensive.

"I mean, no worries if you don't want to…"

She was asking me out on a second date. And she thought I would say no. Silly woman. I jumped right in to quash her doubts.

"No no – that'd be great, I'd love to."

"Really?" she said, grinning and then trying to recover some semblance of cool. My heart flipped as I watched her try to regain it.

"Really."

We had another drink in the bar and chatted a little to Max before stepping out into the warm night air, which was a welcome contrast after the air-conditioned chill of the bar. As we fell into step beside each other walking towards Hoxton Square, I thought how right Lucy felt by my side.

Neither of us spoke at first and I realised we were both wondering where this was going. At least I was. I'd promised myself I wasn't going to sleep with her on the first date but if pushed my principles had been known to crumble under the weight of a gorgeous woman – it's just the way I was built. I wondered if Lucy had made the same promises to herself too.

"Great bar." I broke the silence first.

"Yeah it is." She took hold of my hand again as we walked.

"Do you fancy another drink?"

"I can't, I have to get up tomorrow," Lucy said, frowning. Getting up? This was news. "I have my cousin coming over from Canada and I'm picking him up from Heathrow at midday."

"Coffee at mine then? And I do mean a coffee," I said.

She looked at her watch, squeezed my hand and scuffed her feet on the floor. "I really shouldn't, it's nearly 12 now…"

She was being sensible. At least, I hoped that's all it was.

"No problem," I said. We stopped in front of my blue front door with the number 73 hanging in chrome on the front.

"Well, this is me," I said. I turned to face her, my back to the door. I was all set to try to persuade her to come up one more time but before I had a chance to get any words out, Lucy was pressing me up against the door, pressing her lips onto mine, kissing me. Finally.

I felt her right hand brush my face as she kissed me lightly at first. I kissed her back but let her take the lead. After a couple of minutes when her other hand was firmly placed around my back and our hips were locked together, I felt her tongue slide inside and I drew a breath.

Her kiss became more intense and I lost myself in the moment. We may have been standing up against my front door in a side street in East London, but we really could have been anywhere in the world. All I knew was that a seriously sexy woman had her hands on me and was kissing me into submission. Eventually, Lucy pulled away slightly, kissing me more gently now, running her hand up and down my back, kneading the skin lower down.

When I eventually opened my eyes hers were already open and locked firmly on mine. She kissed me one more time and grinned. I pushed her away slightly and inhaled, but noticed that she wasn't being brushed off that easily. We were still joined at the hip, our breathing ragged, our smiles broad.

"You sure you don't want to come upstairs?"

She stepped back a pace and laughed, running her hand down my face to my breast before coming back in for a kiss. Her face was inches from mine and I was finding it hard to breathe.

"If I did that, I doubt I'd be anywhere near Heathrow tomorrow morning, do you?" she whispered.

"Maybe not," I mumbled. Lucy planted another kiss on me, which my whole body melted into. Both of us thought of pulling away but neither one of us could.

"I should go," she said.

"I know...."

She slipped her tongue inside my mouth and I quivered inside and out. Lucy pressed her thigh in between mine and I wondered how I was going to let go of her tonight, how she was going to do the same to me. Her kisses were getting more urgent now.

I took a gamble and pushed her gently off me, moving her with me as I twisted to face my door. I fumbled with the key trying to get it in the lock as Lucy kissed her way down my neck. Not distracting at all.

Neither one of us spoke about the fact that she was meant to be on her way home right now. Walking in the door, I again nearly tripped over Kate's bike and cursed. Lucy giggled at my profanity as I pulled on her hand and led her up the stairs and into the lounge.

Once there though, I was struck with a case of shyness and was somewhat hesitant of the next stage of the evening. I busied myself by walking to the kitchen to get drinks, telling Lucy to choose something from the iPod as I left the lounge. But when I realised I had no idea what she wanted to drink I returned to find her wheeling through my collection. She looked edible and my fear multiplied.

"Did you find something?"

"Quite a lot about you, I think," she said. She turned her head towards me from where she was bent over. "You've got quite a selection of country on here."

"I could lie and tell you it's Kate's, but I won't," I said, holding both my hands up. "Guilty as charged. What do you fancy?"

"Whatever you're having."

"Beer?"

"Beer's great." She flashed me her killer smile.

I gulped down my nerves and grabbed two Peronis from the fridge. When I returned, Kenny and Dolly were warbling about islands in the stream. I laughed and handed her a bottle.

"Good choice."

"You can't beat a bit of Dolly," she said. "I took my mum to see her at Wembley – she was awesome."

"She is."

The leather sofa creaked as I sat down next to her,

electricity crackling between us as our thighs touched. We both took a swig of our beer then I twisted so I was facing Lucy. Her focus was straight ahead.

"Nice place," she said, putting her bottle on the coffee table and running her palms up and down her thighs. "How long has Kate been here?"

"Since before I went to Oz, so a few years now. Pretty cool though…"

"I'd expect it from Kate. She's quite particular from what I know of her."

"Good cook too, so I can't complain."

"But so are you now…"

I leant forward to put my beer next to hers and then leaned back, taking her hand in mine and entwining our fingers. I twisted into her, kissed her lightly on the lips and felt my whole body react.

"Now where were we?"

She smiled her dazzling smile, kissed me back and twisted her body into mine, crossing her legs and running her foot up my shin. I leaned in closer, cupping her left breast with my right hand and kneading it gently. She responded by stroking my face as we kissed, breathing heavily as she slipped her tongue inside my mouth. I felt her smile as she kissed me.

"You like that?" she whispered. I felt her tongue lick along my ear lobe before it dropped under my ear – her hot breath in my ear at the same time was almost too much to bear. She travelled along my jawline before kissing me passionately on the lips. After a few seconds she pulled back.

"I have to go soon," she said, staring into my eyes.

"Tell me you're joking."

"I'm joking." Her eyes burned with desire.

Instead, she began to kiss me again, swivelling her body until she was straddling my waist, our hips and bodies now locked together. She began to kiss my neck as I ground my pelvis into hers and put both hands at the top of her buttocks, pulling her into me.

Both of us were breathless and even though we were both still fully dressed we were already in good voice – I wondered what the night ahead held. We were now into the advanced stages of frottage and if they ever do make it into an Olympic sport, I hope to be able to represent my country with honour.

I caressed her lips with mine, reaching up under her shirt to try to unhook her bra – I was out of practice and couldn't do it. She laughed, reaching behind herself but I pushed her hand away and tried again with both hands, causing her to fall into me and kiss the top of my head.

As I succeeded, I slid both hands around to the front and pushed up with my pelvis. In response, Lucy slipped her top off over her head and shook off her now unclasped bra to reveal full, gorgeous breasts. I touched them as if they were breakable, making sure to take it all in, running my fingers over her soft skin and dark nipples.

"You're beautiful," I said. I reached up and pulled her towards me again but after a couple of seconds she pushed away and stood up. She held my gaze as she stood in front of me, a blaze of smooth skin and breathtakingly sexy. I was spellbound.

"Shall we?" She held out her hand and I took it without hesitation. "Lead the way then. This is my first time here remember?" she said. I kissed her and tugged on her hand, stopping momentarily as she ran back to retrieve her discarded clothing.

Once in my room we fell onto the bed kissing, Lucy pulling at my shirt. I sat up and went to unbutton it, but she slapped my hands.

"Let me," she said. She expertly slipped each button loose, pushing it back and kissing my collarbone, breasts, stomach. She reached round to undo my bra, managed it first time and slipped it off, bending down to kiss my left nipple as she tossed the bra aside. I sighed with pleasure as she teased my nipple, circling it with her tongue and nibbling it gently. Within seconds she was lurking over me on all fours, her breasts delicious above me. She reached down with her right hand to undo my belt, unzip my jeans, slip her hand inside them and press down firmly. I cried out. Fucking hell, I was so ready.

"Are you always this easy?" she said.

"Not always," I said. Her hand was still on my crotch and I could feel myself pulsing.

"God, you're sexy." I never claimed to be a poet when put in this situation. She smiled though and it seemed like I'd said the right thing.

Lucy slipped off my jeans, then worked upwards from my feet, kissing my legs and licking the back of my knees. When she sunk her teeth into my arse I let out a squeal which made her chuckle. I felt her breath in my ear seconds later.

"Was that a good squeal or a bad squeal?" she asked. I swallowed down.

"Good," I said, my voice cracking. "Just unexpected." I felt her grin beside me before running her tongue over my ear again and my body shuddered.

Next thing I knew I was on my back and I could feel my sweat against the sheets. She slid my pants off, then her breasts were tantalisingly in my face. But before I could touch she put her whole weight on top of me, pressing her naked body into mine. Her skin fully against mine felt glorious and we both let out low moans.

"Jesus," I said.

After teasing me some more she finally manoeuvred her body and reached down between my open legs, slipping through my liquid heat. My whole body rocked and I was overwhelmed with pleasure at the feel of her inside me, her leaning on me, her breath on my face. As she slid in and out I felt my body responding, pushing my hips up so she could go deeper. Within minutes I felt the slow, steady build of an orgasm begin but then Lucy began to concentrate on my clit. I was close.

She began nibbling on my neck and whispered: "Come for me baby."

And that was it. With those few words, she tipped me over the edge. As my body exploded, my back arched and I moaned loudly, Lucy proved herself adept by thrusting back into me and fucking me hard and fast. All manner of kaleidoscopic rainbows played in my head – she was that good. After a few moments I put my hand down to hers to stop her – she went to pull out but I shook my head.

"Stay for a while," I whispered.

"Okay," she said, kissing my breast softly before laying on top of me. I could feel myself hugging her fingers inside, not wanting to let her go. When I opened my eyes, she was smiling down at me. I reached up and kissed her.

"You're beautiful." I touched the side of her face. She smiled but looked bashful.

"So are you." We held each other's gaze for a second.

It was that moment – the time when you've just had sex with someone and you feel the connection. I wanted to stop time and stay in that moment forever, Sky Plus it and play it back again and again – my whole being fizzed with the absolute glory of it. It was wordless, but it just was.

Cut that moment down the middle and it would have had both our names carved through its core – it was ours and ours alone. I knew she felt it too because within seconds she was kissing me again, softly but urgently, wanting to prolong the moment, not wanting reality to bruise it. I kissed her back and the moment stayed. It was going nowhere. This was clearly our time.

I took advantage and reached up and into Lucy while she was still on top of me. She sucked in breath, her body bucked a little, then she kissed me again as the moment deepened. It was this kind of instance that makes people cry out that they love each other in the throes of passion. I concentrated hard on not doing that on our first date.

After a few moments, Lucy adjusted herself on top of me, got her rhythm and I steadied myself as she ground herself into me. It was intense, with pure unrivalled lust driving the show – we'd both been waiting for this, imagined it in our beds throughout the week. I drew her head towards me and fucked her fast, plunging my tongue into her as I did, twisting and thrusting into her wetness with my skilled hand. She responded as I knew she would. This was going to be a long night.

As she clutched my hand and came, her body straining from the effort, she fell into me, her head on my shoulder. I kissed her neck, then gently manoeuvred her over onto her back. She looked pleased with the new situation.

"You didn't think you were done, did you?" I licked her ear before moving down to her delectable breasts.

"I was hoping not."

She breathed out heavily, running her hand absentmindedly through my hair. I carried on kissing down her body, licked her flat stomach, circled her belly button and then I was kissing her pubes, licking her inner thigh, clamping down on her sex. There was nowhere to hide. Within minutes she was arching her body too, releasing herself under my insistent tongue, pushing my head away, telling me she could take no more. I kissed her some more and made my way up to the pillow, kissed her cheek, her mouth and laid beside her. We were silent for at least a minute.

"Wow," I said. I had that utter lack of coherence that only overtakes you right after orgasm.

"Mmmm," she replied. Her eyes were closed.

She shook her head gently and grinned from ear to ear. I trailed my hand up the side of her face and she turned her head to kiss my hand. After a few minutes simply staring at each other, she rolled on top of me and raised an eyebrow.

"Ready to go again?"

* * *

We fell asleep three hours later in each other's arms, legs entwined, both of us fully spent. We extrapolated ourselves soon after though – drifting off in those positions is one thing, but it's only in the movies that they stay like that all night without cutting off their blood supply.

We'd broken all the first night rules – we hadn't sampled each other, we'd taken each other fully. Then again, this was no normal first night and we both knew it. This was something else: we fitted. This was the kind of night that makes you think the next morning you're going to wake up and it will all have been a dream. But I knew it wasn't and as I drifted off that night with Lucy's leg wrapped around me, shrouded in a hazy cloud of sex, I knew there was nowhere else I'd rather be.

Chapter Twenty-Two

The sunlight slithered in under my too-light curtains the next morning way too early for either of us.

"Too bright," murmured Lucy. She looked so damn sexy I wanted to take a picture and frame it for my wall.

"Let me make a call and I'll tell them to turn the sun down," I said. I kissed her cheek. She opened one eye cautiously.

"What time is it?"

I rolled over and hit the light button on my alarm clock. It read 9:05. I estimated we'd had around five hours sleep.

"You've got to be at the airport in three hours to pick up your cousin."

"Shit," she said. She moved onto her back and opened both eyes. "I think my eyes are dead."

"Good job you're an optician then."

She rolled into me and buried her head in my chest.

"Damn my cousin and his terrible timing," she mumbled. After a few minutes of listening to each other's breathing and revelling in the other's body heat, she pulled away slightly and propped herself up on one arm. She looked me directly in the eye and smiled wickedly.

"So who are you again?"

I grinned. "The woman your mother warned you about."

"Ah yes. I've been waiting for your call." She kissed me deeply and we stayed like that for a few minutes.

"This is not getting you to the airport," I said.

In response, she wrapped her leg around my outer thigh and I felt her hand slide from my breast down my stomach and beyond. I sucked in breath and my insides sprawled as she pressed her tongue into my mouth. I stopped talking. Before I knew it, she'd moved her body stealth-like on top of me and was buried deep inside me, fucking me gently, pressing herself into me and making me wonder why all mornings didn't start just like this. I spread my legs and moved my hips, feeling how wet I was and savouring the moment. It wasn't long before I came, more quietly this morning but no less satisfying.

"You were saying about being that woman..." She smiled down at me. 24 hours ago I hadn't even kissed her, now she was lying naked, inches away from my face. Life was a funny thing wasn't it?

"I take it all back. Now I think about it, I think *you're* the woman my mother warned *me* about," I said. "But I distinctly remember she said you'd be blonde so maybe I'm mistaken."

She laughed gently, sliding off me.

"Your mum was far more descriptive than mine."

"Can we stop talking about my mum now?" I said.

"Not appropriate first date pillow talk?"

"Not really," I said. I groaned as she extracted herself from me.

"So how would you rate this first date?" she asked. With my body falling into the bed in my post-orgasmic state, I smiled at her weakly.

"You can come again."

"I hope so," she said. She kissed my shoulder. "But with incredible bad timing, now I have to go. I hate my family, did I mention that?"

"A couple of times."

"You're too delicious to leave." She kissed me again.

"I could come with you."

She sat up and considered it for a moment but shook her head.

"It'd be a bit weird. I don't want him to feel like he's playing gooseberry to a couple who've been up half the night having sex, which is exactly how it would be." She paused. "Have you got dinner at your parents today did you say?"

I closed my eyes and shook my head. "Tomorrow thank god. Today I plan to sleep, eat processed food and watch Match Of The Day. All the while wearing a stupid grin thinking back to last night."

"I'm so jealous," she said.

"You can lie in tomorrow while I face the wrath of my family. And with Kate smirking at me the whole time."

"Have a couple of glasses of wine and it'll be fine," she said. "Besides, won't Kate be too busy fending off your mum's advances?"

"That sounds very weird coming out of your mouth."

"It sounded just as weird when you told me last night," she said. "I'll have to make sure your mum's as crazy about me, won't I?"

"You're planning on meeting her then are you?"

Lucy blushed, realising what she'd said and I felt bad for pointing it out. I stroked her back.

"My mum's going to love you so you have no worries on that score. If for nothing else than you're an optician and in her eyes that is a Proper Job."

She smiled, placated. "I hope so, because I plan on coming back."

"I'm pleased to hear it."

We kissed again, our lips drawn to each other like two halves of the same magnet.

"This was the problem last night, I recall."

"I only came in for a coffee, I've no idea what happened." She grinned devilishly.

"Witchcraft I think. Now go before I take you hostage for the day and tie you up."

"I thought we agreed that was a third-date scenario."

She climbed on top of me and ground her naked body into mine. I raised my eyebrows.

"I'm going," she said, holding up both palms in defence. "I'm just getting my money's worth before I leave."

"Charming," I said. She hoiked herself off me.

"Can I use your shower? I should at least try to look presentable for Chris shouldn't I?"

"Course – take my dressing gown." I pointed to where it was hanging on the back of the bedroom door. "And there are towels on the shelf in the bathroom."

Lying there listening to the water cascade on Lucy's body, it took me back to Ange and how different this felt. That morning I'd woken up tasting regret. Today though, my only regret was that Lucy had to rush off and we couldn't stay like this all day. Still, it would probably stop us becoming a lesbian cliché and moving in together tomorrow.

I mused on my favourable situation, flexing my toes, stretching my fingers and moving my head from side to side in a bid to stretch out my body. I must have dozed off though, because the next thing I knew Lucy was shaking me awake, standing next to the bed shower-fresh in my white dressing gown.

"I'm going to be late and it's your fault," she said. She rubbed her hair vigorously with a towel. As she leant forward, the gown fell open slightly and I could see her breasts through the gap.

"Can you check the tube lines for me on my phone?"

I picked up Lucy's iPhone from the bedside table and obediently opened the underground app. Unusually, all the London underground lines were running fine on this particular Sunday morning which Lucy was pleased about, giving me a thumbs up as she let the gown drop to the floor. She was naked now and I was staring. I couldn't help it. She was gorgeous and completely unselfconscious. I was still a little shy when it came to that but Lucy had no such qualms and why should she, with a body like hers? Petite, toned and tanned. She reached down for her pants from the floor and hopped into them.

"So what are you doing with your cousin today?"

She breathed out heavily. "Sighing, drinking coffee and trying to stay awake." She paused, thinking about it for a second, then shrugged.

"Dunno. We'll probably drop his stuff off at mine and then go for lunch somewhere. And then I'm hoping he's really tired and we can watch a film and go to bed."

In an uncharacteristic burst of daring, I pulled back the covers and got up, grabbing the dressing gown from where she'd discarded it on the floor. Lucy pulled me in for a kiss and I ran my hands up and down her naked back, finally resting on her butt.

"You smell like sex," she said.

"And you smell like my shower gel." I kissed her again. "I was gonna make you a cup of tea – you got time?"

"That would be great," she said.

I gave her a final kiss and headed to the kitchen to put the kettle on.

* * *

After Lucy left I must have drifted off to sleep, because the next thing I knew was someone knocking on my door.

"You up yet?" I let my eyes edge open and saw Kate's face peering round my door. "Can I come in?"

It was more a statement than a question as she walked over to perch on the side of my bed. I rubbed my eyes and pushed myself further up the bed into a semi-sitting-up position.

"You could have at least brought some coffee if you're going to barge in."

"Kettle's on, this is just your wake-up call."

"What time is it?" I rubbed my eyes.

"Twenty to one. Time you were up." She paused. "So…"

I laughed as she raised her eyebrows at me.

"Where's she hiding?"

"Not here. She had to go and pick up her cousin from Heathrow." I yawned before stretching my whole body which caused Kate to get up as I wriggled beneath her.

"Two women in the space of a couple of weeks. Who's going to be in your bed next week we wonder?"

I shot her a look.

"Well, you can tell me all about it over coffee and then we can tell Shirley all about it over lunch tomorrow."

"Ha ha. Just go and make me coffee wench."

Kate chuckled as she backed out of the room, hands together as if praying and bowing as she left.

* * *

I was out in the lounge in five minutes, pulling my dressing gown around me and pressing my nose to it to see if I could still smell Lucy in it. I reckoned I could.

"So young lady," Kate began, putting fresh coffee in front of me. "Shall I put you some toast in while you tell me all about it?"

"Yes please, I'm starving."

"I bet you are."

She went back to the kitchen and I heard the rustle of the bread bag.

"You're being very nice to me," I shouted after her. She shouted something back but I couldn't hear it. I looked at my coffee and added one and a half sugars, figuring if ever there was a sugar day, this was one. I heard Kate open the fridge and moments later she reappeared with the margarine and marmalade.

"I said you're spoiling me," I told her as she sat down at the table.

"Well, then you won't hold back."

I smiled and took a deep breath out. "Nothing to tell. We went out, we came back and she ended up staying. I'm in lust. Anything else?"

Kate picked up her coffee mug and took a sip, blowing on it first.

"So you touched her tits, then?"

"A few times."

We heard the toast pop and I went to get up but Kate pushed me down.

"You need your rest." She delivered the goods in seconds.

"What did you do last night then?" I said.

"I was meant to stay at Caroline's but she ended up working. Again."

"So you were here?" I said. I felt my cheeks colour.

"It's okay, you were very quiet. Ish."

I concentrated on buttering my toast while Kate chuckled.

"Nice flowers," I said, pointing to a bunch of tulips that had appeared overnight, red and yellow tops at the end of milky green stems.

"Nice try."

I took a bite of my toast after smearing it with jam.

"There's nothing else to say. Unless you'd like to see the video?"

"Before the football or after?"

* * *

I managed to shake Kate off the topic of Lucy by letting her moan about Caroline and how they never saw each other anymore. It wasn't difficult.

"I work all week and then she works all weekend," she said.

"She's saving lives and you're trashing them working on your gossip rag. There's something poetic about that, don't you think? Do you think you were attracted to her because her goodness balances out your badness?"

"I'm just pissed off. I'm starting to think she doesn't want to see me anymore and that's more the issue."

"Really?"

"Maybe." She paused. "I dunno. Maybe I'm just being dramatic." She pushed out her bottom lip. "But that's my forte isn't it?"

"It is. And I'd say you are." I sat forward on the sofa. "Hey we can go out together as a foursome soon – you, me, Caroline and Lucy. There's something for you to look forward to." Kate didn't look thrilled.

"Okay grumpy. Let me get myself together..." I said, heaving myself off the sofa. "...And we can go down the pub and you can moan at me through the football."

"Sounds like my perfect Saturday," she said.

Chapter Twenty-Three

The next day we were out of the house by the allotted time and on a bus to my parent's house in the North London suburbs. My head throbbed as the bus jolted along the road, fresh potholes appearing every few seconds to add to my discomfort. I breathed out heavily and Kate patted my thigh lightly. She didn't seem to suffer too much with hangovers, which (along with her washboard stomach) was just another brick in the unfairness wall of life.

However, in my corner this morning was Lucy who'd sent me a sexy wake-up text, letting me know that she wished it was me she was waking up with this morning and not her cousin, hastily adding he wasn't in her bed but rather in her spare room. I was impressed by that fact – having a spare room meant you were officially grown up.

I texted Lucy back, telling her there was nothing I would have liked more than to wake up with her that morning, to smell her skin, feel her touch. She already felt like a part of me; I already felt addicted. That thought made me smile but it also worried me too. The last time I'd felt something this strong was with Karen and look how that ended.

* * *

We arrived at my parents' house to a scene of mayhem. Freddie and Luke were chasing each other round a well-worn circuit of the ground floor – out through the lounge door, down the hallway, into the dining room and then through the lounge: repeat until someone falls over. Stepping into the hallway after Vicky opened the door was to blunder onto a racing circuit and fear for your life. Sure enough, within 20 seconds Luke had crashed into my legs, causing Freddie to crash into him and me to stagger into Vicky.

"Boys! What did I tell you? Slow down!" said Vicky. She struggled to keep the strictness in her voice.

"Hiya by the way," she added, hugging me. She looked her usual coolly turned out self but her eyes and the bags under them also gave away tiredness. I made a mental note to sit myself beside her so my mum wouldn't single out the tell-tale tired luggage on my face.

"Hey yourself," I said, still smiling but also wincing and rubbing my leg. Meanwhile, Jack appeared and scooped up a whimpering Luke in his arms, with Freddie seemingly unperturbed – he was two years old and indestructible. Jack grinned and leaned over to give me a kiss before I planted one on Luke in his arms.

"Sorry if my leg hurt you Luke. Bad leg," I said. I hit my leg and winced in pain. I'd hit it a bit too hard.

"Selfless aunty," Jack said. "How are we, ladies?" He kissed Kate hello.

"Ready for a drink," Kate said, shrugging off her coat.

Jack put Luke down then took our coats as we followed Vicky through to the kitchen. Mum and Dad were in full Sunday lunch flow, the smell of roast lamb searing the air, the heat of the kitchen sticking to our skin as we walked in.

"Girls! Hello!" Dad said. I was touched to see he was wearing his blue apron with white stripes that I'd sent over last Christmas.

Not for the first time though, I wondered when either Kate or I – both being over 30 – would graduate to being ladies in my dad's eyes. Being called girls always grated with me and it was something I was having to get used to all over again now I was back. I would have loved to have brought it up with Dad but it seemed a little churlish. Pick your battles, as Kate had told me when I mentioned it.

We both kissed him and Mum, then Dad opened the fridge and popped his head around it.

"Beer? Wine? G&T?"

"Beer please," Kate said.

"Me too."

Dad took two Stellas out of the fridge and put them on the counter. "Glasses over there," he said, indicating the cupboard by my head.

"I know, I did used to live here."

"Okay," he said in a sing-song voice, not quite understanding my bristling tone. I urged myself to put my qualms aside and settle into this lunch, otherwise it could get uncomfortable for us all.

"Thanks, Dad." A bit more contrite.

"You okay?" Mum said. Her pink top brought out her red hair, although she'd clearly been at the wine already as her face had a slight rouged hue.

"Fine," I said.

"Late night?"

"Not particularly, just a bit tired."

Kate coughed as I passed her the bottle opener.

"You should try some of those herbal pills, worked wonders when I went through that patch last year you know," she said. I grunted at my mum's suggestion and wondered why I'd turned into a surly teenager. My parents were clearly puzzled too but turned their attention to Kate instead.

"So Kate, how are you doing living with Jess? You keeping her in check?" Dad said. He still had a tone in his voice which told me he was a little afraid of the answer he might get. Part of Dad perceives the gay lifestyle as so other to his: orgies, keys in bowls and hazy smoke-filled rooms. How disappointed he'd be to learn it's exactly the same as his, one long conga line of washing up, council tax bills and jam in the margarine.

"I do my best, Ian, but she's a bit of a wild child," Kate said.

"I think you should be asking Jess that about my sister from what I hear," Vicky said. And so began the inquisition of the city slickers from the suburbanites.

I ducked out, leaving Kate and Vicky charming my parents, and took Luke into the lounge where Jack was on the floor with Freddie. I sat on the sofa and put Luke on my lap but he wriggled free just like Tess's cats always had anytime I'd tried the same trick with them.

"So, little sis, how are things?"

"Things are good," I said. "Great in fact."

"Date went well, then?"

I nodded.

"Good for you, it's about time."

"About time?"

Jack shrugged. "Well you know – it's been a while since Karen, hasn't it? Someone new would be nice."

"I suppose so."

"So when do we get to meet her?" He looked overly excited.

"When the second, third and possibly the tenth date is over and I know she doesn't scare easily."

"I'm not talking about Mum and Dad."

"Even so, I don't want to rush this one. She's... I don't know, but I think this could be something."

Jack raised his eyebrows at me. "From the grand dame of understatement, that's almost like a declaration of love."

* * *

We sat down to dinner half an hour later after Kate and I had set the table while Vicky helped Mum and Dad in the kitchen. I don't know why it's always been that way but it has – I set up and wash up but never cook.

Mum was in inquisitive mood and the conversation soon turned to Caroline, much to my surprise. Clearly, other lesbians' love lives were fair game but mine was a different story.

"So Kate, I hear you're courting," Mum said. Vicky and I both choked on our green beans. Meanwhile, Freddie was sat alongside me kicking me rhythmically in the knee, which wasn't all that comfortable. When I tried to stop him under the table, he just kicked my hand instead so I decided to put up with it for now. I kept trying to shift position in a bid to avoid the incoming foot but he seemed to shift with me, needing me to bounce off to keep his stride.

"I am, yes – Caroline."

"Wonderful. What does she do?"

I felt like I was in some sort of surreal sketch show but the canned laughter never came – rather, the whole family was straining their eyes and ears, wondering where this was going.

"She's a nurse, works at the general on geriatrics."

"A nurse. How lovely to be going out with a nurse," Mum said. She was smiling a smile I didn't recognise.

"Good bedside manner, Kate?" Jack said.

"Jack!" Mum said. The rest of us sniggered as Mum gave him a disapproving stare.

"Well you must bring her next time, plenty of lamb left over," Dad said, indicating the not-yet eaten meat. This was all getting far too weird for me.

"She tends to work a lot of weekends but if she's free I will," Kate said. There was a pause while we all looked around, rummaging in our brains for the next subject. I'm not quite sure why but I took the lead against all my better instincts.

"I've started seeing someone too, so perhaps I'll bring her along as well."

Where it had come from I had no idea, but there it was. Out there in the middle of the table along with the roast potatoes, sliced lamb and mint sauce. It didn't have its own dish but right now it was centre stage with flashing lights. I'd told my family I was seeing someone and I didn't even know if I was. Oh my god.

"Really?" Mum said. She was blinking at a rapid rate, chewing her food round and round with no sign of digestion imminent.

"Well, that's marvellous!" Dad said. His voice was now so uncomfortably high he reminded me of Ange. I took a large swig of my wine and forged ahead on the white-water rapids I'd suddenly launched myself onto, water splattering in my face at an alarming rate.

"She's called Lucy, she's an optician." I paused to check Mum's face and sure enough, there was an uplift. I slalomed on. "She's really nice. You'd like her."

All of a sudden my bravado disappeared and my canoe capsized. I took another swig of my wine and focused my attention on Freddie.

"And you young man can stop kicking me." Amazingly, he did as he was told.

"So how long have you been seeing her?" Mum said. I could see the cogs whirring in her brain.

"We had our first date on Friday."

"Friday. Early days then." Her tone implied it was a bit soon to be making grand statements when I'd had one solitary date.

"Yes, but I'm optimistic."

If the word awkward hadn't already been invented, I would have carved it into the table then and there and presented it to my mother, gift-wrapped.

"Well, of course she's welcome any time," Mum said. "Any of your friends are."

And there it was: Kate was courting, I had a friend.

"She's my girlfriend, Mum." I didn't want to give this up even though I knew it was a fight I'd already conceded. Plus, was she my girlfriend after one date? Even I wasn't sure.

"You know what I mean," she said. Her tone and body language told me this subject experiment had just come to close. "Now, who's for more potatoes?"

And with that we were back on familiar Sunday lunch territory, the thorny prospect of my love life being swept neatly back under the carpet.

Chapter Twenty-Four

Before bed that night I decided to write some emails and check Facebook. When I worked in an office I used to check Facebook at least once an hour and at times was worried I was becoming addicted. These days, though, I'd shaken my addiction and now Facebook was just a casual pastime, which was probably more appropriate for someone in their 30s.

I double-clicked on my email and as it hovered into view, a familiar name sat in my inbox, causing my stomach to churn. I shifted on my bed. Karen had emailed me, something she hadn't done since she'd told me to leave and pulled the duvet over her and Paula. But now that Paula had deserted her, had she been lying alone under the duvet and thinking of me? I took a deep breath, slowly wheeled the cursor across the screen and clicked on the email which was innocuously titled 'Hi From Sydney.'

Dear Jess,

I know this is not an email you were expecting to receive but I feel compelled to write to you so I hope you read this and don't just discard it. Hope the UK is treating you well and you're enjoying being back home with your friends and family. Sydney is the same as it always was, but it misses you. I'm not really sure how to start this letter, so I guess I'll just dive right in…

I'm writing to say sorry for everything that happened. I know I treated you badly with the whole Paula situation and I've since had time to think about it and just wanted you to know I was really happy with you and buggered it up. What happened had nothing to do with you, it was all about me and where I was at – i.e., not a good place. Paula filled a void temporarily, but it's only now that I'm in therapy I realise how wrong I was and how much I owe you an apology.

You were nothing but lovely to me and I threw it all back in your face. I hope you don't bear too much of a grudge and that if our paths do ever cross in the future we could say hello. I hope that one day we can even be friends but I know that's up to you.

I just want you to know that I valued our time together and that everything that happened was my fault, all down to me and nothing to do with you. This is all my shit that I'm dealing with now. Paula and I are no longer together in case you didn't know.

Anyway, I hope you're happy doing whatever you're doing. I ran into Tess a few weeks ago and she said you were so that's good. I'm also planning on a trip to the UK in the next few weeks so maybe we could catch up – I'll be in London for a bit. I still love you but I understand I've probably burnt my bridges with you.

Take care, all my love,
Karen xxx

Well. I wasn't expecting that.

Chapter Twenty-Five

After Karen's email I'd managed to get a surprisingly good night's sleep, waking from a dream in which I was being chased by a dragon called Karen when my alarm went at 6.30am. My first thought on waking was 'Karen is a dragon'. This was quickly followed by 'Karen is coming to London'. And then: 'Fuck. Shit. Fuckity fucksticks.'

Lucy had texted me as promised to let me know she was home with her cousin and thinking of me, having recurring flashbacks to Friday night. She wasn't the only one.

I relished these times when it was all about base instincts and all you had to think about was having sex and when you could next fit it in. The lust stages of a relationship were always the easiest – it's when you started trying to talk and brought feelings into the equation that things got complicated.

However, somehow with the knowledge of what was sitting in my inbox, I began to feel guilty. My ex had emailed to say she was still in love with me and she was coming to London, just months after I'd flown home to get away from her. Just when life seemed to be getting back on track, it seemed there were some engineering works on the line.

Throughout my morning shower thoughts fizzed through my head. Should I tell Lucy? Should I tell anyone? Should I just ignore the situation? After all, Karen didn't know where I lived. But she did know where my parents lived and I'm sure if she fished around hard enough somebody would tell her my London whereabouts. I winced as my hand hit a spot that was forming in my hairline – I must be ovulating. The newly forming spot buzzed atop my head, temporarily averting my brain train, but not for long.

I pulled on jeans and a blue T-shirt, blowing out my cheeks in cartoon fashion and shaking my head from side to side. This could be nothing. This could just be Karen playing with me. Remember, she used to do that?

I sat down but I couldn't remember anything about our relationship. All I could remember was that I loved her, she cheated and now she was getting on a plane and coming to London to win me back. Nine months ago I would have leapt for joy and headed right back into the storm.

Today though, things were different. My compass had identified a new direction, one that I was so confident of I'd even told my parents about. If Karen turned up, so be it. She would find a different woman, not one who'd fall for her charms again. Walking to work, I cursed Karen for bursting my perfect Lucy-shaped bubble.

Matt, though, was having no such trouble, appearing to be fully embracing his bubble with gusto when I arrived. I was ten minutes early but he was already in the café whipping up some banana and blueberry muffins when I arrived.

"Morning," he said without looking up, spooning the mixture into the muffin cases. The kitchen already smelt way more delicious than any other workplace I'd been in.

"Good weekend?" he asked.

"Can't complain. You?"

"Very good thanks."

I slung my bag over the hook by the kitchen door and grabbed my newly laundered apron – Matt had done the honours this weekend.

"And by very good you mean?"

This time he looked up, licking some of the mixture off his finger as he did.

"Just that. I mean, she's amazing. Where did Julia find her? She loves sport, she's funny, she's attractive and she's solvent. We had an even better second date. I keep wondering where the catch is."

"On the back of her bra."

"Ha ha."

"So you had a good time?"

"I had a great time," he said, picking up a tray and transporting it to the oven. "And I think she did too. I mean, it's been a while, you know..." He paused. "But I managed not to spill anything down me, I held doors open and..." He shrugged. "We had a good time." He looked shy all of a sudden and I laughed.

"There's no need to be so apologetic about it."

"Julia should really start up a match-making service, she's that good."

I snorted. "Perhaps for straights. Remember she's set me up on quite a few dates and I'm not married yet."

"But you have had far more sex than you would have had without her."

"True, but not all of it advisable."

I was glad Matt didn't know the full extent of my Julia-induced sluttery.

"Anyway, how was your big date?"

"Pretty much the same as yours," I said. "We had a great night and I'm seeing her again, so I don't think I repelled her too much. And I didn't spill anything either."

We grinned at each other triumphantly.

"Well I think that deserves a cup of tea, don't you?"

"I'll put the kettle on."

Matt and I spent the next two hours prattling on about how great our respective dates had been. If Beth had been there she would have clouted us both over the head with a muffin tray.

* * *

That night I called Julia and told her about Karen's email. I could hear her tutting down the phone and shaking her head.

"She's got a bloody cheek. Her other girlfriend's dumped her and now she wants you back and thinks if she says sorry that'll work? I hope you emailed her straight back and told her not to bother coming."

"Not quite."

"What…" she said. The exasperation in her voice was very much evident. Matters of the heart had always been so straightforward for Julia, so her patience often wore thin when life didn't run as smoothly for others.

"You're not…" I could hear the question in her voice.

"No I'm not," I said.

"Well, good."

"But I also don't want to react straightaway – I want to let it sink in for a bit and consider my answer. I'm sure she didn't knock that email up in ten minutes."

"Send it to me, I want to see it."

"Thing is, I don't know what to say just yet. I mean, I don't want to see her. But then again I don't want to reply like a hysterical harlot saying 'don't you come to England'…"

"Why not? It's your bloody country."

"I think the Queen might disagree with you."

"If Liz knew what Karen had done she'd be on your side. Look, I know you still have a thing for Karen…"

"I don't…" I said. Defensive.

"I know you don't in that way, but you're still…" She paused to locate the right word. "Vulnerable."

"I am not vulnerable." I was double-defensive now.

"Trust me, you are. It's a fault of yours," Julia said. "I haven't even met the woman and I hate her. I don't want you meeting her. You've just met someone and you like her – don't let Karen ruin that."

"I'm not going to. But I also can't stop her coming. She's got some fucking timing, I'll give her that."

"Have you told Lucy?" she asked.

"No."

"Don't. It's not very sexy telling someone you've just slept with that your ex wants you back. Just let it ride, reply to Karen saying you're not up for meeting her and to have a nice life. Then you can get back to your life now, not a year ago. You were miserable with her, don't forget that."

"I suppose."

"Don't let this get in the way of now. She's already ruined enough of your life." Julia sounded like she was summing up a case.

I agreed with her that I wouldn't tell Lucy and that I'd mail Karen back putting her off. However, I had a funny feeling that just telling her on email wasn't going to be the full stop that Julia seemed to imagine. She didn't know Karen like I did.

Chapter Twenty-Six

After such an inauspicious start to the week, it went steadily downhill from there, dragging my mood down with it. Lucy's cousin took up her first couple of evenings and then she had a work dinner she couldn't get out of. I arranged to have dinner with Adam to try to drag myself out of my teenage funk at not seeing Lucy. It wasn't going to be easy.

He turned up at the Japanese restaurant we'd agreed to meet at looking tanned and tweezed. He'd clearly had his eyebrows done recently and I found myself touching mine and wishing I had a gay man's beauty regime to fall back on – they always put me to shame. He was dressed immaculately, something I couldn't always accuse him of.

"You look gorgeous, darling," I said.

"Thanks, sweets."

He kissed me on both cheeks and ordered an Asahi beer for both of us. Adam eschewed all gay logic by shunning the gym and drinking carbs. He drew the line at chips and bread, though: "At least there's a point to drinking beer," was his motto.

I asked him if there was any reason he was looking so dapper.

"I've decided it's time to up my game," he said. "I shagged one of my staff last week and that's always a worrying sign."

"Oh my god – you've turned into one of those sleazy managers, well done. I always knew you had it in you." I patted his arm in congratulatory manner.

"It was too good an opportunity to refuse." He shook his head. "He was throwing himself at me at some after-work drinks and he's by far the prettiest man who's ever worked there. I think it's the lure of power." Adam eyed up the dishes as they passed us at eye level on the sushi train.

"Oh yes, shift manager at a call centre – always floats my boat."

"He's Bulgarian." Adam shrugged as if that explained everything.

"Well here's to Bulgarians and the odd things they find attractive."

"Doing my bit to unite Europe."

"Selfless."

"Anyway, he wasn't bad but it's time to move on. He's certainly not husband material and I'm at the time of life where that's important now. I want my husband to at least be able to speak English in full sentences."

"Fussy."

"So my mother would say. It's depressing, though – after ten years in London I think I've exhausted Gaydar. And Grindr. Same old men turning up again and again. So I had a wardrobe de-clutter the other day, finished painting my new flat, then went and blew a stack of cash on new clothes and shoes."

"Intensive. All this is in aid of finding a new man?" I took a swig of my beer.

"Yep. And finding a new job, too – now I've moved, that's next on my list. You've been an inspiration working in a café – I'd love to do that. So I've decided to retrain as a chef."

"Wow, that's great."

Adam smiled as he took a salmon sashimi from the passing food train.

"Want one?" he said.

I took one from his plate, dabbed the top of the rice with wasabi and dipped it in my tiny tray of soy sauce. The wasabi was stronger than I'd anticipated and I recoiled as it hit my sinuses. Adam was oblivious, though – having already demolished his salmon, he was now busy selecting our next trays from the train of food chugging past.

As he filled me in on his future plans, I filled him in on Lucy and he seemed impressed – mainly that she had a motorbike and had turned up at my work in a leather jacket.

"Always been a dream of mine that," he said. "You haven't been on her bike yet?"

"Nope. We've only had one date remember?"

"Get her to take you out and you can live my dream for me."

I promised him I would. However, I wasn't sure when that would be and that was making me sad. Kate, Tess and Julia were all on tenterhooks wondering when it was going to happen but I simply didn't know and I was beginning to worry that what I thought had been a great first date had only been in my mind alone. To my horror, I appeared to be turning into one of those women who pine and analyse constantly.

Chapter Twenty-Seven

By Thursday I was miserable, whereas Matt was buoyant, having met up with Natalie and arranged his next date for Saturday when they were both kid-free. I'd pointed out that was the sign of a sure-thing but he didn't want to get his hopes up or jinx things. Sometimes, women's magazines got it so wrong – all the men I knew were so far off the Cosmo-imagined caveman versions.

Julia could sense my fatalism too when she'd called earlier in the week.

"Why don't you just go round and see her?" she'd asked.

"I don't know her address."

"So call her and ask!" She was getting exasperated. "She's not going to be put off by that is she?"

"No." Sulky.

"And if she is, then you run a mile. If you like her, call her."

"I don't want to bother her when she has her cousin. She texted me and told me she'd try to get away."

"So she's been in contact?"

"Every day." Julia sighed.

"Then stop being so dramatic and get this out of the way before the weekend. I don't want you walking around pining just because you haven't seen her. See her, have a shag and then come on my hen weekend and be happy, okay? And write that email to Karen, too – I know you haven't done it yet so don't try to tell me you have."

London Calling

* * *

Julia was correct. Four days had slunk by and I had been resolutely avoiding my emails, as if not looking at them would make them vanish into thin air. Tonight I promised myself I was going to deal with Karen and Lucy but in slightly different ways: prioritise the women in my life as they should be.

Lucy was obviously thinking the same thing (minus the Karen bit) as she pulled up outside the café at 4pm. When she walked in the door my heart flipped: she was carrying a bunch of white roses and looking gorgeous.

"Sorry, we're closed…" Matt began coming out of the back, not realising I was out there and who it was. When he saw Lucy, he smiled and disappeared into the kitchen.

Lucy's smile lit up the café as she walked towards me. I took the roses she offered and breathed in their scent.

"They're lovely, thanks," I said, blushing. This was ridiculous.

"It's good to see you." She touched my arm lightly and looked bashful. Her eyes sparkled and her skin glowed. "I came to offer you a lift home."

"I only live round the corner."

"Well you can help me push the bike round the corner then." She nodded out the window.

"Okay." All my blood surged down my body. "Give me a minute."

With Lucy right in front of me, suddenly all thoughts of Karen and impending doom had flown out the window. What I wanted right now was right here in the café waiting to take me home.

"I'll be right here," she said. She sat down at the nearest table. "Take your time."

I finished clearing the side, then went into the kitchen where Matt was waiting with my coat and bag all ready. I could have kissed him. I said goodbye and we were off, nearly tripping over each other as we wheeled the bike in the humid summer haze.

"So you got off early today, then?"

We were outside my flat and Lucy began the laborious process of locking up her bike. She walked up and kissed me in reply, then went back to the lock. Okay, if this is how we were going to play it that was fine with me. I could do dark, brooding, sexy – no problem. Lucy's face was a mess of concentration as she leaned over her bike, her butt an invitation encased in denim.

Once inside, I was overwhelmed with all the feelings the week had thrown up – where Lucy was concerned, over-ridingly lust. I took her hand and hauled her up the stairs at speed, stopping only in the kitchen on the way to put the flowers in the sink. Neither of us said a word.

As the water cascaded over my fingers Lucy was right beside me and my blood plummeted down my body to where I needed it most. I drew in a short, sharp breath. Sensing this, Lucy leaned in and kissed me hard on the mouth. I turned off the tap, tightened my grip on her hand and led her to the bedroom.

Once in, I threw my dressing gown off the back of the door and pressed her up against it. I slid my tongue into her mouth and felt cold metal under my fingers as I grasped for her belt. I was in a hurry and she knew it.

Within moments my fingers were buried deep inside her, slamming her up against the door. There were no pleasantries, no small talk. This is what we'd both been thinking about all week long.

"Fucking hell Jess..." Lucy said.

She stopped me so she could get out of her jeans, then took my hand and pushed it back in, looking directly into my eyes. I gulped – this was incredible. As I felt her very core I could feel her sinking deeper into me, spreading her legs as far as she could so I could take her further. I felt her body tense, her hand tighten around the back of my neck and then she threw her head back where it cracked against the door. She opened her eyes in pain and winced.

"You okay? Shall I carry on?" I said.

She opened her eyes fully. "You fucking better." A wry smile.

A few moments later she gripped my fingers tightly, coming against me still half-clothed. I stilled my hand and held her tight, then ran my tongue up her exposed neck. She breathed out heavily. I kissed her lips and guided her to the bed.

* * *

Kate arrived home just as I was coming for around the fourth time that day. The clock showed 18:34 as we heard the front door slam and Kate's footsteps come up the stairs. Lucy reached up and covered my mouth, as she travelled up my body, her tongue having done its work, her fingers now doing the talking. She kissed my inner thighs, my stomach and breasts as she ascended, finally lying down beside me just as Kate knocked on my door.

"Jess? You home? Have you managed to…"

"Yes, but don't come in…" Too late. Kate poked her head around the door.

"I was just wondering…" she said. Her eyes widened as I pulled the covers upwards.

"Oh, fuck, sorry," she said. She was grinning as she shut the door behind her. Lucy moaned under the covers while I just laughed.

"And that's why I've got my own place," she said. "Will we be all over the front page of the Lesbian Gazette now?"

"I think we'd make a gorgeous front page if we were, don't you?"

"Beautiful," she said, kissing me. "But we will have to face her in a minute you know."

"A minute? Can't it be two? Perhaps ten?"

"Perhaps ten."

"Good. Because I don't think I can move right now," I said. We kissed again and I breathed out heavily. I seemed to have been doing that a lot today.

"So that was…" I paused and cocked my head to one side. "Was that what you had in mind when you came to pick me up today?"

"It went pretty much exactly to plan."

"I'm glad."

"I didn't plan to have my jeans round my ankles until around an hour into it but I'm not complaining."

I kissed her again. I couldn't stop. Lucy moved closer into me and I lifted my arm so she could rest her head on it.

"I missed you," she said.

My heart lurched.

"I missed you too."

"Your going away this weekend is terrible timing too. My cousin leaves tomorrow and then I have a whole big empty bed."

"Can you keep it that way till I get back?"

"I dunno, there are normally hordes of women queuing up at the weekends. What'll I tell them?"

I thought for a moment.

"Tell them… Tell them things have changed and you're a one-woman kinda girl right now."

Her eyes widened and she smiled.

"I should tell them that?" she said.

"Definitely."

"Okay then, it's decided."

She gently ran her hand up and down my torso.

"Same goes for you too you know."

"Hmmm?" I said, enjoying the feel of her.

"With the women. I mean, you should tell them the same."

I grinned broadly. "You got a deal."

"And anyway, I think it's me who should be more worried, right? After all, you're going to Brighton, the UK's gay capital, while I am going to be mostly in my lounge."

I closed my eyes, thinking I would much rather be in her lounge – I hadn't even seen it yet.

"I might be in the gay capital but I'm there with a bunch of straight women on a hen weekend, remember? Trust me, it's more likely men will be throwing themselves at me than women. And that'll be fun." I made a face and she laughed.

"I'll just have to send you a picture of my breasts to remember me by then won't I, just in case you fancy a change from the norm."

I smiled at her and kissed her lips. "I think you being in my bed for the past few hours might give me a more vital memory of you. And then next week, no hens, no cousins, just us. Sound like a plan?"

"Sounds perfect."

She slipped her hand behind my head and pulled me in for a long, lingering kiss. After a couple of minutes we came up for air, my senses jumbled as tended to happen with Lucy I'd noticed. She gave me a heated stare and rolled on top of me.

"Now, after I fuck you one final time, what are you cooking me for dinner?" It was official: I'd found my perfect woman.

Chapter Twenty-Eight

Friday arrived way sooner than I wanted and after hastily packing my weekend suitcase and getting a tube to Victoria train station, I looked around for Julia and the rest of the hen party. It didn't take too much effort seeing as they were all already wearing feather boas that her sister and chief bridesmaid Lisa had kindly bought us. As I walked up, Lisa was also handing out train tickets, with instructions that as soon as we got on the train it was time to start drinking.

Julia gave me a massive bear hug of excitement when I arrived amid the clutter of a Friday morning. Today it was a mass of late commuters, discarded papers and perplexed tourists, their heads cocked towards the massive overhead departures board.

Once on the train, Lisa managed to commandeer two opposite tables so we could all sit together. The talk turned to other weddings and also what Tom was doing for his stag. The answer was a trip to Dublin which included paintballing and go-karting. I shook my head as I realised my two normally sane and rational friends had fallen head-first into the stag and hen traps of Dublin and Brighton.

Still, at least I wasn't being dragged on a week to Ibiza as Lisa had first wanted and Julia had vetoed. Glitter and tack she could take no problem; clubbing till dawn was not at all her style. The conversation was in full flow on the other table when Julia leaned over to me.

"So did you see her?" She adjusted her feather boa so it sat neatly on her breasts.

"Lucy?"

"No, Wonder Woman," Julia said. "Yes, of course Lucy."

I nodded.

"And?"

"I did exactly as you told me and got laid."

"Hurrah! Does that mean you're going to be texting under the table the whole weekend?"

"Probably," I grinned.

"Well good," she said, squeezing my arm. "I'm just glad you didn't blow me out to spend the weekend in bed."

"That thought never even crossed my mind."

"Liar," she said. An audible pause.

"What's that look for?"

Julia pursed her lips. "I've got something to tell you and I don't think you're going to be very happy."

"What?" I didn't like the sound of this.

"Well... I did try to keep it from her but it wasn't very easy." She paused. "The thing is, Ange is maybe turning up tomorrow night."

I groaned and put my hands to my face.

"But only maybe."

"And you let me get on the train…" I said.

"She… well… I've started working with her on a case and she's a laugh."

"A high-pitched laugh?"

"She's not that bad," Julia said. "Well anyway, I've been talking about the hen do and she's down in Brighton this weekend visiting a friend, so she said to text her where we were and she'd pop in for a drink. She won't stay all night, just for one. It'll be fine," she added, as much to reassure herself as me. "Anyway, we're all adults here aren't we? And it's my hen do so no fighting."

"Don't worry, I won't be fighting. I'll be hiding in a corner and hoping her mate isn't too butch," I said.

"Mind you, a dyke fight would make a good story wouldn't it?" Julia smiled a little too gleefully.

"I can't believe she might be coming," I said. "This means I'm going to have to get really drunk now, you realise."

"I would hope that was a prerequisite for the weekend anyway."

As if on cue, Lisa stood up from the table opposite and produced a bottle of Cava, a tube of plastic wine glasses and proceeded to fill them.

"Here's to a great weekend girls!" she said. She held her wine glass aloft.

"Cheers!" said everyone.

And just like that, the weekend was off.

* * *

The hotel Lisa had booked for the occasion was on the seafront, halfway between Brighton and Hove. As was customary in Brighton, even though it was a balmy day in London, here the wind whipped around you in great galloping swirls.

Nevertheless, our rooms had curtains that swished and were comfortingly beige, decorated beyond the point of neutrality. Julia and I were paired to share and both flopped on our respective beds when we arrived, already knackered from the short train ride.

"Do you think anyone would notice if we buggered off to France for a couple of days now?" she said. Her eyes were staring at the ceiling.

"Sure it'd be fine," I said. "So long as everyone could still get pissed."

"Thanks, you know how to make a girl feel special."

"You're not the first woman to say that." I gave her a wink.

Julia twisted herself semi-upright on the bed so she was now leaning on her right elbow, chin cupped in her right palm.

"Talking of which – I know you sorted out one lady last night, but did you do the other?"

I raised an eyebrow at her. "I was sort of busy."

Julia made a face. "Well you're not sort of busy now."

With that, she sprung off the bed, unzipped her suitcase and produced her laptop.

"There's free wi-fi here, so do it now before we go out."

I sighed heavily, to which Julia furrowed her brow.

"I'm going round the rooms in hostess fashion. I'll be gone for at least half an hour. So start writing."

With that, she disappeared and I was left alone with a laptop glaring at me. Sometimes I hated Julia and her 'seize the day' zeal.

Chapter Twenty-Nine

The following morning I was back in the same bed, lying flat, feeling the spot in my hairline that was now fully blossomed. I hadn't slept brilliantly, remembering too late that Julia snored like a navvy, especially after a bucketload of champagne. Being that it was her hen weekend I couldn't complain but I had made a mental note to buy some earplugs today.

I plucked my phone from my bedside table and wrote Lucy a good morning text, wondering what she was doing today. Thinking of Lucy gave me goosebumps and I smiled as I pressed send. Julia turned with the grace of an elephant and squeezed open her eyes.

"Tippy tappy tippy tappy. Can you text a bit quieter please?"

"I'm a noisy texter, what can I say."

"I'd hate to have sex with you," she said.

"Bang go my plans for later."

She stuck out her tongue.

"What time is it anyway?"

"Early. 8.30."

"Oh god – what you doing awake? Apart from texting your girlfriend..."

"I get up at stupid o'clock these days, my body's used to being up at this time."

"Well be stricter with it. Tell it to go back to sleep." With that she turned over and pulled the covers up over her head.

I left Julia to it, pulling on my jeans and sweatshirt as quietly as possible and heading out onto the seafront for a morning walk. A beautiful day was dawning over the south coast, the sun sitting low in the sky, gearing up for its starring role later in the day.

At close to 9am the seafront was already bristling with warmth, joggers pounding the concrete alongside pensioners with their yappy dogs. The white shelters that were scattered along the beachfront gleamed in the sunlight and the sea sparkled with energy.

As I walked along past the pier with its rundown feel, past Kemp Town which was yet to wake from its slumber and as far as the marina, I shared my thoughts with the sea.

I'd obeyed Julia yesterday and sent Karen a short, sharp email. After a week pondering I was still no closer to the perfect reply and even putting fingers to keys had brought me out in a cold sweat. I hadn't given much away, just saying the UK was going well and if we ever did meet again, I'm sure we could be civil.

I wasn't going to send her an invitation to visit, which I think she would partially expect. No forwarding address, no love sent back, no apology accepted. I just told Karen that coming home had been the right decision and I was happy – without her, if she read between the lines.

I strode purposefully back along the gently baking seafront, feeling the sun's warmth tingling on my skin. I made a mental note not to bring a jacket out later as I felt the first bead of sweat trickle down my back.

Walking back past the pier I heard Punch & Judy start up their regular sparring match to a group of five enthralled kids sitting cross-legged, necks cricked upwards. I slipped down onto the seafront, walking past the bars tucked under the arches, past the deserted volleyball court, past the market stalls just setting up.

By the time I returned to the hotel it was nearly 10am and there were definite signs of life in the dining room, although none of our party were there. I patted myself on the back once more for drinking water and pacing myself last night. As I'd pointed out to Julia, it was a marathon not a sprint but she'd just told me to bore off.

* * *

After breakfast we headed out for a fish pedicure where we all plunged our feet into individual tanks and tiny fish feasted on our hard skin. If I thought about it all too much it was enough to make me gag, so I tried not to. We followed up the fish by going for lunch at a fancy burger joint. Just as I was tucking in, my phone buzzed in my pocket. It was a text from Lucy.

'Might see you sooner than expected. A mate's just asked if I fancy a night in Brighton as her dad's just moved there. Let me know where you are later and I'll see if I can stop by to say hi.'

I grinned at the phone. Lucy was coming to Brighton! I allowed my grin to spread a little wider. I texted back telling her I'd be sure to let her know, then tuned back into the lunchtime discussion.

* * *

We spent the rest of the afternoon on a mini pub crawl interspersed with shopping. We ended up in a suitably loud bar in Kemp Town, all metallic bar, wooden floors and leather couches. It was a definitely a step up from the hen night hell I'd been expecting, but nevertheless the bar smelt of Saturday night: cheap aftershave, sweet perfume and a glaze of sweat.

By 8pm our party had more than doubled, our table

swamped under a barrage of glasses, bottles, feather boas and glitter. So much glitter in all different shades. Was it just manufactured for hen party purposes, I wondered?

I'd been harangued into wearing a feather boa and T-shirt with 'Team Julia: A Law Unto Themselves' emblazoned on it. What's more, I also had a lightning bolt etched onto my face. Glitter was flecked through my hair too and I'd been attacked by George's make-up bag. In short, I looked like I'd been railroaded into dressing as a slutty lesbian for the night and had been shocked when I went to the loo, pondering my new persona and hoping there weren't too many photos taken. I also hoped that Lucy had a sense of humour.

It was my appearance I was thinking of a few minutes later when I saw Ange approaching flanked by two other women. Dressed to impress in heels, jeans and a shimmering top, she was stunning and had clearly come prepared. Whereas I looked like a sparkly twiglet. Perhaps this was exactly the sort of situation she'd dreamt of ever since I'd tipped her out of my flat that Sunday morning.

I squirmed under the spotlight, although of course Ange paid no attention to me. Instead, she hugged Julia before heading to the bar. I followed her retreating figure in time to see one of her friends turn and meet my eye – clearly they'd been forewarned and were now wondering why Ange had fallen for this nightmare in pink.

Now she was here though – I'd been secretly hoping she wouldn't make it – I hoped Ange would steer clear of me, especially with Lucy showing up soon. She'd sent a follow-up text to tell me she'd arrived in Brighton and I'd given her the address of the bar, warning her to expect a gaggle of drunken ladies.

'I'll just say hello, give you a quick kiss and then I'll go. I'm not going to gate-crash your party completely,' she'd promised.

* * *

Some time later with tequila in full flow, *Footloose* came on and Julia put down her drink and dragged everyone onto the dance floor, some of us kicking, some of us screaming. I tried to look straight ahead or down at my feet as I moved my body side to side. Definitely not to the right, as that was where Ange was.

The song ended and we all clapped and whistled, the whole bar on some merry journey now, no stopping the Saturday night juggernaut. The next song was *Dancing Queen* which got the whole place jumping, but I decided I'd sit it out and so returned to our table with George following me click-clacking in her heels.

"These shoes are killing me. Why didn't you talk me out of wearing these tonight?"

"Because it would have been a thankless task," I said.

"Slap me next time, right?"

"Only if you give me explicit written permission beforehand. I don't want a lawsuit and I know what you lawyers are like."

"Ha ha." She sat down, taking off her right shoe and rubbing her foot. "Sometimes I hate being a woman. I should have followed your lead and worn comfortable shoes."

"Lesbian shoes I believe they're called. And as you don't fit the bill, you're not qualified."

She snorted at that. "Such strict rules…"

I reached into my pocket to check my phone as I sat down. I had a message.

'Hey, should be there any minute as we've left the restaurant and are en route. See you soon!' Lucy was on her way. My stomach lurched.

"Everything okay?" said George, nodding to my phone.

"Yeah great. This girl I just started seeing is in Brighton so she's going to pop in to say hi."

"Lucky her," George said. "Let's hope she's had a bit to drink first."

Abba's *Dancing Queen* came to an end, replaced by more up-to-date tunes which made the dance floor crowd swell. A couple of our girls drifted back to the table and I was just rooting around in my bag for a tissue when I heard a voice saying my name.

"Hi Jess." I'd recognise that voice anywhere.

"Hi," I said.

Lucy was on her way and Ange was sliding into the chair opposite me. Sometimes, my life played out in such an interesting fashion. My heart began to beat faster and I could feel a sweat breaking out down my back.

Ange moved a discarded feather boa from the chair and sat. This was just the sort of situation I'd been dreading after it became apparent Ange was staying for longer than a single drink. If she was going to declare undying love this was really bad timing. I didn't need it twice in one week.

"Good night?" she said.

She gave me a once over, in the way someone might do if they were buying a dining table. It was all she could do not to run her hand up my side to check for dust. She was still attractive, still high-pitched. I winced internally. If we could hurry this up, that would be great. I peered over her shoulder at the door but couldn't see the entrance through the crowd. Still no Lucy.

"Yeah, great. I think Julia's enjoying it and that's the main thing."

"She is," Ange agreed. We both turned our heads to where Julia was still dancing, belting out every word. Ange turned back to me.

"Listen," she said, leaning in. "I just came over to say everything's cool."

She paused as I blinked rapidly. The light in the bar seemed to dim.

"I mean, we're both adults and this situation is a bit awkward but it doesn't have to be. We had a one-night stand, no hard feelings." She really stressed that last bit. "I just thought if we're going to run into each other at Julia's wedding and whatever else, maybe it's best to have everything out in the open."

She took a gulp of her wine, breathed out and stared at me. She'd clearly practised that little speech in her head. She also still had amazing eyes.

"I, well..." I said. "Yeah." Then I shrugged, which was probably not the best body move for that moment. Ange looked rightly put out. I tried to recover.

"I totally agree. We're both adults after all," I said.

She looked relieved.

"It's agreed then," she said, metaphorically shutting the case on this one in true lawyer fashion. Her chair scraped along the ground as she got up. Her friends were looking down the table towards me and I could see this had been a coordinated attack.

"By the way, I'd tone down the glitter in future," she said. Okay, I deserved that.

"Thanks for the tip," I said.

We shared a tiny fraction of a moment of what might have been – me, Ange, together on this hen night – before Ange recalled that she was the wronged party and to stay in control of the situation. Her face twitched with the concentration needed to play this part after so much tequila, but she regained full composure and fixed me with a seductive stare, before turning and moving back up the table.

Julia slithered past the other way as she did and they crashed into each other. Eventually untangled, Ange disappeared to the bar and Julia sat in her recently vacated seat, eyes wide with anticipation.

"So is there going to be a fight? Did she challenge you to a duel? Has she gone to get more tequila so you can see which lesbian can slug them back the quickest?" Julia sat back with a fat grin on her face.

London Calling

"Yes, she's gone to collect up her mates and we're meeting outside to see which of us can pull each other's hair hardest in 30 seconds," I said.

"Marvellous. Lesbian *and* bitchy."

Julia turned to check Ange wasn't re-approaching.

"Isn't this a little obvious?" I said.

"What?"

"Ange leaves and you slither into her seat and grill me. She's come to your hen night, she's your friend. Shouldn't you be impartial, Ms Switzerland? Rushing over to get the gossip says to me that you're taking my side."

"I'm taking the side of drama," Julia said, taking a swig of her red wine. "My life is so horribly predictable, what with being with Tom for a certain amount of years then succumbing to marriage. You try to be different but look at how it's ended up: I'm swamped in glitter and adorned with a feather boa in Brighton. It's not very original is it?"

"Anthropologically rich, though," I said. I sipped my beer and smiled at her. She wasn't having it.

"But you – you have it all. One-night stands, living in Australia, women travelling from across the world to win your heart back…"

"Woman, singular…"

"Whatever. It's alive, it's vibrant, it's not the norm. I'm not special, you are. You shag women and glamorous ones at that. Lawyers, opticians. You're not boring. I'm boring. Straight and boring. Oh god, when did I get so straight and boring…"

Julia put her forehead on the table in despair. I leaned over and unclasped her hands from the back of her head just as Lisa turned up. She was having none of it and got Julia out of her chair.

"I think tequila maudlin has struck," I said, standing up. "Listen lady," I added as Julia's pouting eyes fixed on mine. "You're fabulous. You're not like everyone else. You have a great fiancée who loves you and you're marrying the love of your life – there can't be anything better than that, can there?"

Julia softened as thoughts of Tom flitted through her mind and Lisa took the gap in the conversation to chime in.

"Besides, this is no time to get maudlin. There's still plenty of drinking left to do and we've just decided we're going dancing. Sound like a plan?" Julia perked up and clapped her hands together, doing her best seal impression.

"Count me in!" she slurred.

"That's good, seeing as it's your hen night," Lisa said.

I paused, then fixed my stare on Julia. "Anyway, I've got other exciting news for you too."

Julia was standing unaided now, trying to focus on the evening but distracted by the glitter and sparkles all around.

"What?" she said.

"Lucy's coming."

"Who?"

"Lucy. You know, *Lucy*…" I pronounced her name like it was the first word I'd just learnt of a whole new language. Julia's eyes widened as blocks of understanding slotted into place inside her brain. Once they did, she clapped her hands.

"Here? Now?" I nodded.

"Oooh, this is getting good."

"So remember, play nicely. She's just popping in to say a quick hi as she's out with a mate."

"I'll be good, scout's honour," Julia said, scouting the area for Ange as she did. Neither of us were going to voice that concern but we both knew it was the elephant in the crowded, drunken room. I looked up to check the entrance but still couldn't see any sign of her.

"So I'll go and get a final round shall I," I said, a statement rather than a question. I kissed Julia on the cheek as I wriggled out from the table.

When I eventually got near the bar I recognised the figure

ahead of me as Ange. She was ordering more wine and tequila and I nudged her as I settled beside her, sliding in ahead of a short man in a polka-dot shirt who really should have known better. Ange turned her head and smiled as if recalling some far-off memory. I could see by her eyes there was already a fog building behind them.

"Oh I've just been served…" she said. She put her drinks on a tray.

I waved my hand. "It's fine. I'm ordering a ton of tequila so don't worry."

She nodded, then paused. "You know, there was just one more thing Jess," she said.

"What's that?" I said, turning my head.

She leaned in, put her right hand up to my face and kissed me full on the mouth, sliding her tongue in and causing definite friction through my body. Just as before, it wasn't terrible. The woman could kiss.

I was shocked by her action but certainly didn't pull away. Truth be told, I might even have kissed her back a little. Whatever, I was fairly sure that at its climax, it was Ange who was the first to pull out, not me. When I opened my eyes, she was smiling. Then she leaned in once more and gave me a final kiss, before fixing me with another seductive stare.

"Shame," she said. "We could have been good you know." With that, she put her index finger to my lips, winked, picked up her tray of drinks and casually walked away.

When I regained focus on the room I saw Lucy standing nearby with her mouth wide open, her mate standing beside her mirroring her look of horror. I wondered how much she'd seen but I think I knew. My current lover had just seen Ange snog me at the bar which was not the evening I'd planned in my head.

My heart thumped in my chest as I began to walk towards Lucy to explain, but her face told me she wasn't interested. I stopped in my tracks as her eyes burnt through me, then she turned, grabbed her mate's arm and took off towards the entrance. Ange, oblivious to the mess she'd caused, was already back at our table and sitting down. I looked to her and then to the door to see Lucy disappearing through it without a single look back. I took a deep breath and began to run towards the entrance.

Chapter Thirty

The next morning I woke up and fixed my stare on the ceiling cornice in our room – if it had been restored, they'd done a good job. It was only 7.20am but I was having trouble sleeping and my head was foggy with trouble more than booze. I'd stopped drinking after Lucy's exit, sobered up into the cold, harsh reality that the woman who I'd briefly begun to consider as my new girlfriend had just seen me kissing someone else. Not a great addition to a relationship that was barely a week old. By the time I'd made it to the door of the bar, Lucy and her mate had disappeared and my efforts to find her had been to no avail.

Predictably, Lucy wasn't answering her phone and I didn't even know her friend's name, never mind where she was staying. So, after 20 minutes desperately trying to locate her, I'd slunk back into the bar with my heart and spirits on the floor. Ange passed me on her way out, although she didn't see me. I wanted to kill her at that precise moment, but had no doubt if she knew what her actions had done, she wouldn't be sorry. Karma's a bitch, as they say.

Instead, I texted Lucy an overly long message, asking her to call me back so I could explain and asking her to meet me tomorrow for breakfast. It was a long shot but I had to get this sorted out – I really liked Lucy and I wasn't going to let Ange's mistimed lunge ruin it for me.

* * *

One thing I knew was that sleeping on the problem hadn't helped and, if anything, I was feeling worse this morning. I looked at the inbox on my phone again but it was empty, no word from my... no, I couldn't quite bring myself to say the word. Especially not if it was the most short-lived relationship in the history of the lesbian world. Confirmed Thursday, dumped by Saturday – definitely a personal best.

I swung my legs out of bed and padded to the bathroom slowly and silently, so as not to wake Julia. Once inside, I locked the door and tugged the string of the mirror light. It lit up obediently and I examined my face up close. I'd seen better days. I stuck my tongue out – it was covered in a white film, the taste in my mouth bordering on bitter. I cleaned my teeth to make myself feel better but it didn't work.

I shut the lid of the toilet, sat down and put my head in my hands. What a royal fucking balls-up. I thought about crying, concentrated hard and squeezed my eyes tight but there was nothing. I was too dehydrated to cry. Besides, I wasn't really the crying kind, not even in situations like this where crying would have been totally justified. Instead I felt the heavy weight of resignation in the pit of my stomach. If only I could get hold of Lucy I knew I could solve this. At least, I hoped I could. But if she didn't answer her phone then I didn't stand a chance.

I stood up and filled one of the glasses on the side with water, skulled it, refilled it and drank the lot in one. I took a couple of the Nurofen that were poking out the top of Julia's washbag and swigged another glass to wash them down. Then I took hold of the sink and looked at myself in the mirror, like I was in a Hollywood movie trying to convince myself of my greatness. After eyeballing myself for a few intense seconds, I got dressed and heard the door click shut behind me, leaving Julia gently snoring.

Chapter Thirty-One

I arrived home from Julia's hen weekend later that day completely worn out mentally and physically – keeping up appearances takes its toll. I'd alluded to Julia that something had happened but it wasn't something I wanted to share with the whole group. I'd put on a brave face and worn it all the way back to London. Then I kissed everyone goodbye and exchanged my smile for a frown. It felt better that way.

As I predicted, Lucy hadn't replied to any of my text messages or calls, so I figured I'd leave it for today and would have to resort to doing my grovelling in person over the next few days. Surely such great sex and connection had to count for something?

* * *

When I let myself into the flat I knew immediately that something was wrong – call it lesbian sixth sense. I walked up the stairs, dumped my bag in the hallway and walked directly through to the lounge. It was in darkness but held a snivelling Kate on the sofa, curled up in a ball with a bunch of scrunched-up tissues at her feet.

Turns out Lucy wasn't the only one to catch her girlfriend kissing another woman this weekend – it'd also happened to Kate when she went out for a drink with a mate. There she'd caught the supposedly-at-work Caroline out for drinks with another woman, gazing at each other dreamily over gin and tonics. She'd left the pub but had confronted Caroline this morning with the evidence and she'd come clean, saying she was about to tell Kate. When wasn't precisely clear, but either way Kate realised she was being dumped.

"She was apologetic about it but wouldn't answer when I asked her how long it'd been going on," Kate said. "When I think of all the times she told me she was working and she probably wasn't, she was probably off shagging this bird." She started to cry again, so I handed her another tissue and hugged her.

"Tell your bloody mother that nurses aren't all that."

"I'll let her know." I paused. And then I proceeded to fill her in on my sorry tale of a weekend, culminating in the fact that I was now also, to all intents and purposes, a single woman too. Even the thought of it made my jaw hurt.

"I guess this means it's Sunday lunch with just the two of us again," I said.

Kate nodded, blowing her nose into a tissue and throwing it on the floor.

"God, I bloody hate women and I hate feeling like this."

She looked so small on the couch, her peroxide blond hair a shaggy mess, her eyes puffy and red. She asked for details of my tale of woe, so I filled her in on the minutiae of my weekend which took her mind off of her own troubles for at least five minutes.

"And you kissed her back why?" was all she kept repeating. I told her that Ange had caught me unawares, to which Kate raised her eyebrows.

"I would say you have some serious work to do to resurrect that one," she said. I hoped this was just her mood talking and that by tomorrow, Lucy would see that it was just a silly mistake and we could carry on from where we left off.

However, Kate pointed out the crucial fact that Lucy didn't

know who Ange was and had no idea of the events surrounding that kiss. To her, she'd just walked into a bar to say hi to her new lover and found her snogging somebody else.

With that realisation crashing down on my cheery take on the situation, I got up, punched the wall and kicked the skirting board a few times until Kate told me to stop or she'd put my rent up. Instead, I made us both a coffee even though I wanted something stronger but Kate talked me out of it. Then I cut us both a slice of chocolate cake and together we sat and bemoaned women.

For both of us, it looked like it was back to the drawing board, but while that decision was out of Kate's control, mine was within my own grasp. I just had to make Lucy believe that what she'd seen wasn't really what she'd seen. Either that or I had to invent some way of turning back time and ironing out the whole sorry mess.

Chapter Thirty-Two

The next day at work Matt was full of the joys of spring, having sealed the deal with Natalie over the weekend at his place and now all he saw on the horizon was a life full of sex. To say he was chirpy was an understatement. Beth too was crackling with lust after pulling some bloke at a party. It seemed that while mine and Lucy's relationship was going down the toilet, my colleagues had been busy shagging themselves senseless, which did nothing for my mood.

The night before, Kate's troubles had gone some way to relieving my own. However, this morning, surrounded as I was by a cloud full of optimism, the weekend's events seemed more ominous than ever. They were an ash cloud following me around and waiting to burst. I knew I had to work fast to shore up the damage but I was also too scared to act. I concentrated on making the best ham and mushroom paninis I could possibly muster and sunk my mind into my work. Denial turned out to be a comforting companion.

* * *

Tuesday followed Monday with stunning predictability and my mood descended further. I was short with Matt, flung my phone across the room when it flashed up as my mum's number and not Lucy's, and spent the evenings lying flat on my bed, staring at the ceiling and chastising myself for my lack of action. If Kate had not been so concerned with her own situation perhaps she would have talked me out of my slump but this wasn't a high point in our cohabiting partnership.

However, by Wednesday Matt had seen enough. As soon as the lunchtime rush had dispersed, he sat me down with a coffee and demanded to know what was wrong.

"Nothing, I'm fine." I kept my eyes on my coffee cup and fiddled with the teaspoon. Matt gave me a look.

I hadn't wanted to voice my story because the café was riding along on a wave of love. Eventually, though, I told him the whole sorry affair and sat with a settled frown, my shoulders slumped along with my spirits.

"You're a daft git, you know that?" he said.

"Am I?"

"Yes, you bloody are."

"Thanks," I replied. He got up and gave me a hug which I reluctantly accepted, before sitting down again opposite me at the table.

"So what are you going to do about it?"

I shrugged.

"Jess..."

"What?"

"This situation isn't going to change unless you do something. You're waiting for Lucy to walk through the door but she's not going to is she? You have to walk through her door and make things happen."

I sighed. "Easier said than done."

Matt laughed. "True. But if you really want this to work, don't you think you owe it to yourself to at least try? And don't you think Lucy deserves more, too? Nobody said it was easy."

"Thank you, Mr Coldplay."

Matt touched me on the arm and I looked up.

"Why don't you take the bull by the horns? Leave now, go home, get changed and go to her work. At least then you'll know one way or the other and can move on. For my money, I bet Lucy is watching the door just as much as you and every day that passes she's a bit sadder."

"You think?"

"I do."

Maybe he had a point.

Chapter Thirty-Three

So it was that I hung up my apron around 3pm and headed home. Now here I was, climbing the stairs to the top floor of the 243 bus, dodging the chewing gum glued to the penultimate step. I was on my way to Lucy's opticians and laying my heart on the line.

En route to the bus I'd stopped at the flat to have a quick shower, change into my favourite shirt and jeans and beautify myself so that I looked as irresistible as possible – a must in these situations. Eye liner, mascara, lip gloss and spot cover; I'd also brushed and flossed, tweezed some stray lashes from my brows and practised sucking in my stomach for the big speech. Even though I didn't have a big speech.

However, right now, watching the afternoon slip by and feeling my heart beginning to pound, I wondered why I hadn't prepared a PowerPoint presentation or brought some of those enormous flashcards to explain exactly how I felt. It seemed they would have done the job far better than me, who was likely to stumble and blush bright red. I needed something gold-plated and watertight in this situation and the simple truth that she was an old flame who still fancied me wasn't good enough.

As I stepped off the bus, the afternoon seemed to have increased its heat, but the sun shining down this afternoon wasn't the sun I'd soaked up of late. Rather, it seemed to me a burning star from a mean-spirited galaxy, intent on making me sweat. Not that I needed any help with that today.

As I turned into the road that housed Lucy's opticians I took a deep breath and ran my tongue along the front of my top teeth. I was now standing ten metres from the front door but propelling myself forwards was proving tricky, all my regrets, what-ifs and time itself weighing me down. I looked up at the black-and-white signage over the entrance and before I had a chance to change my mind, I pushed the door to her shop. A little bell rang, causing the blonde woman at reception to look up. She wore a name badge that read 'Nicola'.

"Can I help you?" she said. I noted her green shirt was neatly tapered to her body.

"I'm a friend of Lucy. I wondered if she was in today?"

I hoped I sounded casual and I think I pulled it off as the blond woman smiled warmly, looking me up and down in one eye sweep.

"She is but she might be with a client. Let me just check for you, take a seat," she said. She pointed at some red velvet chairs to my left. "Sorry, your name?"

"It's Jess," I said. My heart was now beating far too fast for my chest and I wondered if it might jump out at any moment or simply stop from over-exertion. It would be a terribly inopportune moment for that to happen. I drummed my fingers on my legs while I waited, and when I got bored with that I twisted my body around to check out the rows of glasses in clear cases lining the walls. Unlike Specsavers, some of these had very fancy price tags and I wondered if I could get a discount for my mum. Yes, even in this situation, that's what I was thinking. Sometimes I truly disappointed myself.

But not as much as I'd disappointed Lucy, which was etched all over her face when she appeared ten minutes later. She was dressed in what I perceived to be funereal black trousers and grey shirt, with white Converse boots to offset the gloom. Her dark hair was just as I remembered but her smile had vanished, replaced by a stoicism that it pained me to realise was my fault. As she neared me I got up, put my left hand behind my neck and stood in just about the most awkward position I could. I wasn't sure what the protocol was in this situation. Last week this woman had been in my bed but now she was looking at me with a face that said 'Say what you've come to say and then get out'.

"Hi," I said.

"Hi," she replied. Behind her, I saw Nicola glance up and clock the situation. Did she know? Had Lucy told her if I wasn't out the door within five minutes, she should come over and evict me?

"Thanks for seeing me." I was aware I sounded like I'd made a last-minute appointment to get my eyes checked. "You're looking good." I knew this was a weak line before it came out of my mouth. Why hadn't I prepared a speech?

Lucy sighed. "Why are you here?"

"I want to talk to you about what happened."

The silence with which she greeted this was disbelief-flavoured. I ploughed on.

"I just wanted to tell you that it wasn't what it looked like. I knew that girl…"

She spluttered. "And that's meant to make me feel better?"

There was no intonation in her voice as she said this, no sarcasm, no rising incredulity. It was flat with no emotion and I knew that wasn't a good sign. Lucy had probably already made up her mind about me. Player. Idiot. No good.

"No, I suppose not."

My voice was now drained of its initial optimism, now as flat as hers.

"It's just – it's not how it seemed and I just wondered if you had time for a coffee? So I could explain to you what happened. Do you have five minutes?"

My voice had taken on a slightly begging tone now I knew,

but that's what I felt in my heart. At that precise moment I would have gone down on one knee to beg her for forgiveness. I knew Lucy was the woman I wanted but it wasn't until she was standing in front of me that the full force of that truly hit me. Our connection was more than just physical and I had to keep hold of it. Lucy had to understand, had to see it my way. But looking at her face, it didn't seem like that was happening.

"Do I have five minutes? I went out of my way to see you on Saturday. It took half an hour from the restaurant to the bar. Then when I got there – and I'd told you I was coming, that's what really gets me – you were kissing someone else."

Her voice was full of emotion now and I could see she was fighting back tears. She sat down on one of the two red chairs and I sat down on the other one. Lucy bowed her head, took a deep breath, gripped the side of the chair so that the velvet crushed all around the tips of her fingers. She pulled her head up and looked me straight in the eye.

"You made me look a fool. I'd been going on to my mate all night about you, how great you are… Were." Ouch.

"I drag her out of our way on our night out to say hi to you – I was literally only going to stay for half an hour, one drink and then go – and I get there and you're at the bar kissing someone else. And not just a peck, but a full-on, tongues-in snog."

"It's not what it looked like…" I said.

"No, I think that's the thing. It was exactly what it looked like. It might not have meant a thing to you but you can say what you want – you were snogging that girl…"

"She was snogging me…" I said. My voice was now at Ange range. Bloody Ange.

"And you were snogging her right back. Or did I get that wrong? Were you pushing her away, telling her to stop?"

I dropped my head in shame and stared at the plush beige carpet.

"Were you?" she said. The bell rang and a customer walked in, glancing curiously at the two women on the red velvet chairs who must have appeared to her to be having some kind of heated altercation. Her face told me that no pair of glasses was worth getting this worked up about. If only she knew.

Having this conversation in public wasn't part of the plan. I'd thought we could go for a coffee, chat about it, I could explain it'd all been a huge mistake and within half an hour we'd be ordering cake and laughing at the insane mix-up.

In the far-off distance I dimly heard Nicola talk the woman through the range of products available and heard her unlock some glasses cases along the walls. But my focus was on Lucy, who was wiping away a tear and gripping the chair. I put my hand out to touch her leg and she didn't pull away. I realised I'd really hurt her but the injustice of the whole situation made me want to scream. I decided to be honest, lay all my cards on the table.

I reached over and took hold of her right hand with both of mine. She flopped forward, putting up no resistance. I opened my mouth. Closed it. Opened it again.

"Lucy, I'm so sorry. This was nothing, absolutely nothing. I knew you were turning up that night and I was looking forward to seeing you. I really was. And then Ange turned up..." Lucy was looking directly at me but she didn't flinch. She held my gaze and wiped away a tear.

"Ange is a woman I had a one-night stand with a few months ago. She's one of Julia's work colleagues but I didn't know she was going to be there that night – I swear that, I would have told you. Anyway, she turned up and it was the first time I'd seen her since I tipped her out of my flat a few months ago so it was a bit awkward..."

"And so you thought you'd kiss her to make it better?" Lucy's face now seemed to be twisted into an impossible angle and my gut wrenched.

"We spoke earlier in the evening and we sorted it out – she's coming to the wedding so we agreed to be adult about it and call it what it was. A one-night stand, nothing more, nothing less. I actually felt better about the situation, believe it or not."

At that precise moment, Lucy didn't look like she cared.

"And then... and then we were chatting at the bar, she'd had a few tequilas and she just... she just lunged at me and kissed me. That's it. And, no, I didn't push her away, but that's probably because I was so shocked at what was happening. I'd been really looking forward to seeing you too – I bored the whole hen party to tears with how great you are. And then you saw that..." I paused, but didn't let go of her hand.

"Look, I know you owe me nothing and we haven't known each other long. But I think we have something here, something worth giving a go. And what happened on Saturday night was a drunken snog I had no control over. Honestly." I squeezed her hand to emphasise that point. She made no movement. I carried on.

"I was looking forward to you turning up. I raced up and down the street looking for you afterwards but I couldn't find you. I left loads of messages on your phone. I was desperate. I wanted to find you, to explain. But you'd gone."

She was still listening, still looking at me, still looked like she wanted to believe me. I was making my unplanned speech up but I had the punchline all worked out. I just had to hope she played along with it too.

"Before I left for Brighton we had a couple of great dates... So let's turn back the clock, pretend Brighton never happened and I'll show you I'm into you and nobody else. I'm not a player... I'm really not. You're the first woman in a long time who's made me feel... something. I don't want to lose that."

Her face remained impassive, giving away nothing, although she took some time to fish in her pocket for a tissue and blow her nose. I caught the line of her leg through her trousers and remembered kissing it only a week ago. It could have been in another time zone from where we were now.

Another customer came in and Lucy looked up and said hi to the man who was in his forties with thick grey hair like a Hollywood film star.

"That's my next customer, I have to go," Lucy said, indicating the film-star guy. She got up and adjusted her shirt, pulling it down at the front and back before running her fingers through her hair. I could tell she wanted to go to the toilet to check her appearance before seeing her client.

"Before you go, I really want to see you again," I said. I stood up. Lucy looked pained, and then like she might punch me. I continued talking before she could put any of her plans into action.

"But I know you probably need some time. So let me take you to dinner on Saturday night. I'll meet you at Athena bar first for a drink at 7.30. If you're not going to turn up, text me by Friday lunchtime. Deal?"

She looked at me and my stomach flipped. She was gorgeous and I wanted to kiss her there and then, but thought that might be deemed inappropriate. She pursed her lips, sighed and I wondered if she was going to turn me down. Please don't turn me down…

"Okay."

"Okay?" I was taken aback.

"Okay." She gave me thin-lipped smile. "I'll text you one way or the other. I've got to go."

And with that she turned and greeted the man. I watched her walk with him through to the back of the shop, gave Nicola a weak smile and heard the bell go as I left. I'd said what I'd come to say. Now I just had to wait and see.

Chapter Thirty-Four

I got home about an hour later and assessed the situation – I didn't think I could have done much more. I hoped I'd conveyed my feelings to Lucy without coming across as too much of a desperado. Above all, I hoped she knew I was genuine. I threw my clothes on the bed and changed into some blue shorts I liked to wear around the house and a well worn T-shirt to go with it. After my exertions, I needed comfort.

I went into the kitchen, flicked the kettle on and took a couple of biscuits from the recently installed biscuit jar Kate had introduced to the kitchen "for sugar emergencies". A Caroline-induced measure, the emergencies seemed to be happening most days but I for one was grateful as I poured some boiling water into a mug, watching the bag try to swim in the heat.

I took my tea and biscuits through to the lounge and sat on the sofa, pulling my phone out of my pocket. I had a text. I took a deep breath, realising that every text from now until Friday was a possible dream-killer. This one, however, was from my brother Jack asking if I was free for after-work drinks tomorrow. I texted straight back saying I was around. My brother in town and kid-free was a rare occasion.

Five minutes later another text arrived, this time from Kate telling me not to wait up. I imagined Kate would be throwing herself into her social life this week, which is what she did when she suffered a break-up – I'd witnessed it before. And that suited me just fine, as tonight would be a night of solace. I drank my tea, ate a Jammy Dodger and fired up Facebook. I wasn't about to update my status with anything relationship-wise, but I was keen to see if Karen had replied to my email. She had. Super.

I clicked on the message, saw my curt reply flash up and then her reply, still jovial, still coming. Bugger. The gist of it was she was glad we might be able to be friends, she was coming to London for two weeks and she'd message me when she was around and perhaps we could go out and "catch up". Just like that. Like nothing had happened between us at all. Apparently, in Karen's brain we could now be friends in the time-honoured lesbian tradition. Friends with benefits if she had her way.

I shook my head and gulped my tea. There was no need to panic, she didn't have my address and there was a half-full biscuit tin in the kitchen. No problem was insurmountable. Apart from Lucy telling me to bugger off.

I rang Julia who was no help at all, being as she was currently engaged in a war with Tom's mum about seating plans, photographers and the wedding cake. Julia had asked me to make it and I was quite looking forward to it. However, Tom's mum thought wedding cakes should only be ordered from professional wedding-cake makers and not from some casual acquaintance who also happened to be a lesbian.

"That's when I really exploded at her," Julia said. "What on earth has you sleeping with women – and we'll get to how that's going in a moment – possibly got to do with your ability to bake? Answer me that?"

I told her to just ignore it and I would make her the best cake possible. She told me to make the icing grey and the inside red like they did in Steel Magnolias just to piss off her future mother-in-law.

I wiped some dust from the remote control as I filled

Julia in on the Lucy showdown. She seemed sure Lucy would show but warned me that spurned women needed extra-special wooing and I was going to have to pull out the big guns if I wanted success. I agreed that nothing less than full-on gallantry would do, along with champagne and an obscenely expensive restaurant. Julia promised to email me a list of recommendations seeing as she frequented such establishments far more than I did these days.

"I'm keeping you as a plus-one for the big day, though – I have faith. But you do know that chances are Ange will be coming to the evening?"

"Don't remind me. Between that and Karen's imminent arrival, I'm suddenly the most desired lesbian in London – by everyone apart from the one person I actually want to desire me."

Chapter Thirty-Five

The next day at work and the Polish builders were in fine form, teasing Beth about her new sparkly apron as she cleared the tables. Artur in particular seemed to be paying her close attention and I saw her blush bright pink as he smiled at her. Was he too late to win Beth's heart? He should have moved quicker.

I chatted to the morning coffee crowd and was outside taking a breather just before the lunch rush when who should walk past but Caroline. Surprising, seeing as she knew where I worked and if I was her I'd be giving anything Kate-related a wide berth. She caught my eye and carried on walking, but within seconds was back in front of me, eyes to the floor. She fiddled with one of her ear piercings before speaking.

"Hi," she said. She finally worked up the courage to look at me fully.

"Hi," I replied. A tight smile.

"Look, I know you probably hate me and I would too in your shoes. Believe me. I know I hurt Kate but I didn't mean to. These things just…" A shrug. "Happen."

She looked at me directly now. I shrugged back. She took a deep breath.

"But anyway, I didn't stop to talk about Kate."

"You didn't?"

"Nope." A definite shake of the head. "I was going to walk on by but thought I owed it to Lucy not to."

Lucy. Now it was my turn to look down.

"Like I said, I never meant to hurt Kate and I'm sure you didn't mean to hurt Lucy either. But you did. However you'll be pleased to know I'm in your corner. I stuck up for you."

I nodded solemnly but avoided her gaze.

"Thanks," I mumbled.

"You're welcome." Definite sarcasm. She shook her head again.

"I do need to know though – was it what you said? Because I'd like to think so. But Lucy's a good mate and I don't want to see her pulled into some mindfuck shit. But I told her you're genuine. Am I right?"

This time I met her gaze.

"Totally. I really want this to happen and Brighton was... A stupid mistake."

Caroline took it in with a slow nod.

"She's upset but she also really likes you. She told me about yesterday, in her shop."

I kicked the pavement and took a gulp of air.

Caroline continued. "All I'm saying is that Lucy is a brilliant girl. Honest, caring, gorgeous..."

"I know..."

Caroline touched my arm. "Let me finish. She's a babe. And if you're being truthful and you're not going to lead her on, then I'll put in a word for you." She paused. "So are you?"

"Being truthful? I told you, yes. And I told Lucy too." I sighed. "I hope you can persuade her." I gave her a defeated smile.

"I think you did a good job yesterday judging by what she told me last night. But I'll nudge her further along with a call later." She returned a sad smile.

"Thanks," I said.

She leaned in and gave me a kiss on the cheek.

"Take care. Might see you around sometime."

I nodded and watched her walk away.

London Calling

* * *

I ground my way through the lunch rush and sank tiredly into my chair with my soup and tea at around 3pm. I'd been constantly checking the door willing Lucy to walk through it but even I knew that wasn't wise.

Conversely, Natalie did walk in for Matt and he took her and her son to a table where he charmed her with coffee and him with cake. He also did that trick where you make a coin disappear behind your ear. I was impressed and so was Natalie.

She stayed for just over half an hour, just on her way home from the school run and clearly smitten with Matt, judging from the number of hair flicks and giggles she threw him. They made me smile and feel rueful all in one go, quite some feat. Still, at least I'd had no text telling me to bugger off, which had to count for something.

I left Matt to lock up and went home: I needed a shower and change before meeting Jack to watch Liverpool's must-win Champions League match. Even though my brother was a West Ham fan, I'm sure he wouldn't begrudge me that. With perhaps a tiny moan.

* * *

Jack walked into the Blue Moon pub at 7pm. It was filled with a mix of hipsters and suits, clearly suffering a personality crisis for all to see. It was a traditional pub with dark wooden furniture, the obligatory brick-red patterned carpet and a scattering of odd memorabilia. It was as if someone had come back from a car-boot sale and thrown their swag in the air, leaving it wherever it randomly landed. I'd nabbed a table on the far side of the bar.

Jack was wearing a navy blue suit, black shoes, cream shirt and a gold tie. His dark hair was in need of a cut and he was cultivating a splattering of grey at his temples. He took a couple of moments to spot me and smiled when he did, walking over to the table and hugging me hello.

"I'm not late, am I?" he said, checking his watch.

"Nope, bang on time."

"Cool. Drink?"

"I'm okay," I said, indicating my pint. "Do you want food?"

Jack gave me a look of disdain.

"Eating's cheating," he said. He went to the bar to get his drink and returned quickly with a pint of Guinness. He took off his jacket, threw it on the bench beside me, loosened his tie and sat down on the chair opposite.

"Nice day at the office, darling?" I said.

"As usual. Exciting day in brokering."

"To what do I owe this honour then?"

"Honour?" He looked perplexed.

"I've been home nearly nine months and we haven't had a drink in that time."

He shrugged. "We... I mean I... I dunno. I just thought it would be good to have a drink. Catch up, just us two."

I touched his arm. "I appreciate the thought."

"So how was your day?" He sat back in his chair and loosened his tie a little more.

"You know, coffee, cake, sandwiches. The usual. My entire workforce is loved up so that's a bit of a challenge but apart from that."

He gave me a quizzical look.

"Hang on, so were you last time I saw you."

"Long time ago."

"Just over a week."

I nodded.

"So what happened?"

I filled him in on the sorry details of the weekend, Jack

swigging his pint, jaw slack, not knowing whether to laugh or cry. I told him about the optician showdown and he shook his head.

"Makes me glad to be married. I don't have to go through any of this shit again."

"You are lucky, believe me," I said. "Your wife's beautiful and sane, two qualities that don't often go together in one woman."

"Not sure about the sane part…"

"Talking of your lovely wife, how is she? And the boys?"

"All good. Luke is loving nursery and Freddie is roaming the house smashing everything in his path. You couldn't get two more different characters if you tried."

"Cute though," I said.

"Very. But also like a mini demolition firm you never hired. As for Vic, she's good so yeah, can't complain. Sometimes my life seems complicated but not half as complicated as yours…" He gave me a brotherly grin.

"I know. I really want to give this a shot and also I want her to come to Julia's wedding with me."

My brother gave me another quizzical look.

"You want Lucy to go to the wedding with you?"

"I do."

"Well you can't take her if Ange is there. You wouldn't want to go if the woman you caught your girlfriend kissing a couple of weeks earlier was there too, would you?"

He was looking at me incredulously and I realised he was right. There was no way I could take Lucy to the wedding and there was also no way I could go alone, as Ange would be there and I didn't want to lie to Lucy.

"You have to get Julia to un-invite this lunatic," Jack said. For once, he'd hit the nail on the head.

"This lunatic happens to be her work colleague though."

"So? You're one of her oldest friends. Tell her to lose the

invite in the post. You can't take both of them to the wedding."

"I wasn't planning on *taking* both of them."

Jack made a face at me. "You know what I mean."

And I did know exactly what he meant. In all my haste of trying to win Lucy back I couldn't believe I hadn't thought about this obvious fact. I pushed it to the back of my mind for now though and decided to deal with it later.

We chatted on and Jack got up to get us two more beers just before the match kicked off. The Lucy thing was still whirring round my brain and I wasn't focusing, so when someone said my name, I jumped. It was Lucy.

"Hi," she said. It was only two letters but it sounded delicious coming out of her mouth.

"Hi – what are you doing here?"

She'd caught me unawares but she looked delectable as usual, in a summery beige trouser suit with a crisp white shirt that gleamed.

"I'm here with some people from work. Leaving do..." she said. She motioned over her shoulder to a table with two women and a man, one of the women I recognised as being receptionist Nicola. She was wearing the same green shirt I noticed, unless she'd decided green was her colour and bought more than one.

"Right," I said. "You look amazing. How are you?"

She looked me directly in the eye.

"Feeling a bit better today thanks." She paused. "What about you?" she said, seeing two pint glasses on the table. I realised she might think I was here on a date and hastened my reply.

"I'm here with my brother, he works around here. Just catching up," I said. I pointed towards Jack who'd just begun heading back to our table. He put the drinks down, along with the two bags of crisps he'd also bought – "Dinner" – and smiled at Lucy.

"Hi, I'm Lucy," she said, holding out her hand before I had a chance to make introductions. Jack's eyes widened ever so slightly but he did well not to react.

"Jack, nice to meet you."

"You too," she said.

"Is this your local, too?"

She flashed him a gorgeous smile and I felt inordinately proud.

"One of many. I work locally and we like to spread our trade around."

"Keeps them on their toes."

Jack and Lucy ran out of smalltalk and there was a pregnant pause.

"Well, I'd better get back, I was meant to be buying the drinks. Nice to meet you," she said to Jack to which he nodded. She turned, then stopped and turned back.

"Oh and by the way."

I looked up expectantly. "Yeah?"

"See you Saturday. Let me know when and where."

It took me a few seconds to register what she'd just said.

"Really? You're coming?" I said. I was unable to stop a relieved smile spreading across my face.

She nodded slowly.

"I'll drop you a text tomorrow," I said.

"Great."

With that, she flashed me a shy smile before walking to the bar while I sat back, grinning. See you Saturday. She was going to see me Saturday. Jack looked like he was about to high-five me but I stopped him. Neither of us could stop smiling, though.

"So that's Lucy. I can see the appeal," he said. "Nice work."

I scowled at him and he held his hands up in defence.

"I'm just saying she's good-looking and seems nice. That's a positive thing to say about your sister's new girlfriend, isn't it?"

"Let's not jump the gun."

"She said she's seeing you Saturday, which means unless you spectacularly fuck that up, I think it's back on. And she clearly wants to continue now that she knows what a gorgeous brother you have."

"Ha ha."

"Just get Julia to lose the other wedding invite and I predict a long and happy life for you both. Otherwise, don't say I didn't warn you."

The Champions League music began on the telly opposite us.

"Shut up and let's watch the game," I said. He shook his head but dutifully turned his chair around.

"This doesn't have to be difficult sis, so don't make it difficult. She likes you, you like her, simple."

"Oh look, it's the football," I said. He shook his head and settled back in his chair, stretching out his long legs in front of him.

Chapter Thirty-Six

The following day my head felt like it had been burgled, thanks to the five pints Jack and I had consumed the previous evening. Matt knew this and so insisted on having the radio on at high volume in the kitchen as he was putting together the day's specials. I left him to his own devices, preferring to deal with the customers and their breakfast orders.

We made it through the morning rush and I relented and had my third coffee of the day and a bacon sandwich, which perked me up considerably. I was just about recovering near the end of lunch – but even at 2pm the queue was still out the door – when my mum arrived. She gave me a little wave, bypassed the queue and came to the end of the counter where we served the coffees.

"I'll have a tea and a sandwich when you're ready," she trilled, taking up a window stool and stowing her bags on the hooks provided underneath the ledge. She was dressed in traditional summer wear, no doubt bolstering M&S's coffers into the bargain.

"Bit busy," I said. I served some salmon and oriental salad to an anxious-looking woman in her mid-twenties.

"No rush!" Mum called back. She produced a Daily Mail from her bag and waved at Matt, who waved back. It took half an hour for the queue to die down and for Matt to give me the green light to take a break, not that Mum seemed to mind.

"Catching up on the world's happenings," she said. As she folded her paper in two I put two paninis and our drinks on the window bench, then undid my apron. I was sweaty after a busy morning and I saw her giving me a once-over. She'd have to lump it: I wasn't in the mood.

"You should have called, you know we're still busy at lunchtime," I said. She flapped her hand at me, in a 'don't be stupid' gesture.

"It's fine. Anyway, no rush – thought I'd come and say hello before going home. I had a coffee and a doughnut to tide me over earlier in Marks so I wasn't famished." She was in a cheery mood.

"So did you get anything exciting?" I said.

"Some tops. Did I tell you me and your dad are going to Mexico?"

I shook my head.

"Saw an advert in the paper and thought, why not, we've never been. So I thought I'd pick up some things. Got your dad some new shorts, too."

I nodded, glad of the chance to sit and listen, chewing my food. My hangover was still lingering around the edges of my brain, curling it upwards slightly.

"I did have another reason for stopping by," Mum said. She glanced around the café to check if anyone else was listening and I braced myself. Either somebody was dying or she was going to mention something to do with my sexuality, I knew the signs. Change of breathing, slight uncomfortable stance, dry throat in constant need of clearing. True to form, she cleared her throat and shifted in her seat.

"I was thinking that you could invite your friend around for the barbecue we're having."

She said it in almost a whisper.

"Barbecue?" I said, stalling and giving my brain time to take in this information.

"Day after Julia's wedding, it's meant to be a nice day. So I thought me and your dad, Jack, Vicky and the boys, you and your friend."

"Lucy."

"Yes, Lucy. The whole family." She smoothed out her trousers and smiled at me.

I didn't know what to say. I could see this was a major step for Mum and she was trying desperately to make it all sound normal. She wasn't even raising her pitch too much, which surely deserved a small round of applause. And how else were things meant to move forward if I didn't try to meet her halfway, to normalise the situation for both of us?

"That'd be great, Mum," I said. I took a sip of my coffee and held her eye contact. She smiled again. Now I just had to make sure Lucy was still my girlfriend following Julia's wedding. Should be easy.

"Super," she said, relieved. She studied my face a little harder. "You look tired. Everything okay?"

"Fine. Blame Jack."

"Jack?"

"Dragged me out for drinks last night and I've only just recovered. It's been a long, slow morning shall we say."

Mum laughed. "I won't feel sorry for you then, serves you right."

Her face contorted slightly and she went back into serious mode. I wondered what else she had to say and braced myself mentally.

"I don't want this to be a one-off either," she said.

I scrunched up my forehead as a question, my mouth too full to do anything else.

"You bringing Lucy to ours. I want…" She paused. "I want you to feel you can bring her anytime. If she's your partner then she's welcome."

I felt myself welling up. Mum put her hand on my arm as

if she knew, or perhaps she was feeling the same and needed to steady herself and her thoughts. If she was feeling as nervous as me, she was doing an incredible job of covering it up.

"I don't want to be shut out of your life anymore and I don't want you running off to Australia again. I want... I want us to be a family."

I didn't know what to say. So I put down my panini and hugged her. In return, she squeezed me tight right back.

"Thanks Mum, really," I said. "It means a lot. I'll definitely ask Lucy."

I kissed her cheek and sat back down in my chair. Her face was flushed red and I could see the fair hairs on her cheeks, her face a little more crinkled than it was five years ago. My mum was getting older but she was still learning, still trying to live her life outside the brackets, no matter how much safety they afforded her. I beamed proudly at her and she smiled back. We'd shared a moment and it wasn't something I thought would ever happen, never mind when I woke up so hungover this morning.

"Shall I get us some cake?" I said.

Mum nodded enthusiastically.

"Another tea would be lovely too."

Chapter Thirty-Seven

Later that day I texted Lucy to confirm our date tomorrow, telling her to meet me at Athena for a drink in town first. She texted straight back to say she was looking forward to it. I smiled at my phone and pictured her in her opticians, all slick and professional. Then I pictured her naked in my bed and found I had to walk at a slightly quicker pace.

I shook my head at myself as I ambled along: whatever the state of play in my personal life, my libido had never deserted me. Julia had often commented that I had many of the attributes of a straight man: "Their sole topic of conversation is how much they're getting and what's the score." I told her that was a little harsh, but thinking about it now, what else was there apart from food?

By texting straight back though, Lucy was being true to her word that she wasn't a player. Now I just had to prove to her I wasn't either, but I had some catching up to do. I'd booked into a Michelin-starred restaurant in town called Hexagon that Julia had recommended: "divine lamb" apparently. I was planning to open the night with bubbles at the super-swanky Daphne's, a champagne bar awash with velvet and glamour. She didn't know it yet, but Athena was a diversion tactic.

Sweeping Lucy off her feet was the plan: I'd run it by Kate and Julia and both had agreed it would work for them. Julia had even offered herself for a trial run, but reneged when I told her it would mean she'd have to put out.

As it was still just after 5pm and another hot, sunny day, my plan was to walk along the canal, meet Adam for a drink after work in the sun and then get home early for my beauty sleep for the next day. D-day was nearly here.

* * *

"I'd recognise those legs anywhere."

Adam's voice broke the silence as he leant down to kiss me and sat next to me on the bench. Being straight from the office he was dressed smart, in grey trousers and a baby blue shirt with a lightweight grey jacket. Neither of us ever did understand why you had to dress smart in a call centre – it's not like you were ever going to meet people face to face. Really, you could come in dressed in your pyjamas and it wouldn't make a jot of difference.

"You look very gay today," I said.

"Why thank you." Adam put his pint of cider on the floor beside him.

"Any special occasion?"

"Coming to meet my special gay friend. I thought them was the rules?"

"Gotcha," I said.

"What you drinking?" He arched an eyebrow.

"Diet Coke."

"What happened?"

"Nothing – I've got my big date tomorrow and I don't want to be hungover."

"Oh, is that all? Lesbians." He tutted.

"What's my sexuality got to do with it?"

"Everything. Drama dyke, that's what you are. And gay men get the bad name."

He winked at me, then looked ahead into the throng that were gathering on the canalside in the evening haze. I sipped my drink and screwed up my eyes in the sunlight.

"So what's going on, then?" I said. Adam had called the night before to say he had big news. Big news that needed a face-to-face meeting.

"I've met someone. I think this could be it."

"Blimey." I twisted in my seat to face him. "Spill."

Adam took a deep breath in and rubbed his hands together with glee. He seemed excessively pleased with himself.

"He's an architect…"

"Get you…"

"…own hair and teeth, solvent as far as I can tell. Well, he has his own flat at least."

"Which you've seen?" I said.

"Course. Gotta try before you buy."

"Big cock?"

"Don't get me started." Massive grin.

"So what's this mystery man called?"

"Stuart."

"Shame. I was hoping he'd be called Steve. Adam and Steve."

"I've never heard that before," Adam said. He rolled his eyes while I chuckled at my own joke. Then he stretched out his right arm behind me on the bench and leaned back, closing his eyes to soak up some rays.

"Own hair and teeth. You're certainly going up in the world."

"Aren't I though?" he said.

"So when do I get to meet him?"

He opened his eyes and looked at me.

"When I get to meet yours, honey."

"Ah."

"Don't gimme that *ah*. You'll be fine. Just don't let her pay for anything tomorrow, don't tell her she's a cunt and all will be well. She wouldn't be going out with you if she wasn't interested, now would she? Especially after she caught you snogging someone else."

He began to laugh, his body convulsing slightly on the bench beside me. I nudged him in the ribs and gave him my stern look.

"Too soon for jokes?" he said.

"She's not even going back out with me yet, so I'd say yes, definitely too soon. Anyway, change of subject. When are you seeing Stuart again?"

"Tomorrow too, we're going into town. Might see you there."

"Well if you do, walk the other way please. I have enough hurdles to overcome."

"Surely a visit from your super-stylish gay friend would tick some key lezza boxes though?" he said.

"One thing at a time. I've got to get her to like me again before asking her to like any of my friends."

"True, tough call."

Adam rolled his neck from left to right, loosening up the muscles held tightly in one place from spending a day behind a computer.

"What else is going on in your life then?"

"Nothing much. Looking into cookery schools but apparently the competition for places is fierce now everybody wants to be a chef. Jamie, Gordon and all that bollocks have made it seem all rock 'n' roll. I bet the drop-out rate is phenomenal once they realise they have to chop carrots for ten hours a day for the first month."

"I bet you're right."

I sipped my drink while Adam chatted on about work, Stuart, cooking and when he was going to hand in his notice. But running in the back of my mind the whole time was Lucy in those grey trousers, Lucy's deep brown eyes, the surge of love I experienced as Lucy held my hand. I was just thankful we weren't in that terrible Mel Gibson film where Adam would be able to read my thoughts.

* * *

I got home at around 8pm, having managed to steer clear of alcohol and stopping at the local Tesco on the way home to see if there was anything in their reduced section. When I got back I stuck my chicken pasta in the microwave, then went through to the lounge where Kate was lying flat on the floor, her eyes wide open and staring upwards like a doll in a horror film. I wasn't expecting her so I jumped.

"Is it a mirage?" I said. Kate responded to the intrusion by closing her eyes and covering her face with her right hand.

"You okay?"

"Yes, just pondering the wreckage of my life," she said.

"Good, nothing serious then. Want a cup of tea? I just put the kettle on."

"No thanks. I've got a drink on the go."

I looked and saw a half-drunk bottle of Peroni on the side table.

Kate was sat back on the sofa when I returned with my food, with some new band making doleful noises out of the iPod speakers. She'd finished the beer in my absence so got up to get another.

"Not out tonight then?" I said when she returned. Her normally just-so hair needed bleaching, she had dark rings around her eyes and was looking gaunt. As well as drinking to excess, Kate's break-up routine didn't involve much food.

"Nah, I'm knackered. And I need to give my liver a rest, I reckon." She bent a leg underneath her body and hugged a fluffy cream cushion as she settled into the sofa.

"With more beer?"

"Just a couple."

I grabbed a magazine from the coffee table to rest my hot food on and plonked it on my lap.

"How's things?" I said.

She sighed. "Okay."

"Sounds it."

She shrugged. "I'm all right. I think part of me is really going through the motions of a break-up. Deep down I knew Caroline and I weren't right for each other but it sucks to be cheated on." She shrugged again and swigged her beer. "But I'll get over it, I'm a big girl. I just need to get out of this funk and then it'll all be fine."

I decided not to tell her I'd seen Caroline. Maybe next week.

"You will get a shag again, you know," I said. I twirled my fork in my food.

"And so will you, probably sooner than me," she said. "All ready for tomorrow?"

"As I'll ever be."

"I'll be thinking of you. I'm out with Vicky."

"They must have had a conference," I said.

Kate looked puzzled.

"Vicky and Jack," I said, swallowing down. "They must have had a 'must take sisters out' pact. Jack did me on Thursday, now it's your turn."

Kate chuckled. "Judging from Vicky's tone I think we're out to get drunk, so don't expect much from me on Sunday."

"I'm hoping I'll be otherwise engaged come Sunday morning," I said.

"Hope springs eternal," Kate replied. "Have you heard from any of the other women you're currently spinning around by the way?"

"I ill-advisedly snogged one and I've told the other to bugger off, so I'm hoping that's the end of it." I sounded indignant.

"Hmmm…"

"Hmmm?"

"I mean, let's just hope so for your sake. But should Karen turn up at our door with a bunch of roses, I'll take them and seduce her on the spot. I can now I'm single you see – all for you, an act of pure friendship."

"You're making me feel so much better."

"That's what friends are for."

"I'm glad you're finding this all so amusing," I said, chewing. "But if Karen does show up, you have my permission to snog her and then punch her. Whatever, just make sure she stays as far away from me as possible."

Chapter Thirty-Eight

The next day dawned and the hot weather had broken, replaced by lashing rain and white cloud. Julia called, in meltdown having checked the long-range weather forecast and worked out it was going to be raining the following week for her wedding. I assured her the last time the weather people had been correct was, well, never, and that there was plenty of time for the rain to disappear. After all, it was going to be June by then and the sun and June were best friends.

I did have the small matter of uninviting Ange to bring up but I figured perhaps another day, as the tone of her voice told me she didn't need anything to send her an octave higher. I'd broach it later in the week. Today was 'operation Lucy' and my full attention was going to be given over to that.

* * *

The day buzzed by in a blur of pottering, tidying and clothing decisions. I settled on my new blue shirt, dark jeans, brown boots and belt before trying on myriad outfits and ending up back where I began. If tonight went well, I saw my life changing for the better. If I fucked it up by snogging another woman at the bar – surely lightning couldn't strike twice? – I was doomed to a life of Miss Havisham-style spinsterhood. The decision was mine.

Before heading out, I logged on to Facebook to send Tess a

message giving her an update. Tess had started seeing someone too, as had Tom. It seemed like it was the time of life for my friends when they were mating and settling down.

Out of habit, I checked my email too and saw that Karen had sent me another message, telling me she was flying tomorrow and would let me know where she was staying when she landed. I bristled – this was not what I needed tonight. Why couldn't all these women just leave me alone to get on with my life?

I pulled the door of the flat shut and stepped out into the damp air. The rain had let up but the pavements were still dark grey and the air was thick with the smell of wet tarmac. I began the short walk to the tube, untangling my iPod headphones as I walked with the sound of my boots echoing on the concrete. My phone buzzed in my pocket. I thought about leaving it for a second but then reassessed as it might be Lucy. I pulled it out but saw it was Jack calling. I pressed the green button and instantly knew something was wrong.

"Hello?"

"Jess," he said. His voice wavered.

"What's wrong?" I said. I was now at a standstill, knowing the news wasn't going to be good.

"It's Vicky. And Kate." My stomach dropped. "There's been an accident. I think they're okay but they've both been taken to hospital. I need to get there and was wondering if you could come and look after the boys? I tried Mum and Dad but they're not there and they're not answering their mobiles."

"Sure, sure, no problem at all. I can come now."

"Great."

"What happened?"

"Car crash that's all I know."

"Oh my god, oh my god. Are they all right?" I looked around at the world, functioning normally as if nothing had happened as Jack's words seeped into my brain.

"Yeah, I mean alive... I don't know anymore..." His voice was wavering again.

"Look, make a cup of tea and I'll get a cab over right now."

"Okay. Don't be long."

I spun on my heel and walked back towards home and the cab office that was round the corner. My mind was flooded with warped images of crushed metal and worse, shattered people. I tried to rub them out but they just kept coming back. Vicky and Kate were in hospital. My brother's wife and my flatmate. This wasn't good.

Once in a mini-cab, I called Lucy to tell her tonight was off and the reason why. She was very understanding, offering to come with me and wanting to know if there was anything she could do.

"I don't think so," I said. "I'm just in a cab there now so I'll give you a call back when I know more." I paused. "Actually, there is one thing you could do."

"What?"

"Could you ring the restaurant and cancel?"

"Sure, which one?"

"Hexagon."

"Blimey," she said, sounding surprised. I smiled at the other end.

"I was trying to woo you."

"It would have worked, too," she said. I could hear the smile in her voice. "But another time. I'll cancel, no trouble. But please call me when you know more."

"I will. And I'm really sorry."

"Don't be stupid."

* * *

When I arrived at the house the boys were happily ensconced in front of the telly, oblivious to what else was going on. Jack looked pale and his eyes were red when he opened the door in jeans and a black Polo shirt. I hugged him tight and he let me. He put his finger to his lips and led me through to the kitchen. Last time I'd been here was for the barbecue, when Vicky had been alive and well. I swallowed hard and rolled my neck from left to right.

"So what happened?" I asked, putting my jacket on the back of one of the kitchen chairs. Jack sighed and ran his fingers through his thick black hair, shaking his head and flexing his jaw.

"I dunno – I mean, they just left. Kate was over today and they were going into town – dinner somewhere, drinks… They got a cab to the station, I was going to run them but Vicky insisted getting a cab was easier with the boys. And then I get a phone call just before I called you. I don't know much more apart from they're at the hospital. I don't know how they are, if they're okay…" His voice cracked when he said the last bit and I took his hand.

"They're going to be fine, Jack, this is Vicky and Kate we're talking about. Tough birds. I'm sure they've just got some scratches and bruises on them and they've taken them to hospital as a precaution. Walking wounded. Walking, chattering wounded."

He smiled at the last bit.

"I hope so but you know what some of these mini-cab drivers are like…"

"Don't be daft," I said. I was making myself believe my own words. "Look, why don't you get your coat on and get going? Did you get through to Mum and Dad?"

"No, they're not answering."

"Well I'll do that. What about Maureen?"

"I'm picking her up on the way."

I hadn't stopped to consider how Kate and Vicky's mum would be feeling till then. Wretched, I would have thought, seeing as she buried her husband a few years back and now both her children were in hospital.

"Go. Just call me when you know anything, okay?"

Jack nodded. "I fed the boys, so they just need their milk."

I stroked his arm. "Don't worry. Just go."

* * *

The boys seemed oblivious when Jack hugged them extra-hard as he left, so I got them some milk and we settled down to the end of Bob The Builder's latest quest before putting them to bed. Freddie was a little teary his mummy wasn't there to kiss him goodnight but I assured him she'd be back when he woke up. Luke threw a slight paddy about his pyjama choice – he wasn't a fan of pandas. Together we selected a pair with monster trucks on them and he seemed happier as he climbed into his tiny bed. I kissed them both, tucked them in and felt my feet sink into the plush landing carpet as I retreated out of the bedroom.

"Aunty Jess?"

I poked my head back around the door.

"Yeah?"

"Will you get mummy to come and kiss us goodnight when she gets in?" Luke said. My heart lurched.

"I'll make sure she does," I said. "Night now."

"Night."

I walked across the hall and stood in the doorway of Jack and Vicky's room, staring at their purple and white boudoir, their bed still strewn with a few garments that Vicky had rejected for her night out. I rested my head against the white doorframe and sighed. It was going to be a long night.

* * *

I tried Mum and Dad again but still no answer, so I left a message for them to call me on my mobile. Then I went back into the lounge and sunk into the brown leather couch, curling my feet up underneath me and flicking idly through the channels.

The programmes bounced off my brain like raindrops off an umbrella, so I settled on a music channel so my mind could relax. Lucy called half an hour later, making me jump out of my skin.

"Hello?"

"Hi. Any news?" Her voice sounded sexy even though my mind was elsewhere.

"Nothing and I'm going mad. I mean, I know Jack's probably still dealing with stuff but I just need to know how they both are…"

"Listen, let me drive over to you now, then at least I can give you a lift back if you need one. I'm not doing anything except worrying about you so I may as well be with you."

I smiled. "You're worrying about me?"

"Call me stupid."

"I wouldn't do that," I said. I felt a warmth flow through my body. It seemed like I wasn't the only one invested in this relationship after all.

"Text me the address. I'll get my shoes on and be ready to leave in five."

I did as I was told, then went into the kitchen and grabbed a cold bottle of Heineken from the fridge – I could count on my brother for these small things. My stomach growled and I realised I hadn't eaten. I stuck my head in a few cupboards before finding the chocolate biscuits. Perfect.

Just as I took my first swig of the beer, my phone went. I could hear it but I couldn't see it. Where had I put it after speaking to Lucy? The ringing was insistent and I spun around in the kitchen, trying to locate it. Eventually I saw it on top of the fridge, grabbed it and pressed the green button. It was Jack.

"How are they?"

"They're all right. Shaken, bruised, a little broken in places but okay. Poor Maureen is the most shaken up of all three of them…"

"I can imagine," I said. Relief flooded every tiny corner of my body. "So how broken is broken?"

"Kate's got a broken arm and they've both got broken ribs as well as cuts and scratches but from what I can make out they were lucky. Cab got hit by a kid driving too fast and the driver took the brunt of it."

"Is he okay?"

"Still critical."

I breathed out hard. "Fuck."

"Yep."

"But they're okay?" I said. I leant against the fridge, dislodging a children's party invite.

"Essentially, yeah. They're going to keep them in overnight just as a precaution in case they're concussed but I think they'll be released tomorrow."

"Great news," I said.

"Listen, I better get off, I need to let other people know. Can you hang on there till I get home?"

"Course – take your time."

"Thanks."

I pressed the red button and took a swig of my beer, picking up the party invite and putting it back in its place. They weren't dead. Thank you Jesus, even though I believe you to be a mythical character.

Chapter Thirty-Nine

Lucy arrived true to her word about half an hour later. I opened the door and was thrown by her beauty again. She still looked date-ready in sleek grey trousers, a white shirt and waistcoat and I realised that I probably did too, having been en route when the drama began.

"Hi," I said. I shyly stepped aside, ushering her in. She echoed my feelings as she stepped uncertainly into the hallway, casting her eye around the house.

"Have you heard anything yet?" she said.

I shut the door and told her the good news which seemed to break the ice. We wouldn't normally have hugged so soon but this occasion seemed to call for it, so we did.

"What a relief – it's the not knowing that's the killer sometimes isn't it," she said, covering her mouth as she said it. "Not *killer*, but you know what I mean…"

"I know what you mean," I said. I took her hand and lead her through to the kitchen. "I've been going mad imagining all sorts of scenarios but luckily they're alright."

"Both of them?"

"Yep, sounds really lucky. Better than the driver – he's still critical."

"Shit."

"I know." I breathed out heavily. "Still, makes you realise what's important doesn't it?"

She nodded solemnly.

"Nice house, though," Lucy said, changing the subject deftly. "Lovely big kitchen. Perhaps I should consider moving to the burbs."

"Tempting, until you remember you'd be living among suburbanites."

"True," she said. "Still, you'd be living in an actual house with a garden which would be terribly novel."

There was a pause in conversation as we assessed how to handle this situation. Tonight was meant to have been a straightforward wooing mission replete with champagne and candlelight but now the game plan had dramatically altered.

"Drink?" I indicated my bottle on the table.

"I better not," she said. She dangled her car keys from her right index finger.

"Tea then?"

"Tea would be good."

She pulled out a chair from the kitchen table and sat down as I filled the kettle, suddenly self-conscious being on show in such a brightly lit, sanitised space. There were no expensive drinks, low lighting and fancy food to hide behind in Jack and Vicky's kitchen. I was exposed but it felt good to have Lucy there. I placed the kettle back in its base, flipped the switch and turned to her, holding the counter top with both palms outstretched behind me.

"So tonight hasn't gone exactly according to plan..."

"No." She paused. "Bit like us so far would you say?"

"You could definitely say that," I said. I was glad of the noise of the kettle to drown out my quickening heartbeat. "What did you do after I called?"

"Called the restaurant and then I went down to the Tesco near me and bought a meal for one like a saddo. I also learnt there's some terrible telly on Saturday night so driving here was light relief, believe me."

"I wouldn't know, I was watching Bob The Builder."

"Probably better than the dross I sat through," she said.

I put her tea on the table, handed her a Twix and sat down opposite her.

"So…" I said, smiling at the absurdity of the situation.

"So…" she said.

"You look great."

"I ditched the heels when I knew we weren't going somewhere posh. So you didn't get the full effect."

"You still look great."

"So do you," she said.

"Even in my stressed state?"

"Even then."

"I'm glad you came." I reached across the table and took her hand in mine. "And just so you know, I meant everything I said the other day – everything," I said, emphasising the last word.

She sighed. "I know."

"So can we start again?" *Please say we can start again.*

"I hope so. I'd like to…"

"But?" There was definitely a but.

"But… I don't know. It was such a good start, Jess, then it truly went pear-shaped. I'm scared what's next."

"You and me getting to know each other better I hope."

She gave me a weak smile. I took both her hands in mine and fixed her with what I hoped was a sincere stare – because it truly was, that one look held everything I had.

"Look, I get it… I totally do. But I'm going to do everything I can to ensure that you do trust me fully – because you can. You need to know that I'm all in. Have been from the moment I met you. Even though you did play hard to get by running off to Australia for a couple of months."

That raised a smile and I squeezed her hand tighter.

"Whatever it takes Lucy, I'm willing to do. Even if it means sounding like I'm in some corny Hollywood rom-com.

Even if it means taking you for dinner every week at Hexagon till I'm bankrupt," I continued. "Even if it means learning a song and dance routine for your family."

She was smiling now. Smiling was good, right?

"I really like you, Lucy."

She didn't take her eyes off me the whole time I was talking, so I took a chance, leaned over the table and kissed her lips gently. She raised her hand to my face and kissed me back. After a minute or so we eased apart and I touched her face, amazed that I was getting another go with this beautiful woman. Somewhere, somehow, it seemed that the love gods were on my side. I leaned in for another quick kiss before taking her hands again.

"So that's a yes?"

She smiled again. "That's a yes."

I squeezed her hands again.

"But now we're giving it another go, I have one more thing to ask you. Are you free on Saturday to come to Julia's wedding with me?"

"It's not in Brighton, is it?"

"No, they're having it at Marylebone so they can pretend to be pop stars."

"And that woman isn't coming?"

Well, yes.

"Ange? Nope, negative," I lied.

Lucy's face relaxed and she smiled. "In that case, I'd love to."

"Great," I said. I made a mental note to tell Julia not to invite Ange but pushed such negativity out of my mind. Tonight was a good night. Kate and Vicky were still alive and Lucy was my girlfriend.

* * *

Jack arrived back just after 11.30pm, having dropped Maureen off. He looked exhausted but relieved and filled us in on the details of the crash, uncapping a cold beer on the bottle opener that was attached to the wall. Both Kate and Vicky were asleep by the time he left and he said the doctor had advised super-strong painkillers for the next few weeks.

"And no sex with broken ribs apparently."

"I'm sure that was top of Vicky's worries," I said.

"She couldn't hit me when I said it, it hurt too much to move her arm," he said, laughing.

"My sensitive brother."

Lucy just smiled. "So glad they're both okay, though," she said.

"Yeah, me too." He paused. "Anyhow, you're both looking lovely tonight – were you going somewhere?"

"Well we were meant to be going out to dinner…" I said.

"Oh shit," he said, putting his hand up to cover his mouth.

"It'll keep," I said, fixing Lucy with a killer smile. "It'll keep, right?"

She nodded. "It'll keep."

"Glad to hear it," Jack said, holding up his beer bottle.

"A toast. To the fabulous ladies in my life."

"To all of us," I said.

Chapter Forty

I called Julia the next day and told her about Kate and Vicky's accident, which stopped her in her tracks. I could tell from her quickening breathing that she was revving up to tell me her next tale of wedding woe.

"Shit that's awful – is Kate home now?"

"No, later – I have to ring Jack after midday to find out the latest. Lucy's going to drive me up there and bring Kate back though, so that's good." I dropped it in casually, waiting for the response that duly arrived.

"Lucy? Hang on a minute, rewind please. Lucy? Who hates you?"

"She never hated me."

"I think she bloody might have."

"Well, anyway..."

"...Oh my god, it was meant to be your date last night!" The penny had dropped.

"It was, but we didn't end up going. Instead I went to babysit the boys and Lucy came over and drove me home."

"So much to take in!" said Julia, thrilled that someone else's life had more drama than hers. "It's like a scene from some corny rom-com. While sister-in-law lies fighting for her life, the love of your life comes to help you with the kids and holds you in her arms while you sob into your beer."

"That's exactly what happened, did you install cameras again?"

"Ha ha," she said. "So tell me then."

"Tell you?"

"What happened?"

"Nothing. It was just... Nice."

"Jess." Julia sighed impatiently. "How many times do I have to tell you that nice is not a word. Strike it from your vocabulary, it serves no purpose at all. What did she say? After your big speech in the opticians and everything – did she bring it up?"

I shrugged, always effective in a phone call.

"Not exactly but I think it's smoothed over – it wasn't really the time to go into detail but we did talk. It was just good having her there and being driven home. And before you ask, she went home because she had to work in the morning. We're taking it slowly this time."

"You are like a corny rom-com," she said. I could hear her smiling down the phone and I couldn't help but smile too.

"Well I don't care if we are. I just want a quiet life now and for things to get back to normal."

"Not till after next weekend I hope."

"What's happening next weekend?" I said.

"I'm eloping and leaving Tom at the altar after he reveals to me that he's allowed his mother to book a wedding singer whose speciality is *Wind Beneath My Wings*."

"I love that song."

"Don't you start."

"Let's not drag Bette into it."

"Or a wedding singer," Julia said.

"Anyway, while we're on the subject..."

"Of wedding singers? I'm only accepting Adam Sandler, just so you know. And he has to have his comedy nose on too."

"I'll make sure that his agent knows. Nose, geddit?"

"Ha ha."

"Anyway, about your wedding," I said.

"You're not getting out of it now." There was a firmness in her voice.

"I'm not trying to. It's just... well, now Lucy and I are back together, I'd like to bring her..."

"...Which I told you was fine ages ago. I never scrubbed her off the list, I always had faith. Love will conquer all."

"Now you're sounding like a wedding singer."

"Whatever."

"The thing is, now Lucy's coming, I really don't want Ange to. It might be a bit... awkward."

"Ah."

"Yes, *ah*. So I was wondering. Is there any way you can un-invite Ange?"

I paused, letting my request sink in. I knew in the friend stakes I would win this one but I also knew I was putting Julia in a very awkward situation.

"Is that a yes then?" I said.

She sighed. "I'll add it to my ever-growing list of things to do. Un-invite work colleague because best mate shagged her and is bringing new girlfriend."

"You're a star."

"I know."

"And before you say it, I know it's an imposition and I'm sorry."

I heard someone saying something to her in the background at the other end of the line and knew our time was up.

"You have to go?"

"Hang on," she said, covering the phone so that the voices were muffled. I studied my nails, noting they weren't quite as horrendously bitten as normal and silently congratulated myself.

"Yes, turns out I do," Julia said, coming back on the line.

"No worries. Let me know if there's anything I can do to help."

"Just the cake – and give my love to Kate and Vicky."

Chapter Forty-One

Kate didn't look like she'd been in a car accident. Rather, it looked like she'd been in a fight that she'd lost badly, her face showing cuts and bruises. Her right arm was also in a cast and she was clearly in a world of pain with her ribs. When she sneezed she creased her face up so much I thought she might stay etched like that. She told me she was on pain-relieving tablets but that she'd had to ask for a significantly higher dose as they hadn't even touched the sides.

"So I ended up getting ones that are five times the dosage of the over-the-counter ones," she said. "Now when I move, I can still feel my cracked ribs wriggling about inside me but at least they're not stabbing me with every breath. The nurse warned me about taking too many of them but I spoke to my mate Bruce who's a doctor and he told me to take as many as necessary – they just say that to scare you. Who knew?"

Kate was clearly triumphant she'd got one over the medical profession. She was stoic about the accident though, just glad Vicky was okay and they were both still alive.

"Never did get my promised steak and red wine. The things Vicky will do to get out of paying," she said.

I drank my tea while Kate told me her mum had promised to cook up all her childhood favourites over the coming week. She also confessed she must be feeling a little woozy as she was still quite enjoying being taken care of and being at home.

"I'd normally be climbing the walls by now," she said.

"Clearly what being in a near-death experience does to you," I said. "Give it a week though and you'll be pining for me."

* * *

I could see she was in good hands and so left her watching Columbo after a while, kissing Maureen goodbye and going to visit her other daughter.

Vicky was in bed asleep when I got there so I sat with my brother in the garden while the boys chased each other around in a tiny toy car and a mini fire engine. I was transfixed and Jack saw me watching.

"Don't you wish we'd had those in our childhood?"

"You read my mind," I said. "Is it terrible to be a jealous aunty?"

"Natural I think." He got up from his chair. "I'll go and put some coffee on shall I?" He didn't wait for an answer.

"Look at me, Aunty Jess!" shouted Luke. He drove by on his emergency vehicle.

"That's a fab truck you've got!" I said.

"Mummy and Daddy bought it for me."

"Aren't you a lucky boy."

He pedalled by, not listening but making a siren noise as he rushed to his next emergency. I wondered if he would actually become a firefighter in his future – if he did, he'd have no end of boys and girls chasing him.

My phone beeped in my bag, so I fished it out – it was a text from Lucy asking when I'd be back as she'd finished work. I told her to come by my place at 6pm and we'd work stuff out from there. It was 2pm now so I figured another hour here and my familial duties were done. Jack appeared with coffee just as I'd finished texting.

"Lucy?" he said, putting the drinks on the table.

I nodded.

"It was good of her to come and get you last night."

"Yeah it was. Did you get hold of Mum and Dad by the way?"

He nodded. "Eventually, they'd been out at a hoe-down or something."

"A what-down?"

"This is what people do in their dotage it seems," he said. "They were round this morning to see Vicky and they're coming to take the boys to the circus in a bit."

"Do they know that Dad'll be more excited than them?"

"They will do in an hour," he said. "So at least we get a little time if Vicky's awake. And if she's not, I get a couple of hours of peace. It's a win-win."

Chapter Forty-Two

I got home around 3.30pm and nearly called out Kate's name until I realised she wasn't home. I got to work tidying the place up, straightening piles of magazines, plumping cushions, hoovering, dusting, changing bed sheets. Then I flung myself in the shower and buffed myself to a shine. By the time 6pm rolled around I felt like a new woman – lucky, as she was turning up any second now.

Lucy appeared ten minutes later on my doorstep looking just as polished and positively edible. Her short dark hair was slicked back and she wore jeans, a green T-shirt and black leather jacket. She was a soft butch at times and it made me swoon – I'd always had a penchant for them but had never even kissed one until now.

I kissed her lips almost as soon as she appeared, going with my gut rather than reason. She didn't seem offended, smiling and then asking if she could come in. I was embarrassed when I realised she was still on the doorstep.

"Only I know how this can go and last time I didn't even get up the stairs before you had your hand in my pants," she said.

"Of course, of course," I said, making way for her to get past me. This time, I was determined to be more chivalrous. We got to the kitchen and I got two cold Peronis from the fridge, opened them and we went through to the lounge, Lucy taking my hand as we did.

"So," she began, sitting down on the leather couch. I was delighted to see the cushions still retained their plumpness.

"So," I said.

"Here we are again."

"Seems so."

"So what do you fancy doing tonight?" she said. "And before you answer, I think it should involve leaving the house." She smirked and took a swig of her beer.

I shrugged. "There go all my ideas then."

She leaned in and kissed me. It was a long, slow, lingering kiss. It felt safe, warm and it spoke of reconnecting. I was very happy to be reconnecting with Lucy as I opened my eyes.

"I was thinking a gig," she said.

I raised my eyebrows and nodded. "A gig. Novel."

"You've been to gigs before right?" she said, a smile playing on her lips.

"A few."

"Well there's a band playing in Camden that I really like and there's a restaurant opposite that's good – sound okay?"

"Sounds like you've thought about this," I said.

"Well, I've had all afternoon and I thought you might be a little preoccupied. And it's a good job you said yes because I've got the tickets." She reached into her pocket and pulled them out. "Ta-da!" she said.

"It's definitely a go then," I replied.

* * *

Half an hour later we were on the tube, sitting sideways watching brick walls whizz by through murky windows. Emerging out onto Camden's damp, grizzly streets, Lucy took my hand and led me through the maze of drug dealers, Saturday night police and the myriad of people waiting to meet their mates at Camden tube.

She took me to a US-style burger joint that was new and eager to please and we ordered burgers which came loaded with toppings, crisp fries and home-made mayonnaise. The waitresses were far too efficient to be working in Camden and the beers came in chilled glasses – it was just what the doctor ordered. I congratulated Lucy on her choice of pre-gig food and promised that I still owed her a fancy dinner, to which she smiled broadly.

Neither of us could finish the food but we both left full and happy and strolled up the road to the gig venue as if we'd been together for ages. Her warm hand in mine made me feel invincible.

The band were sound-checking as we walked in and a piercing guitar twang bounced around the venue, making me wince. I put my finger in my right ear and frowned.

"Can't they do that earlier?" I said. Lucy just laughed.

"Come on old lady, let's get you a drink."

I followed her to the bar, my feet squelching through a thin layer of lager already coating the red vinyl flooring. She was amazingly quick at the bar once again – I made a note to ask for her tricks – and we walked over to the side of the stage with pints of lager in plastic glasses. Gig glamour at its finest.

When the band eventually began they turned out to be purveyors of jangly indie-pop, replete with fiddles and tambourines as seemed to be the trend these days. Lucy stood behind me and put her arm around my waist as they launched into a full-throttle number, kissing the back of my head as I settled into her embrace. I felt like I was flying.

When the gig finished we had another beer before I suggested Lucy came home with me. She shook her head and my stomach fell.

"I think it's about time you came home with me, don't you?" she said. I grinned.

We kissed as we left the venue, giving the doorman a cheap thrill. Then Lucy hailed a black cab and we sped off into the night.

Chapter Forty-Three

The next morning was a white-cloud day. In Australia, white cloud doesn't exist as a weather description but in the UK it was a particular favourite. When I woke up I wasn't sure where I was, the surroundings unfamiliar to me. But I soon acclimatised when I turned over and saw Lucy lying beside me still sleeping, her dark hair tousled from sleep and her face creased with red lines from where she'd ground herself into her pillow. Her bedroom was more opulent than I'd anticipated, with cushions, a shiny bedspread and expensive-looking curtains hanging at the windows.

Lucy's flat was the top floor of a large stone house that contained four other apartments. Her front door opened into a spacious hallway, off which were two bedrooms and a bathroom. From the hallway a small staircase led up to the top level which contained a spacious living room, plush kitchen with a skylight sucking in the light and a small balcony high up in the sky overlooking lush green gardens.

To say I was impressed would be an understatement. Lucy's descriptions of her flat previously had been 'small, two-bed, okay for now'. The reality was she had something of an eye for interiors and rather than being a pokey bolt-hole, this was a bright and airy two-bed flat with stairs. In London, stairs were a talking point.

I gently eased back the crisp white duvet – I think she might have been expecting company – and levered myself out of bed, careful not to wake her. After going to the loo, I crept silently up the stairs, gratified to note they weren't horror-movie stairs: no creaking at all.

At the top, my feet relishing the soft carpet, I walked into the lounge, through to the kitchen and filled the kettle. In contrast, the slate kitchen tiles were cold on my bare feet and I hopped around as the kettle sprung to life. I wandered out into the lounge and surveyed Lucy's bookshelves, always a window into someone's psyche. There was a multitude of what my mum would call 'hippy self-help' books, alongside a slew of city guides and travel books as well as most of the must-reads from the past decade. Well-travelled and well-read, I concluded from my snooping. Or at least likes to give that impression.

"Well, what's the verdict?" Lucy said. I jumped. That's the trouble with un-creaky stairs; they can work against you too.

"You scared me," I said. "I didn't mean to wake you."

"You shouldn't have got up then," she said. She walked over and put her arms around me before planting a kiss on my mouth.

"Morning," she said.

"Morning," I replied. She was still warm and smelt delicious – she could easily become my favourite smell.

"It's rude to come back to a girl's house and then leave her alone in bed the next morning while you snoop around her apartment you know."

"Is it? Perhaps that's why all the rest have run off," I said.

"Perhaps so."

She took my hand. "Anyway, come back to bed." She was already walking and pulling on my arm.

"I put the kettle on," I protested, walking with her anyway.

"It's not going anywhere."

Lucy led me down the stairs and back into her bed. She didn't say another word but she didn't have to. As she lowered herself on top of me I could think of nothing else but this moment and her beauty inside and out. Looking into her eyes and feeling her breath on my face, I knew she was feeling it too. Emotion swelled inside me and I concentrated hard on not being swept away.

Lucy, meanwhile, channelled all her energy into me: kissing me, loving me. I was completely uninhibited as I stretched out while she kissed my body all over, then slid down the bed. Once there, she slowly licked and nibbled her way along both my inner thighs, before running her tongue along the top of my navel.

I writhed under her gentle touch until she eventually took her tongue to where I needed it most, teasing me, biting me and then finally licking me up and down, immersing my clit in a pool of warmth. When I came, I bucked so hard that I cracked my pubic bone into her nose – only then did we laugh. Occupational hazard of oral sex if you're too good at it.

She wasn't finished, though. After moving back up to smother both breasts with kisses, Lucy kissed me deeply, passionately. *Oh my.* Then she held my gaze as she moved her fingers over my clit in a glorious rhythm before finally filling me. I thought I might pass out from sheer bliss when I came again.

She slid her tongue into my mouth and we kissed deeply, her weight on top of me feeling a perfect fit. When I opened my eyes, her eyes were on me, watching, waiting. The moment was solid with emotion and Lucy opened her mouth, then closed it. Instead, she kissed me again before sliding off me and flopping down beside me. The silence that followed was spine-tingling. I broke it first, touching her face with my hand.

"That was... amazing," I said. She returned my gaze and nodded. Words still left unsaid hung in the air. Amazing really didn't come close.

She turned her head on the pillow, stroking my face and smiling. She decided to change gear.

"So I was thinking," she said. "It's Sunday, what can we do. First plan was to seduce you – I think that's done."

"Gold star," I said. I was still getting my breath back.

"Then I thought, well we could do a little more seduction. Or perhaps save it till later. Do you fancy going to the flower market? I keep meaning to go but never do and it's only half ten. I could make us breakfast and we could be there by 12 – what d'you think?"

"Hmmm."

"Is that a good hmmm or a bad hmmm?"

"It's an 'I can't really think right now' hmmm," I said. "But sounds good."

"Cool," she said, flopping down on her back beside me. "I'll go and make that tea, shall I?"

"You're going to make someone a lovely wife."

* * *

Lucy whipped up tea with bagels, salmon and cream cheese, impressing me no end. We ate it on her balcony at her tiny wooden table, nestled among a throng of pretty plant pots after I'd struggled into my jeans and staggered up the stairs, my legs still wobbly from exertion.

Before I tucked in she produced lemon wedges and squeezed them over the salmon – she clearly had thought of everything. She'd also tamed the back of her hair since she got up and was wearing some red shorts that could almost be classed as hot pants, along with a Pineapple Dance Studio T-shirt. She assured me she'd never been to Pineapple Dance Studios in her life, but her sister-in-law was a big fan and this was what she'd bought her last Christmas.

"I think it looks cute on you," I said.

"You'd think anything looks cute on me right at this moment," she said. I laughed. Very true.

"So what does your brother think of his dance-crazy wife?"

She paused and I could see her picturing them in her head.

"He loves it. She even got him to go to dance class with her and now they go to salsa every week. Salsa in Leeds." She shook her head. "I still can't imagine it. Particularly as my brother's an engineer. But now an enlightened engineer, clearly."

As I chewed my bagel and drank my tea, I could hear the trains rattling by down below at the end of Lucy's garden. Above us, the white cloud was holding steady, the sun still too lazy to reveal itself. No matter though: this was a beautiful, tranquil scene. This was how Sunday mornings were supposed to be, how they were depicted in novels, films and songs. A lazy morning of sex and brunch with someone special. Life felt truly magical at that moment.

"This is beautiful, you know," I said.

"The bagel?"

"This whole thing. The food, the setting, being here with you. It's like I've stepped onto the set of some Richard Curtis film."

"I'll try to rustle up Hugh Grant to join us for lunch later if you like," she said.

"I'll just stick with you if that's okay."

Lucy's phone ringing interrupted our conversation and she ran into the lounge and retrieved it from the sofa. Her face lit up as she answered.

"Hey, Mum." Pause.

"No – just having brunch." Pause.

"Yeah a bit late." Pause.

"Well I have somebody here." She turned to me and flashed me a smile. "Her name is Jess, I might have mentioned her to you." My eyes widened and my cheeks flushed. She'd been talking to her mum about me? Blimey.

"She's just eating the bagel I made her. You want to talk to her?"

Alarm spread across my features and I tensed up as she walked towards me. What on earth was I going to say to her mother? As she reached me Lucy kissed the top of my head, put her hand over the receiver and whispered in my ear: "I'm joking."

My body slumped with relief. I was going to have to get used to Lucy's sense of humour.

* * *

We made it to the flower market around 1pm, after Lucy's best-laid plans took a left-turn after we finished breakfast, she got naked and stepped into her shower. It seemed rude not to follow her.

A while later we hopped on the No.8 bus from Bow, taking us as far as Brick Lane after which we sauntered up Shoreditch High Street hand in hand, taking in the pop-up tea shops and high-fashion stores that seemed to spring up overnight and leave as quickly as they arrived. A right into Hackney Road, a right into Columbia Road and we were there.

The flower market happened every Sunday from 8am–2pm, although I had never made it down there before 12pm and today was no exception. The only people who turned up at 8am to my knowledge were either market-stall holders or clubbers who hadn't made it home the night before.

I loved the atmosphere of the flower market, the wonderful bouquet of all those flowers filling your nose and the vibrancy of the place. The market was set up on the street with a narrow aisle down the middle of stalls on both sides. Behind the stalls the pavements cracked and heaved as crowds zigzagged in and out of the market and into the shops behind, seeking out gifts, piping hot seafood, strong coffee and pots for their new plants.

I took Lucy's hand and we dived straight into the market which was thick with people. Now, coming up to the final hour of the day, flowers were starting to be knocked down in price and bargain-hunters were on the prowl. You had to pay attention to exactly where you were going, otherwise you could get your eye taken out by someone's sunflowers or Gladioli.

We scoured both sides, admiring the white roses, tulips, irises and a host of enormous fauna that neither of us had any clue about. Lucy settled on a mixed bunch that would bring a splash of colour to her muted lounge.

We giggled as we ducked out of the market scrum and into the pub, past the clubbers and found two seats at the bar. Lucy ordered a pint of cider – "the sun's coming out so let's be summery" she told me – so I ordered one too and we settled into our stools, perching the flowers on the bar. The whole time we were there the morning was still on my mind and when I caught Lucy's eye I could tell it was on hers too. When she kissed me at the bar I could tell something had shifted and only for the better.

When we got back to mine I got a text from Kate telling me she was staying put for the week, the doctor having signed her off and her mum quite prepared to look after her. Apparently she'd talked Vicky into coming over too so she could keep an eye on both her girls during the following week and spoil her grandsons into the bargain. Suddenly, the accident had perked up Maureen's week and mine, too. A flat to myself was always a bonus.

I also had a missed call on my phone from a London number I didn't recognise. While Lucy was in the loo I scrolled through my phone seeing if any of my friends fitted the bill but I couldn't find a match, so figured they'd call back if it was urgent. Right now, I had a gorgeous girlfriend to deal with and nothing was going to distract me.

Chapter Forty-Four

Back at Porter's the next day I was still happy in my love bubble and recollections of yesterday were doing nothing to keep my mind focused on the job at hand. After the market, we'd bought dinner and a movie but only managed to drag ourselves from bed to eat it at around 8pm. Matt was babbling on about his weekend with Natalie and how they'd gone suit shopping for the wedding. He no longer owned one having burnt all his suits in a fit of pique when he exited the world of finance.

"Are you coming to the whole day or just the evening?" I didn't know how good a friend Natalie was to Julia.

"The whole thing. I wasn't, but someone's dropped out so I got promoted. Nice timing eh? I'm quite looking forward to it, actually – our first public outing as a couple and it's going to be lovely being cooked for and waited on. The venue looks dead posh."

"If it's to do with Julia and Tom, I've no doubt that posh probably doesn't quite do it justice. Our girl likes the finer things in life and so do I when she's paying," I said.

"Wonder if we'll be on the same table. You're not doing a speech or anything are you?"

"Nope. I managed to duck out of bridesmaid duties on account of me being a lesbian."

"They don't allow it?"

"The manual says it's against lesbian law. Plus Julia knew

I would have laughed in her face."

"She might have really wanted you to be her bridesmaid," he said. He pulled his best liberal frown.

"She'll get over it. Anyhow, her sister and other mates stepped in and they all look far better in a dress than me, take my word for it."

"I think you'd look lovely in a frock. Especially peach. Or perhaps lemon yellow."

"Remind me not to come to you for fashion advice, Porter."

Matt's help for the morning was Jane, a mum he knew from Charlie's school. She popped her head round the corner.

"Can one of you come and help, please," she said. "There's quite a queue."

"I'll go." I said. I wiped my hands on my apron but Matt was right behind me, queues being his pet-hate. We rattled through two Americanos and one skinny latte before the café door opened again. As I turned to look up I did a double-take, stopping mid-pour of my latest latte. I wheeled back around to face the machine and felt my heart drop to the floor with a splat. Karen had just walked into the café, looking tanned and relaxed.

I concentrated on finishing my order as I felt Karen approaching the counter, surveying the board on the wall to the left of me like she was just any other customer. Jane asked what she'd like and she ordered a double espresso as I knew she would.

I nudged Matt who was standing next to me making a pot of tea.

"Can you finish this order – it's done, the blonde at the counter just needs to pay. Skinny latte."

He looked at me puzzled but took the takeaway cup from my outstretched hand.

"Sure. Everything okay?"

I nodded and retreated into the kitchen, feeling Karen's eyes on me as I did. I wasn't sure what to do or how to act. I'd known she was coming to the UK but I hadn't truly processed how I might feel when I saw her. Well here I was, hiding in the kitchen, heart racing, stomach gurgling. Meanwhile, Karen was standing outside drinking a double espresso. Great start.

I gripped the workbench in the kitchen as Matt walked back in.

"What's wrong?" he said.

I shook my head and he looked concerned.

"What's up? You're scaring me."

"I'm scaring myself if it's any consolation."

"Not really." He tilted his head to one side.

"Karen's just walked in."

"Karen?"

"From Australia. Karen. Who broke my heart. The reason I came back to the UK and now here she is in this café when she's meant to be back in Sydney and I'm meant to be getting on with my life. Which I am by the way. Over her and moving on."

I was beginning to get angry. I could see Matt was a little taken aback by my reaction and he wasn't the only one. So this was how it was going to go down.

"How dare she. How dare she just waltz back in here and smile at me. She's got a fucking nerve."

"Did you tell her you worked here?"

"No but it's a small world. I've told people back in Oz and she clearly pumped them for information. I mean, my mates wouldn't have said anything but if you want to find something out bad enough, you usually can." I sighed.

"Is there anything I can do?" Matt said.

I shook my head.

"Want me to eject her, tell her she's not welcome in these parts?"

I smiled grimly. "Yes please." I sighed again and leaned my forehead into my right palm.

"I guess I'm going to have to go out there and face her."

"Probably right," he said. "I mean, you could stay in here and make the rest of the stuff for lunch but I have a hunch that even if you did that, she might come back another time. I've seen enough films to know that's the way these things work."

I dropped the tea towel I'd been clutching onto the counter-top.

"I'm not going to deal with this now though, we're busy..." I said.

"That doesn't matter..."

"...No, it does. She can't just march back into my life and have everything on her terms. I mean, what the fuck is she doing in here before 7.15 in the morning anyway? That's almost stalker behaviour." I paused. "No you're right. I'm going to confront her and tell her to do one."

"Whatever you think," Matt said.

I walked back towards the kitchen door.

"One other thing," he said. I turned back to Matt and the concern was etched all over his face, his hair falling in his eyes. He needed a haircut.

"Just remember you've come a long way in the last year. This woman is from the past, so don't let her drag you down."

I pursed my lips and nodded.

* * *

I went back out into the café a few minutes later and Karen was sitting by the window, legs rested on the ledge, intently people-watching. She had a paper laid out in front of her but I knew she wasn't reading it. Karen never read papers but she liked to be seen with them, she thought it made her look intellectual. I indicated to Matt that I was going over to her and he gave me a thumbs-up. The rush had died down somewhat so now was the best time to get this over with before the 8 o'clock rush began anew.

I wiped my hands on my apron and walked over to where Karen was sitting, trying to contain my nerves and act as if this was an everyday occurrence even though my heart was pounding in my chest.

"Hi Karen," I said. I pulled out the stool next to her. She acted startled even though I was sure she'd been monitoring my progress since coming out of the kitchen. I had to remember she was manipulative. Lesson one.

"Jess. Hi," she said. She broke into an unsure grin I knew all too well.

Her teeth were still straight out of a Colgate advert and her smile still lit up the room. Shame the morals and ethics behind it all were such a let-down. She was wearing denim shorts and a baby blue T-shirt and she looked fresher than you might expect, seeing as she should surely still be jetlagged. She seemed stumped as to what the social etiquette of the occasion was: how do you greet an ex-lover you broke up with so devastatingly in the past year?

I could see she was weighing up giving me a kiss or a hug but that wasn't on my roadmap so I sat down solidly on my stool, making sure my non-verbal signals were clearly stating 'Stay Away'. She seemed to get the message. Instead, Karen went into charm overdrive.

"It's so good to see you, you look fantastic. And I love this café! It's like the ones back home," she said.

"Yeah it is." I paused to look her in the eye. "And of all the cafés in London, you happened to pick this one by chance?"

She seemed taken aback and I could feel my face reddening. Damn my rushing blood and its inappropriateness.

"Well I… I emailed to tell you I was coming. I tried to call you too last night to see if you were free."

My mind whirled.

"You tried to call?" So that was the number I didn't recognise.

"Yeah. I called your mum first and she gave me your number."

"My mother." I sighed.

"But I emailed too and you emailed back," she said. She was giving me her perplexed look.

"I emailed you back saying we really had nothing to say to each other. You made your feelings towards me perfectly clear last year."

She frowned and licked her lips. Surely she couldn't be this dim, to expect to waltz back into my life as if nothing had happened? My mind briefly wondered if she was a psychopath – I was sure I'd read about this kind of behaviour attributed to them in a Sunday supplement. It would explain a lot.

"Look, last year was last year. If I could turn back the clock I would – you were an amazing girlfriend and I was too stupid to see it. Especially seeing as Paula ran off with someone else three months later…"

"So if she hadn't done that, you'd still be back in Oz and we wouldn't be having this conversation?" I stuttered audibly as I said it, amazed at her audacity.

"No, I didn't mean it like that…" she said.

I shook my head and crossed my arms over my stomach.

"I can save you the trouble, anyway. You had your chance with me but you threw it away and as far as I'm concerned, that's that. There's nothing else to say and I don't really know why you're here – what do you expect to happen? I live here now, that's it."

"And I've got an English passport from my grandparents. I could live here too," she said, her Aussie accent really pronounced, her level rising at the end of her sentence.

She'd clearly thought this out and expected me to be on-board straight away. What Karen wanted, Karen got and she wasn't used to being told no. I knew – I'd met her parents who'd created the blueprint.

"What?" I said. "What are you going on about?"

I could feel my voice rising and I didn't want to get caught up in her soap opera, not this early in the morning. So I shifted in my seat, took a deep breath and regained my composure.

"You dumped me, you slept with my flatmate and wrote me out of your life. Now I live here and I'm happy." I swept my arm out to indicate the café and she obligingly followed its arc, looking around as silently directed.

"I love this job, I've got a good flat and I've met somebody else."

I thought about Lucy, about her beautiful body lying in my bed, about the fact I was in love with her. Oh god, I was so in love with her. I felt guilty, like I was cheating by even talking to Karen.

"I still love you," Karen replied, looking into my eyes. How ironic. I snorted, surprised at my bullishness. All my nerves had evaporated now, replaced with indignation. She really was something.

"You don't love me, you just want what you haven't got. If I flung myself into your arms, you'd be off looking for the next challenge. Because that's what life is to you. A challenge."

"I don't know why you're saying all this." She looked hurt and confused.

"Maybe you should ask your therapist, I'm sure she could fill you in." I sighed and got up. "And I don't know why you're here in my café before 7.30am. If you wanted to see me, why come now? Don't you think it's a bit weird?"

She shrugged. "My sleep's all fucked from jetlag so I was awake."

"Well go back to bed," I said.

"I don't want it to end like this."

I shook my head and pushed the stool under the bench.

"It's not ending like this, it ended nearly a year ago. That was it. Go back to your life in Sydney. I'm sure there are plenty of other suckers who'll fall for you."

She looked visibly wounded at that last comment and hung her head, defeated. For a brief moment I felt sorry for her, but then I remembered where I was and who I was with. Show no weakness or she'll jump on it.

"You must have had quite a chat to my mum if she told you where I worked too."

"Oh I knew where you worked – Tom told me in one of his 'She's doing great, leave her alone' speeches. He gives them to me on a regular basis, you'll be pleased to hear."

I smiled at that as Karen pushed her coffee cup aside.

"Look Jess, I get it. I get that you don't want me back, that you don't want me around. But I'm here for the next two weeks and I'm back in London at the weekend. Can't we at least meet for a drink? Just to chat, catch up."

"I don't…"

She held up her hand.

"And before you say no, I'm going back to Sydney. I'll leave you alone after that. What do you think?"

"I think no."

She looked crestfallen.

"I have to get back to work," I said.

"I'll give you some time to think about it," she said as I walked back to the counter.

I turned and looked her straight in the eye and my stomach flipped. A part of me would always love Karen even after everything. However, I couldn't show her that even though it killed me a little bit. Do we ever fully get rid of the taste of old lovers?

"Don't bother. Have a nice life," I said. I turned and walked towards the counter, catching my breath as I did and collecting some plates and cups to give myself something to focus on.

I don't remember a time when I'd been so decisive and where I knew exactly what I wanted, with no doubt in my mind. I wanted Lucy, I didn't want Karen and I wanted to look forward and not back. Matt eyed me as I made my way behind the counter and into the kitchen with the dirty crockery. I heard the till ping as he took the money from the customer he was serving and then he appeared in the doorway.

"All good?" he said. I put the dishes in the dishwasher and stood back up, feeling a little lightheaded as I did so. I nodded slowly.

"Yeah, I think it is." I paused. "Can you check if she's gone, though?" He poked his head out the door then swiftly returned, nodding.

"Then yeah, I really hope it is," I said.

"Good," he said. "I'll say one thing though, you can really pick them."

Chapter Forty-Five

Kate called to tell me she wasn't coming to the evening of the wedding – her ribs were too painful and she was still looking less than wedding-friendly. It was 3pm on Friday and the lunchtime rush had died down. Beth had been clucking all day about her new man, although I noted she was still flirting with Artur – old habits die hard.

I took my mobile outside and leaned up against the alley wall to the right of Porter's, having to plug my left ear with my index finger whenever the traffic became too loud for me to hear. I'd looked all over my mobile and I'll be damned if I could find the volume control for phone calls.

Kate told me she was also staying put at her mum's for another week, so I persuaded her to come to the barbecue with us on Sunday. She was only too pleased to say yes to this, being it meant she was there to witness my inaugural outing with a girlfriend at my parents' house.

"Don't. At least I can't worry about that right now, I've got too much else to get through before that."

"It'll be fine. Ian will dazzle her with his burgers and Shirley will talk really quickly because she's so nervous, perhaps even more than you."

"Hmmm," I said.

"Well, she might be."

"Why you suddenly on her side?" I was frowning.

"I'm not, but you have to admit this is out of her comfort zone too."

"Yeah, well, that's Sunday. Before that I've got Julia to calm down and I've got to get the cake to the venue in the morning."

"You made it already?"

"Yep, last night."

"Take a picture – I want to see it."

"I will."

"Is Julia stressing?" From her tone she already knew the answer.

"Somewhat. She's demanded I come over tonight and be with her – me and some of the hen party."

"Bet Lucy's thrilled with that."

"Not Ange," I replied curtly.

"Just saying. Has she uninvited her now by the way?"

"I hope so. Anyway, I'm leaving her in the hands of her bridesmaids after a couple of drinks and coming home to my lovely empty flat."

"Charming!"

"I miss you really, you know that."

"I know you're lying through your teeth and you're loving having the place to yourself."

"Only a bit. I missed your bacon sarnies this weekend," I said.

"Talking of Lucy, all going well?"

"Very well thanks."

"I suppose I should be grateful not to be there to hear you shagging all the time," she said. "One good thing about this accident is it's taken my mind off my barren love life. Even the thought of sex makes my ribs ache."

After finishing the call I pressed the red button, clearing my throat as I walked back into the café. Matt was on the customer-side of the counter pulling the sole few baguettes to the front, making the offerings look fuller after the lunchtime decimation.

"Listen, go home, we can tidy up," Matt said as I stepped behind the counter.

"No it's fine, I can help shut up."

"I know but go and see Julia, get some rest and I'll meet you here at nine to move the cake tomorrow," he said.

He was clearly in full clean-up mode – I'd witnessed it many times – as now he picked up a damp cloth and began cleaning the milk spout of the coffee machine. He was the only member of staff allowed to do this as Beth and I burnt our fingers every time, so he'd banned us.

"If you're sure. Tell you what, I'll do it if you bugger off early next week in return. Deal?"

Matt smiled. "Deal."

"How's the cake looking by the way?"

"Still there," he said.

"That's a start. What you up to tonight?"

"Polishing my shoes and choosing my tie probably. Exciting stuff."

I went into the back to grab my bag and then reappeared.

"Thanks for this," I told Matt, giving him a kiss on the cheek. He was still cleaning the nozzle, a man obsessed.

"See you in the morning." I paused. "See ya, Beth!" I shouted into the back. She called back a muffled response and I walked out of the café into the afternoon sunshine, glad to get some fresh air. The city was still sizzling in the sun, office workers abandoning their jackets, dogs with their tongues hanging out of their mouths as they tried to get moisture into their hot bodies.

Today as I walked home across Hoxton Square in the milky light there were all manner of people and colours strewn across the grass readying themselves for the weekend. I guaranteed they didn't have as busy a one as mine.

Chapter Forty-Six

Saturday June 5th and my first thought on waking was 'cake'. I'd arrived at Julia's the night before expecting a stressed scene but was greeted at the door by a serene-looking bride-to-be. Tom had vacated to a nearby hotel to be with his best man and friends, under strict instructions not to get drunk. Julia seemed to be taking her own advice too, a bottle of grape juice open on the kitchen table.

Three of the hens turned up and we ate Chinese food and drank white wine spritzers, although Julia limited herself to two as she didn't want to be hungover in the wedding photos. French manicures and eyebrow teasing featured after a while, nestled in among talk of photographers, flowers and wedding cars as well as Julia intermittently screaming "I'm getting married tomorrow!" and hugging the nearest person a little too hard.

I'd ducked out around 9pm, went home and chatted to Adam about his new squeeze who was apparently proving a good fit, mainly because he was enthusing about Adam's cooking skills no end. After I hung up the phone to my gushing gay man, I had another call but I was in the kitchen with the kettle on and it rang off just as I got there. When I checked the number it was one I didn't recognise. I scrolled through and realised it was the same number from the other night. It looked like I had a new Australian stalker. Terrific.

* * *

But this morning, there was no time to worry. I threw on some jeans and a T-shirt, peering out of my curtains to check it was still sunny – it was. Julia and Tom's wedding day was going to be glorious and it was also going to have the best cake in town. So long as we didn't drop it.

I postponed my shower, downing a cup of tea and some toast then pulling on my trainers and walking over to the café where Matt was standing behind the counter with a coffee and a copy of The Sun, confusing customers because the cafe was very much shut. When I banged on the door he looked up, shaking his head from side to side until he realised who it was. Then he broke into a grin and raced round to open the door.

"People keep wanting to come in, maybe we should open up on a Saturday," he said, closing the door and locking it behind him. He was dressed in his uniform of jeans and a polo shirt, although he had a certain twinkle in his eye this morning.

"Or maybe you should drink your coffee out the back."

"It's not sunny round the back," he said. "What do you think of opening on Saturdays?" He looked like a little kid who'd just had a brilliant idea and I frowned at him.

"I think it would probably be a waste of time and you might sell ten coffees and a couple of buns. But we could try it if it makes you happy so long as I don't have to work every week."

"I could employ Saturday staff," he said.

"Let's see if it works first, shall we?"

"Yeah, you're probably right."

"Do I get a coffee then?"

"Course," he said, putting his mug down on top of Dear Deirdre.

"So you look very perky today. Did you get laid last night?"

He grinned. "Might have. And this morning."

It was my turn to grin at him.

"Am I the only one?" he asked.

"Having coffee?"

"Who got lucky," he said, bumping my hip with his.

"Unfortunately today, yes. Lucy was out last night so I woke up alone this morning."

"Shame."

"I didn't know you were a fan of Dear Deirdre either," I said, changing the subject. "I'm learning a lot about you today."

Matt smiled as he ground the beans, a noise I hated so he didn't leave the machine on too long.

"Who isn't a fan of Deirdre?" he shouted over the din. "You can trust women called Deirdre. They're not going to steer you wrong, are they?"

"No?"

"No, Deirdres are solid," he said.

"I only know two – this one and the one on Coronation Street."

"I rest my case."

"I'm not sure about the photo-stories though," I said. I tilted my head to one side where a half-naked woman was sitting astride a man, telling him she was worried about her blow job technique. "Are picture instructions the way to go with sex problems?"

Matt laughed. "Absolutely – stop being so bourgeois. You don't get shit like that in The Guardian, do you?"

"I have to admit you don't."

He added milk to my Americano and brought it over as another customer knocked on the window. Matt made a motion like he was slitting his throat.

"Are you telling him we're shut or we're about to kill him?"

"We should go through to the back, shouldn't we?" he said.

"Probably," I said, picking up the paper as we walked.

The plan was to shift the cake to the venue – Julia was having her reception at The Landmark Hotel, opposite the Marylebone registry office where they were getting hitched. In the kitchen were huge cardboard catering boxes for transporting all the cupcakes, which we began to fill, shifting the cakes from the fridges to the boxes.

When the cupcakes were done, we carefully lifted the layers of chocolate cake with white icing into their Tupperware containers and then set about transporting the whole lot to the car. The whole operation wasn't as painful as I'd anticipated and we were back before 11am, with the wedding at 2pm.

Matt dropped me back at the flat and I threw myself into the shower and began panicking about my wedding outfit – dressing posh always had this effect on me and had done from a young age. My mum loved to regale anyone who'd listen about my childhood tantrums whenever she tried to get me in a dress or put my hair up in a bun. What can I tell you? Clearly, like Lady Gaga says, I was born this way.

Chapter Forty-Seven

I put the radio on loud in my bedroom and did my hair, praying for it to dry obediently today. Miraculously, it obeyed. Then I dressed in my white trousers and shirt, blue chequered tie and blue and white jacket. I had meant to buy some white shoes to go with the ensemble but ran out of time so my blue ones would have to do. It took away some of the 'Richard Gere in *An Officer And A Gentleman*' look but I didn't mind my reflection in the mirror. Lucy was due in five minutes and I hoped she thought the same.

I was fiddling with my hair and adding extra lip gloss when I heard the door and I grinned at my reflection before racing to the door. I opened it with a broad smile, expecting to greet Lucy. The smile soon evaporated as I saw Karen standing there with a packet of TimTams. She knew I loved TimTams.

"Wow, you look very smart," she said, giving me the once over and whistling her appreciation. "Actually, scrap smart – more like stunning," she said, her Aussie accent giving the sentence that expected twang. Unlike me, she was dressed casually in jeans and a red T-shirt with black flip-flops on her feet. Her toe nails were painted silver and her hair was artfully styled, even though she was trying to appear casual.

I sighed. "You never cease to amaze me. Are you stalking me now?"

"Nah, I just followed you home the other night and went to give you these today in the café but it was closed. So I thought

I'd drop them off here." She offered me the packet of TimTams and I took them. They were double-chocolate, my favourite.

"You know I could have you arrested."

"For giving you TimTams?"

"For following me home."

She laughed nervously and shrugged.

"Well, thanks," I said, turning to put her gift on the bottom of the stairs. "But if that's it, I have a wedding to go to." I didn't want to get into histrionics right now, I just wanted Karen to bugger off before Lucy arrived.

"That's why you're so smart," she said. "Julia's wedding, right?"

Julia had told me she was planning to get married while I was still with Karen and I was surprised she'd even listened. I'd been upset when I thought I probably wouldn't be able to go but Karen had stepped in and solved that one, so I did have something to thank her for.

"Yeah and I'm expecting my girlfriend, so it'd be good if you'd go. Like, *now*."

"Girlfriend?" She sounded surprised.

"I told you I was seeing someone."

"There's seeing someone and then there's girlfriend," she said, putting her hand in her jeans pocket and leaning against the doorframe. Then she put on her serious face.

"Look Jess, I know you weren't thrilled to see me the other day but I thought you'd have had time to think about it by now. We were good together, you know that. You've only just started seeing this other girl, so what is she to you? Give me a chance to make it up to you," she said, reaching out her hand and brushing my shoulder. I instinctively slapped it away.

"Karen, listen for once in your life for fuck's sake. I've moved on and you should too. Now stop phoning me, don't come round here again and don't come to the café, goddit? We've been over for a very long time."

At that moment a black cab steered into the street and pulled up. Lucy stepped out, wearing a deep purple dress with a grey jacket and heels, looking drop dead gorgeous. I took a deep breath – this was not the scenario I had in my head this morning with Karen on my doorstep. I looked at Karen and I think she read my mind – ex-lovers have their benefits. Suddenly, she seemed to get it and stood down, stepping away from the door and turning to smile at Lucy. When she reached the door Karen held out her hand in greeting as I held my breath. My life couldn't get much weirder than this moment.

"Hi, I'm Karen," she said.

"Lucy," my girlfriend replied, eyeing me, then Karen before shaking her hand. "Nice to meet you."

"You too," Karen said. "Right, well... I'm off. See you around, Jess."

Karen nodded at me and walked away down the street without looking back.

"Yeah, see ya."

I watched her retreating figure for a couple of seconds with a gut feeling that this time it was for real and I felt a momentary tug on my heart. But then Lucy's lips were on mine and I snapped back into reality.

"You look gorgeous," she said. She stepped back to assess the full package.

"So do you," I said. And she really did. The colour brought out her gorgeous eyes and her legs were stunning. I drew in breath and didn't notice the blocks of reality falling into place in Lucy's mind.

"Was that Karen – *the* Karen?" she said, flicking her head left. I turned, picked up the biscuits and pulled her inside.

"Yep," I said, not looking at her and walking up the stairs. Lucy followed but I was scared to look round and see her face. I didn't need to, I knew she wouldn't be smiling. The kiss from a minute ago seemed a long way off.

"She's here? Not in Australia?"

"On holiday. She came to give me some TimTams, would you believe."

"That old chestnut," Lucy said. She didn't sound amused.

At the top of the stairs I pulled her to me and kissed her full on the lips but she wasn't being put off that easily. Instead, I felt her pull away and eye me suspiciously.

"I promise you, she's the last person I expected on my doorstep this morning."

"So long as she wasn't just leaving?" Lucy said. She raised an eyebrow.

I laughed, shocked, which was probably not the best response when your girlfriend asks you that question, just in case you're ever asked.

"God no," I said. "I've been out with the cake all morning, only got back an hour ago. The door just went and I thought it was you. Instead, there was Karen."

I squeezed her hand but she pulled back slightly, eyeing me with caution. To be honest, I couldn't say I blamed her. I knew this was a lot to take in.

"You're sure?" she said.

"Positive. She just has terrifically bad timing."

"You didn't know she was in the UK?"

"I'd heard she was coming over via some friends but London's a big place. Then she turned up in the café the other day…"

"She turned up in the café?" Lucy's eyes widened.

Shit.

"Er, yeah. She turned up in the café," I said. Shit, shit, shit.

"And you didn't think to mention it?"

I was scared to look at her but knew I had to. I sighed heavily, took Lucy's hand and looked her directly in the eyes, which were filling with suspicion. This was not how today was meant to go at all and I didn't want to be the girlfriend who ruined Lucy's beautifully applied make-up. I had to make this right.

"No, I didn't mention it and I'm sorry. She turned up and she wanted to catch up but I told her no. I didn't say anything because, well, things are still too raw after Brighton. I didn't want anything rocking the boat and thought I'd dealt with Karen and told her to bugger off. I wasn't hiding anything from you, honest."

Now it was her turn to sigh and she dropped my hand.

"That's not the way it seems to me."

Her face shone with disappointment again and I felt crushed.

"You have to believe me," I said.

"I do believe you." Her shoulders slumped. "But things aren't really plain sailing with you, are they?"

I had to admit they weren't.

"First you snog someone else on your best mate's hen night. Then I turn up to go to said best mate's wedding and you've got your ex on the doorstep, just leaving."

"She never even came in the door..." I stuttered.

"...Bringing gifts for you too. Despite all the evidence though, I want to believe you because I like you. But this is..."

She breathed out heavily, then motioned with her hand between us.

"You and me, we're good together I think. It's just you seem to have a whole line of exes queuing up who still think the same and I'm not prepared to share. It's not me."

"It's not me either," I said. "You're who I want. Only you. Ange was a drunken idiot and so was I to let it happen. As for Karen, she's over here on a two-week holiday and that's just bad timing but she'll be gone soon." I sighed heavily. "So can we start this day again? Please?"

I knew my voice was sounding a bit pleading but I figured it was what the situation needed. I took her hand in mine and squeezed. Lucy wanted to believe me and that was half the battle. She looked at me and smiled weakly.

"Are you going to be more trouble than you're worth?" she said.

I looked into her eyes. "I'm going to really work hard on being trouble-free from now on," I said. I leaned in to kiss her and she let me, which was a good sign. I stood back and assessed.

"We okay?"

She nodded slowly. "We're okay."

"Great, because the taxi's coming in five minutes and we have a wedding to go to."

Chapter Forty-Eight

Despite Julia's protestations of hating weddings, I didn't think I'd ever seen a more radiant bride. She floated down the aisle in her white satin and lace dress, and seeing two people I cared about deeply saying 'I do' made me realise that not all weddings were bad. They were two of my closest friends and I couldn't have been more thrilled.

Lucy squeezed my hand tight during the vows which I took as a good sign that Karen was forgiven, if not forgotten. Julia caught my eye and winked as she walked down the aisle with her new husband and a photobook flashed through my mind of all the times we'd spent together and our friendship, which had lasted over 20 years.

Outside, I hugged her parents and introduced them to Lucy, then fell in with Matt and Natalie, Andy and Jason. We stood in the foyer of the grand old town hall and watched the happy couple pose for pictures, parents and immediate family looking on proudly, cousins looking detached and disinterested. After 20 minutes we trooped out onto the huge concrete steps and into the sunshine, breathing in the traffic fumes from the Euston Road.

"Bloody starving," Jason said, looking at his watch. He looked dapper in a dark grey suit with paisley grey cravat. He was also wearing black shoes that were shined as if he were in the army.

"Terrible time for a wedding, lunchtime. Do you think they're going to feed us soon?"

"Think of the calories you're not ingesting," I said.

"I can't, I'm too hungry."

"You're such a bad gay."

"And we had a big breakfast," Andy said.

His boyfriend looked suave too although he'd favoured a baby blue suit with matching tie, cream shirt and cream shoes which looked expensively Italian and probably were. In a break for individuality, Andy had shaved off his goatee too, meaning the pair looked less a homogenous mass and more two stylish queens.

"Four hours ago that was," Jason said. His whining made both Lucy and I smirk.

"Well you should have brought that banana shouldn't you? I believe I did mention it when we were leaving the house." Andy rolled his eyes as Jason sighed. "Anyway, it's your appetite that nearly meant you couldn't get into that suit. So remember, dust is your friend. Eat dust."

"I don't think a banana would have cut it – and bugger dust, I'm in the suit now," Jason said. "Anyway, let's talk about something other than food. What do you do, Lucy? And don't say you're a chef."

"I'm a chef," she said. I sniggered.

"You're not are you?"

She shook her head, laughing.

"She's good," Jason said.

"I know," I said. I put my hand around Lucy's waist.

"I'm an optician," Lucy said.

Jason raised his eyebrows in approval.

"Lawyers, opticians, you get them all don't you," he told me. Andy stamped on his foot.

"Ow!" he said. "What was that for?"

"So how long have you two been seeing each other?"

Andy said, changing the subject.

"Not long, a couple of weeks," I said.

"Ah, young love. We were like that once weren't we dear?"

"Yes, when you didn't used to beat me up." Jason was still hopping on one foot and looked wounded.

"So hard done by," Andy said.

Julia interrupted which I was grateful for after Jason's bungling attempts at conversation. She told us to get over the road if we wanted canapés before Tom's family scoffed the lot. Jason didn't need telling twice, attempting to cross the Euston Road Frogger-style before realising his mistake and walking to the crossing like the rest of us.

Once at the hotel, we were shown through to the special wedding suite and greeted with champagne and canapés by waiters attired in black and gold – this was more like it. Huge chandeliers hung along the centre of the room and everything seemed to sparkle – table settings, flowers, candles, the works.

Sunflowers were spread throughout the room and on every circular table, with all the chairs covered in white fabric and golden bows to match. Even the wooden floorboards seemed to shimmer as sunlight splattered itself over them, lighting up the room and the atmosphere.

I spied our cake over to the side, its virgin icing looking regal and for all the world a fruit cake but I knew the truth. It was surrounded by tiers of our golden and white cupcakes and even I had to admit it looked impressive. We both grabbed a glass of champagne from a passing waiter along with a mini-Yorkshire pudding smeared with horseradish and topped with beef. I allowed Lucy to steer me to the seats by the far window, shaking off our entourage in one swift move.

"I just need to sit down a minute, these heels are killing me," she said.

"Already?"

"I think they need adjusting. Or maybe I shouldn't have worn new shoes."

My heart leapt as she sat down beside me and steadied herself on my knee: her touch did things to me I never remembered happening before. I ate my canapé, wiping my hand on the serviette and then stroking Lucy's back. She fixed her heel back into place, then kissed me briefly, before sitting back, legs crossed and exposed, sipping her champagne. Her skin looked silky smooth and my eyes couldn't help but be drawn to it.

"Pretty fancy, eh?" she said, her eyes sweeping the venue. "The last wedding I went to was in a hall in Hull."

"You don't get much fancier than this. This is where footballers get married," I said.

"Do you think there'll be thrones?"

"We can only hope. There was a mention of a wedding singer, which I'm hoping proves true."

"Well it's a thumbs-up to free champagne." She paused. "Do we know who's on our table?"

"I think Andy and Jason, Matt and Natalie and some of Julia's nicer cousins. At least she promised me they would be the nicer ones."

"That's bad."

"Why?"

"They all drink. You don't want that at a wedding, you want a few tee-total aunts on your table or at least a pregnant couple where the man has to not drink too out of sympathy," Lucy said.

"Don't think any of my aunts are tee-total I can promise you. You'll just have to flash your cleavage at our waiter and I'm sure he'll bring us more wine if we run out."

Lucy slapped my leg, then looked serious for a moment.

"What?" I said. She frowned, shook her head and turned to look at the crowd again. I nudged her.

"What?"

"Nothing…"

"Tell me." She sighed and swivelled to face me.

"It's just… Are you sure Karen just turned up this morning. Nothing else to it? Nothing you want to tell me?"

I shook my head. "Nope, nothing else, I told you."

"She didn't show up to try to win you back?"

I shifted in my seat, then took Lucy's hand. "Who knows why she showed up, I gave up trying to read her long ago. But she did and I told her to go away. That's it."

"You sure?"

I held Lucy's gaze, the last couple of weeks whizzing through my brain.

"You're the only woman I want. Truly."

It didn't matter if Karen showed up on my doorstep every day – Lucy was the one I wanted now. There had been plenty of times when Karen would have been welcomed but not now. Besides, I was sure she'd soon have bigger fish to fry – she normally did. She hadn't stopped chasing what she couldn't have, which was always the biggest prize.

Lucy hadn't taken her eyes from me. I loved this woman and she was sitting here asking me if everything was okay with us. All because of Karen. Damn her. I needed to reassure Lucy. Needed to let her know the truth. Surely she knew the truth by now? We hadn't verbalised it, but the feelings were on show for everyone to see. I locked her gaze once more and cleared my throat. If you can't tell someone you love them at a wedding, when can you?

"Lucy, I…"

"There you are! Sitting down already?" Matt's voice boomed out beside us shattering the moment. I looked up and smiled weakly.

"Not interrupting are we?"

Lucy and I shook our heads rapidly, overcompensating for the moment that was now gone.

"No, all good. Just getting a bit soppy with all the romance around us," I said. I squeezed Lucy's hand and took a sip of her drink. "Tell you later," I mouthed. She smiled.

Weddings seemed to bring out the best in people, with everyone looking like they'd just stepped off the pages of Vogue. Even jeans-and-polo-shirt Matt looked suitably stylish, with a black suit, crisp white shirt and black tie, going for the rock star minimalist look. It suited him. Meanwhile, Natalie looked radiant in a blue and cream number beside him.

"So the cake looks good," Matt said.

"We haven't tasted it yet," I replied.

I spotted Julia honing into view so I waved over Matt's shoulder. She made her way towards us, raising her eyebrows to the heavens in the manner of a super-diva.

"How are we? All good?"

"We're great darling," I said.

"How are the canapés? Taste all right?"

"Wonderful," I said. "You've got an eyelash just there," I told her, pointing under my right eye. She went to her left. "Other side... Got it."

"Good," she said. "Look at all these bloody people! At my bloody wedding!" We all laughed.

"It's going really well," I said. "And you look beautiful." She blushed and smiled at me.

"This place looks amazing too," said Matt. "They've done a great job."

Julia nodded, assessing the venue.

"Yeah they have haven't they? Mind you, they should the price they charge... Well, I better go circulate – apparently everyone wants to talk to me, no idea why." She scanned the room. "Have you seen the champagne man?"

Lucy spotted him out of the corner of her eye. She slid sideways to pluck a fresh glass from his tray and delivered it to Julia's hand.

"I like her a lot, have I mentioned that?" Julia said, before floating off to the next group in a cloud of white lace.

* * *

I guessed there were around 80 guests invited to the wedding, who all played their part in creating a picture-postcard wedding vista of love and romance in an opulent setting.

As we sat down I looked over to the top table where Julia and Tom were grinning at each other, their magnum of Verve Clicquot diminishing by the second. Jason stopped griping once the food came out and Julia's cousins turned out to be a hoot, along with her Aunt Dawn and Uncle Alan who seemed inordinately excited to be on a table with a lesbian couple *and* a gay couple.

"So terribly London!" I heard her telling her husband with a thrilled look on her face. Alan went on to describe three other gay people he knew in his life, all very decent sorts he was pleased to report.

"The thing with lesbians these days though is that it's a choice, isn't it?" he said. "I mean, time was when the uglier women chose that route because women are so much more accommodating and can look past appearances. But look at you – you're not at all ugly, you don't have to be a lesbian, it's what you want to be. And I think that's great," he said.

"Yes, it's all sorts these days, Alan – not just those with mullets and motorbikes," I said. As expected, the irony passed him by.

"Exactly!" he said. "And you're not a mechanic or a labourer – you're a baker!" he said, his eyes bulging at the fact that a lesbian could bake. Alan took a bite of his dessert to calm himself down and I followed suit, wondering where the conversation was heading next.

"And what does your friend do?" He nodded towards Lucy.

"She's an optician."

"You see," Alan said, astounded. "Takes all sorts. Just wonderful."

I looked around just to check I wasn't being filmed for some candid camera joke, but apparently I wasn't. Alan was not a figment of my imagination and he really did say all of those things.

* * *

On the way to the loo Julia waved and beckoned me over. I pitched up in front of the giddy bride on her big day, the toxic mix of wine, champagne and bonhomie working their magic.

"How's it all going? How's the food and your table? I gave you one nearby so you'd get served quickly," she said.

"Great. And your Uncle Alan — he's a rare find. Him and Dawn think they're sitting with London's A-gays like they're in the pages of some Saturday supplement."

"Glad he's being entertaining. I thought he might be," she said.

"He told me he thinks it's great that lesbians don't have to be ugly anymore."

"Oh my god!" Tom said, covering his face with his hands while Julia threw back her head with laughter.

"I love him! I love him even more now. How great are Alan and Dawn? I wanted to have them on the top table with us but Tom told me that wasn't protocol."

A waiter drew up beside me, placing full glasses of champagne along the top table. I shifted my head left.

"I better go to the loo before the speeches start," I said.

The toilets were posh and full of jauntily-angled mirrors

as I expected. I dried my hands on a proper mini hand towel, putting it in the dark wicker bin provided – "imagine the laundry bill" my mum's voice chimed in my head. Smoothing down my trousers in one of the full-length mirrors, I decided the scorecard didn't read too badly. My hair was still fairly buoyant, my make-up in place and the spot count was zero. No wonder Karen had looked so dejected when I told her to bugger off, on top of Lucy turning up looking stunning.

I allowed myself a smile as I took a deep breath and got back out there, sliding into the seat beside Lucy just as Julia's dad was clearing his throat to start the speeches.

Chapter Forty-Nine

The disco got started around 7.30pm. By that time, my tie was loose around my neck and Lucy had abandoned her heels.

"Going ethnic," she said, whatever that meant. We put our bags and redundant shoes under our table and went for a boogie as *YMCA* came on, at which time half the wedding decided to do the same which I knew would appal Julia. She'd tried to stipulate no cheese for the first half of the disco but I'd told her if she wanted people to dance, that was the wedding law.

The song had just finished when I saw Mum and Dad walking in with a card and gift in their hands. Mum had been thrilled with the evening invite and had been chattering about the night for weeks now. I told her two days ago I was bringing Lucy – perhaps that's why I saw a touch of apprehension on her face as she scanned the room for us. She was dressed in my favourite outfit though, a coral floaty number. Dad had opted for his trusty grey suit, his thick hair looking newly trimmed.

I whispered to Lucy they'd arrived and took her hand, walking over to where Shirley and Ian had halted their progress. I waved and Mum waved back, relief flooding her face as she saw someone she recognised. She knew Julia's mum too, seeing as we'd been to school together, so she was next on my list to introduce them to.

"Hiya," I said, kissing Mum on the cheek and reaching up to do the same to Dad. Lucy had dropped my hand and was standing at my side smiling.

"Mum, Dad, this is Lucy," I said. I looked at my girlfriend who held out her hand and gave my parents a full-beam smile.

"Really lovely to meet you. Jess's told me a lot about you."

"Oh, I hope not too much!" Mum said. She looked relieved that Lucy was a normal human being, one head, no scales.

As Lucy shook my dad's hand, I mentally stepped back and took a snapshot in my head of this historic moment: my parents meeting their first girlfriend. The room began to slither around me as I wiped out all background distractions, everything else a blur as I clicked my mental camera and saved the crystal clear image to disc. I snapped another just for good measure, then focused back on the whole room, the noise levels revving up as I floated back. Smiles all round, nobody had died and Mum was asking me a question which my ears were not attuned to.

"Sorry?"

"I said has it been a lovely day?"

"Great," I said. Lucy was giving me a strange look but stepped in to cover my tracks.

"It's been amazing – the food was great, the speeches short and the toilets have proper hand towels," she said. "Plus the weather was amazing too, I'm sure they got some great shots in the grounds."

"So lovely, isn't it, love?" Mum asked Dad.

"Grand," Dad said.

I guided Mum and Dad to the presents table to leave their gift then manoeuvred them through the crowds to Julia's parents, Christine and Dave, who were thrilled to see them.

"They seem really sweet," Lucy said as we left them.

"They have their moments," I said. For all their past misdemeanours they'd been gorgeous to Lucy and my doubts about tomorrow, about them meeting Lucy, about them integrating her into their lives all melted away. Perhaps change was possible, for me and for them.

"You really look like your mum too," Lucy said.

"Well take a good look because that's your future," I said, the words tumbling out of my mouth before I could stop them. Lucy was still smiling at me though, clearly not that easily scared off.

"Well, she's not bad for an older woman..." she said.

"You're not finishing that sentence," I said, my brows shooting upwards as I dragged her to the dance floor.

* * *

An hour later and we were still twirling with Matt and Natalie. Jason and Andy had retired injured – sore foot so Jason said, although I had a sneaking suspicion it was more to do with the free bar.

I looked at my watch as Aretha demanded a little more respect and considered what a perfect evening it had turned out to be after such an inauspicious start. After some sweet-talking Lucy seemed to have gotten over the whole Karen debacle and I was hugely relieved. I looked across at her now and grinned at her screaming out every word of the song along with the rest of the crowd. As I looked over her shoulder I spotted Ange at a table at the back of the room, sipping white wine in a red dress and chatting to a woman with short cropped hair.

Ange. Super. Time stopped and the music went muffled in my ears as panic surged through my body with torrential force. I was going to kill Julia.

Lucy caught my gaze and swivelled to look. I tried to grab her arm to dance with her, but too late – she'd already turned, already seen, and was now already turning back to face me, her face hardening by the milli-second.

"What's she doing here? I thought you said Julia had told her not to come?" she said.

Matt and Natalie danced on, oblivious to what was happening as I took Lucy's hand and escorted her off the dance floor in the opposite direction to where Ange was sitting. We stood on the edge, literally and metaphorically, one foot on hard wood, the other on plush carpet.

"She told me she had but it looks like it slipped her mind."

Lucy stopped and assessed the situation. She could see the anguish on my face and I hoped she believed this was definitely not in my plans for a fun night out. On the contrary, Ange had been the furthest thing from my mind. However, I had to take charge of the situation now.

"I can't very well go and tell Julia off on her wedding day, so it looks like we have no choice other than to be grown-ups and ignore it."

The look on Lucy's face told me she didn't like this plan and that right now, she didn't much like me. I swear, if she'd had her shoes on, she'd have shown me a clean pair of heels and been out the door. I gave up a silent note of thanks for lady shoes.

"That's your plan? What if she comes over?"

I looked pained and tried not to shrug even though I had no control over Ange's movements.

"If she comes over we'll deal with it. She's nothing to me Lucy and you... Well, you're the opposite of that."

She wasn't going to be coerced into smiling that easily.

"Let's not let it ruin our night. I say we get a drink, have a chat with the boys and then dance some more. Look at it like we've just run into her in a lesbian bar by chance, which could easily happen."

Lucy seemed to like this approach and I could see her assessing this new tack in her brain. I ran with it.

"It's a big bar, granted, far bigger than usual but what can I say – lesbianism is getting more and more popular these days."

She looked around to where Ange was sitting engrossed in chat, then looked back at me.

"And yes, you might not think that every woman here is a lesbian," I said, indicating some aunts and a granny in front of us, "but looks can be deceiving. I guarantee you everyone here is a lesbian. Even those that look like men."

Finally, a smile and a laugh. I grabbed her hand.

"Come on," I said. "Let's get a drink. What do you want?"

"I'm coming with you, you're not safe going to the bar on your own," she said.

I smiled wryly.

"And I just need to know before we get to the bar, are there any other of your exes waiting in the wings to pounce? I just need to mentally prepare. Karen this morning, Ange tonight — we haven't had the big 'this is how many people I've slept with and this is how many actually meant something' conversation. So please do let me know if I'm missing someone crucial who's about to jump out of the shadows and seduce you."

She paused for breath and held me with a penetrating stare. For a second it felt like there was nobody else in the room but Lucy and I, her waiting for an answer, my mouth dry and unresponsive. She frowned.

"I don't know about you but I need a stiff drink. Tequila?"

It was more a statement than a question so I nodded meekly and we walked to the bar.

"Yes, love?" asked the bartender. Lucy turned and ordered two tequila shots and two beers.

"Make that three tequilas," chimed in Julia, draping her left arm around my shoulder as she leant her weight into me dramatically. Lucy adjusted the order while I put my arm around Julia's extremely skinny waist.

"Hello bride," I said. "How you holding up?"

"Surprisingly well. And this whole centre of attention thing? I could really get used to it."

"You seem like a natural."

"It really is amazing. Everyone wants to talk to you, everyone pays you a compliment, this is what being famous must feel like. So I've told Tom that has to be our first goal as a married couple. To get famous and then people will be nice to us and take our pictures all the time."

"Did he agree?"

"He had to, I'm the bride!" She looked especially pleased with herself.

"Here we go, ladies," Lucy said. She put tequila shots in our hands along with a lemon wedge each, then licked her left hand just below the thumb, sprinkled salt on it and grabbed her own shot. She waited for us to do the same and then proposed a toast.

"To love," she said, looking directly at me.

"To love," we both chorused back, before licking, drinking, sucking.

"So how's it looking from a guest perspective? Eight out of ten? Nine? Six?"

"Eleven," Lucy said. She swigged her beer to wash down the tequila. "It's been a great day."

Julia grinned broadly.

"I think so, too. Tom told me we have to go soon but it seems weird leaving our party before everyone else so I told him to bugger that – sod tradition, I want to dance. So we're staying. Shall we dance?"

I looked over to the dance floor and made out Ange shuffling in the far corner so decided to give it a miss.

"You go, your public awaits. We're just going to check on Mum and Dad."

Julia nodded and then looked sheepish.

"Oh, and by the way, Ange is here." She grimaced at us both. "Sorry, in all the rush I completely forgot to un-invite her. My fault but can I request you kill me later?"

"We know, we've seen her." I couldn't quite keep the irritation out of my voice but tried to disguise it with a smile.

"On that note, I'm going to run away like I was never here. Thanks for the drink," she said. She kissed us both on the cheek before bolting towards the dance floor where Bon Jovi were singing about Tommy and Gina holding on to what they got.

I looked at Lucy, still looking gorgeous in her dress, her hair slightly more dishevelled than earlier.

"We good?" I said.

She blew out a breath but nodded too.

"We're good."

"I like your forgiving side you know," I said, rubbing her arm.

"Forgiven, not forgotten. You might owe me more than one posh dinner now to completely erase the memory."

"However many it takes."

I leaned forward and kissed her.

"Shall we?" I said, holding out my hand. She took it and we stepped onto the dance floor together.

Chapter Fifty

We got in at 2am, drunk, happy, drama-less. Somehow, we'd managed to avoid Ange all night, although we did come perilously close at one stage during the slow dance portion of the evening. Luckily, Julia and Tom had seen the danger and stepped in between us – seeing as it was the first slow dance Lucy and I had ever had, I was lost in the moment.

And somehow, despite a stack of evidence to the contrary, it had been a good night. Great, even. It had also sparked my internal romance fire, so that by the time we got back to Lucy's place, images of the evening kept flicking through my mind like an old-fashioned picture book: Jason and Andy, Matt and Natalie, Julia and Tom, Lucy and I. But mainly Lucy and I.

Now the next morning, despite everything that happened I'd made it through and here I was lying in Lucy's bed gazing at her sleeping form. The past few weeks had meant me swimming against the tide, like a salmon battling upstream. The odds were against me but there was no way I was stopping because this was my stream, the only one I had. I hoped I'd seen off the other fish because all along, there was only one other I wanted and this was crystal clear. I loved this woman and I was such a ridiculous textbook case I almost laughed out loud. As if sensing my swell of love, Lucy slowly opened one eye and peered out.

"How long have you been staring at me?" she said.

I laughed. "Only since I woke up."

"And when was that?"

"About two hours ago."

"Liar," she said. She stretched out her left arm above her head. I leaned in for a quick kiss and she moved in closer.

"Okay, definitely no longer than half an hour."

"I could have you done for stalking."

She wrinkled her nose to stop a sneeze. It didn't work. I decided her sneeze was adorable.

"Only you don't normally spend half the night having sex with your stalker, do you?" I reached behind me for a tissue. She took it gratefully and sat up to blow her nose.

"Only if you're that woman from Abba," she said.

"What?"

"She married her stalker. The blonde one."

"A blonde stalker?"

"*No* – the blonde one from Abba whatever her name is."

"Did she?" I said.

Lucy nodded. "She was a recluse, though. He was probably the only person she ever met," she said.

"Well that makes it all fine then," I said. "Anyway, all ready for today?"

"Totes." She grinned.

"Glad you are."

She laughed and rolled her eyes at me. "You give your parents a bad press you know – they both seemed lovely to me."

"First meeting, best behaviour."

"You're terrible, Muriel."

I stretched my left leg under the cover and yawned.

"It was a good night last night though, wasn't it?"

"It was."

"Romantic."

"Uh-huh, especially the last bit," she said.

"That bit was definitely my favourite."

"The wedding bit wasn't bad either."

She trailed a finger up my arm and I felt a tingle down my whole body as she leaned in to kiss me deeply, thoroughly, expertly. After several minutes passed we pulled back and I stared into her lucid gaze, emotion flowing between us. I went to speak but the words slipped around in my throat. I felt a rush of love and knew I was about to put my heart on the line. Goddamn my romance Tourette's. With no impediments in my way, the way forward appeared clear, direct, a lawn freshly mown. All I had to do was launch myself onto it. So I did.

"I love you," I said. Pure and simple, my eyes never leaving hers. I'd known it since I first laid eyes on her all those months ago, since she lit up my life. And so it was out there, a weighty three-dimensional declaration, fully formed with sharp edges.

We both froze, me caught in her full beams and wanting to duck, her assessing the situation. After what seemed like an eternity, she ran her thumb down my cheek and kissed my lips gently, before pulling back.

"Was that what you were going to say yesterday at the wedding?" she said.

I smiled. "Might have been."

She kissed me again, then paused.

"And despite all rational logic, I think I love you too," she said. She sighed deeply and laughed. I guess I deserved that.

"Only think?"

She smiled at me. "Work with that for now."

We stared at each other, me rolling around our new status in my mind before we both broke into massive grins. I was in love with her and she thought she was in love with me. Yeah, I could definitely work with that for now.

THE END

Want more from me? Sign up to join my VIP Readers' Group and get a FREE lesbian romance, **It Had To Be You!** *Claim your free book here: www.clarelydon.co.uk/it-had-to-be-you*

Would You Leave Me A Review?

If you enjoyed this slice of sapphic London life, I wonder if you'd consider leaving me a review wherever you bought it. Just a line or two is fine, and could really make the difference for someone else when they're wondering whether or not to take a chance on me and my writing. If you enjoyed the book and tell them why, it's possible your words will make them click the buy button, too! Just hop on over to wherever you bought this book — Amazon, Apple Books, Kobo, Bella Books, Barnes & Noble or any of the other digital outlets — and say what's in your heart. I always appreciate honest reviews.

Thank you, you're the best.

Love,
Clare x

Also By Clare Lydon

London Romance Series
London Calling (Book One)
This London Love (Book Two)
A Girl Called London (Book Three)
The London Of Us (Book Four)
London, Actually (Book Five)
Made In London (Book Six)
Hot London Nights (Book Seven)
Big London Dreams (Book Eight)
London Ever After (Book Nine)

Standalone Novels
A Taste Of Love
Before You Say I Do
Change Of Heart
Christmas In Mistletoe
Hotshot
It Started With A Kiss
Nothing To Lose: A Lesbian Romance
Once Upon A Princess
One Golden Summer
The Christmas Catch
The Long Weekend
Twice In A Lifetime
You're My Kind

All I Want Series
Two novels and four novellas chart the course
of one relationship over two years.

Boxsets
Available for both the London Romance series and the
All I Want series for ultimate value. Check out my
website for more: www.clarelydon.co.uk/books

Printed in Great Britain
by Amazon